SWITCHBLADE

switch·blade (swĭch´blād´) n.
a different slice of hardboiled fiction where the dreamers and the schemers, the dispossessed and the damned, and the hobos and the rebels tango at the edge of society.

THE JOOK
GARY PHILLIPS

I-5: A NOVEL OF CRIME, TRANSPORT, AND SEX
SUMMER BRENNER

PIKE
BENJAMIN WHITMER

THE CHIEU HOI SALOON
MICHAEL HARRIS

THE WRONG THING
BARRY GRAHAM

**SEND MY LOVE AND A MOLOTOV COCKTAIL!
STORIES OF CRIME, LOVE AND REBELLION**
EDITED BY GARY PHILLIPS AND ANDREA GIBBONS

PRUDENCE COULDN'T SWIM
JAMES KILGORE

NEARLY NOWHERE
SUMMER BRENNER

PRUDENCE COULDN'T SWIM

JAMES KILGORE

PMPRESS

Prudence Couldn't Swim
By James Kilgore

Published by:
PM Press
PO Box 23912
Oakland, CA 94623
www.pmpress.org

Cover illustration by Mark Maddox www.maddoxplanet.com
Interior design by Courtney Utt/briandesign

ISBN: 978-1-60486-495-3
Library of Congress Control Number: 2011927952
10 9 8 7 6 5 4 3 2 1

Printed in the USA on recycled paper, by the Employee Owners of Thomson-Shore
in Dexter, Michigan.
www.thomsonshore.com

P rudence couldn't swim. She liked to sit by my pool in a skimpy bikini, her body glowing with creams, lotions, and oils. When I came home that Thursday afternoon, I saw her in the water for the first time. She lay face up under the surface, her legs bent like a frog's.

I kicked off my sandals and jumped in feet-first. My favorite Christian Dior sunglasses floated away as I grabbed her hand. Her fingers were limp but warm. I dragged her to the edge, let go for a second, and scrambled onto the deck. As I knelt down and slid my hands under her armpits, I thought I heard her laughing. No such luck.

Her knees banged against the concrete, then her toes caught on the rim of the pool. I'd never been much good at handling women who were alive and breathing, so I shouldn't have been surprised that this wasn't going well. I gave an extra tug and her body slithered onto the scorching concrete. Her skin seemed to sizzle as I laid her down and began the battle to bring my wife back from the dead.

This woman had cost me a fortune—plane tickets, clothes, entertainment. Prudence longed to live in style. I tried to give her that, though I don't know how much she appreciated my efforts. Our union did have its benefits though. I strutted through crowds while gawkers puzzled at how a hare-lipped, balding white man could hold onto this ebony trophy girl. I would remember those times. Now, soaking wet and frantic, I wasn't sure it was all worth it. People would probably say she played me.

For the first time ever, I put my lips to her mouth. I held her nostrils shut, like what I remembered they said to do on the radio if someone wasn't breathing. This once-forbidden fruit felt so natural.

I breathed in and out three, four, five times. A trickle of water ran from her nose. With the flat of my hand between her still-shining breasts, I pushed quick and hard. The purple polish of her toenails flashed in the corner of my eye as her feet bounced in rhythm to my futile thrusts. She'd spent hours with little balls of cotton between her toes getting that polish just right.

I alternated between lips and chest, my cheek finally collapsing onto those once-glorious tits. I was too out of breath to cry. Prudence was gone. What thrills did life hold for me now?

CHAPTER 1

The first issue was getting out of those clothes. I hated wet cotton clinging to my chest. I stripped down to my boxers in the patio, then raced to the bedroom. A pair of black Dockers and a black cashmere sweater helped me regain my composure for a few seconds. But no change of clothes could solve the problem of what to do with this dead body. I rushed back out to the patio and covered Prudence with a green wool blanket. I didn't want to witness whatever changes go on with a dead person. Red Eye would know what to do though he was hard to catch. He hadn't quite gotten the hang of cell phones. He owned one but rarely turned it on and never checked messages. Even his parole officer had a hard time tracking him down. I tried his landline. No reply. He didn't believe in answering machines or voice mail.

"If God intended me to get the call he would have kept my ass at home," was his explanation. Typical convict logic. After his five years in the pen what could I expect?

When Red Eye wasn't home, he was usually at Leon's Sports Bar, a none-too-fancy place on the fringes of Hayward. Red Eye bet on anything—football, NASCAR, the Olympics. He bet on European soccer, though he didn't know a corner kick from an off side. He solved that problem by always betting on teams with red uniforms. In fact, he always bet on red. I once caught him with $100 riding on a ping pong match. He'd backed the Chinese player against the Malaysian because the Chinese guy wore a red shirt.

"And the guy comes from Red China," he'd pointed out to make it more convincing.

I could phone Red Eye at Leon's but the conversation might get awkward and Leon loved to eavesdrop. Better to go there. Still, before

I could go anywhere, I had to do better than leave Prudence lying under a blanket. How long did a body take to start stinking? The last thing I needed was the stench of my now-former wife enveloping the neighborhood. I hadn't lived here long and I was trying to keep up a respectable front. It was all disintegrating fast.

The more I thought about it, the worse it seemed. How could this vibrant, beautiful woman suddenly turn into a rotting heap of flesh?

I wrapped the blanket all the way around her and dragged it across the patio, a little like a husky pulling a sled. Her once-mesmerizing bumps and curves thudded over the sliding glass door frame. At least hers was a bloodless death. I didn't have to worry about stains. Still, dead people did empty their bodily fluids at some point. I hoped that moment wouldn't come too soon. I'd spent over $4,000 recarpeting the living room just a few weeks before. Cream color. I didn't want anyone's emissions, not even Prudence's, to scar my investment. Just for insurance I rolled the body, still in the blanket, onto a little throw rug. Hard to hide blemishes on cream-colored carpet.

I slid this odd-looking parcel across the living room, down the shining hardwood hallway to the guest bathroom. There wasn't much space in there. I had to bend her a little and wrap her around the toilet so I could close the door. As I twisted her ankle to get the required angle, her face popped out of the blanket. A few minutes of death had hollowed her eyes and caved in her cheeks. That tiny scar on her cheek, her only blemish, had somehow grown. I threw a towel over her head before that image got too deeply etched in my memory. I retreated quickly and shut the door, hoping she wouldn't flop into some ungainly position. She deserved better than that.

I rushed to the liquor cabinet and downed two shots of Wild Turkey. The burning liquid temporarily purged her sunken eyes from my mind. I couldn't recall why I'd brought her inside. Oh yes. I didn't want to leave her by the pool while I went to find Red Eye at Leon's.

As I searched for my car keys, another little light went on inside my head—the one that said "you could be in a world of trouble here."

Prudence didn't leap into the heated pool in a suicidal fit. She had help. Someone pushed her. Maybe they were trying to set me up. Running to Leon's looked a little less appealing. If I was going to run, I'd have to run farther than that. Whoever did this had probably phoned the police the minute I walked through the front door. I had to cover some tracks. Fast.

I exchanged the Wild Turkey for Chivas Regal and weighed my options. Two shots of the Chivas halted the tremor in my hands. Scotch was more powerful than bourbon in such situations. I'd save the Wild Turkey for later.

I phoned Leon's and asked for Red Eye.

"He just stepped out," the bartender told me.

"Is he coming back?"

"Hard to say," he replied. "He usually does but you never know."

"Can you give him a message?"

"We don't do messages," he responded. "We're a sports bar, not an answering service. Besides, too many people shoot the messenger, if you get what I mean."

"There's been a death in the family. I need to get him urgently."

"Sorry, Bud," he answered, "we've heard that one. Try Philly Joe's on E. Twelfth and Fifth. It's his other haunt. 651-4893."

"Thanks"

I dialed as far as the four when I heard the sirens coming. I put down the phone and grabbed the broom. Time to hide the evidence, though I wasn't sure why. I went outside and swept away all the little pieces of green wool I'd trailed across the patio, then hosed down the pool deck for good measure. A quick run of the vacuum cleaner over the living room carpet restored some order. It's hard to weigh your options in a messy house.

If the cops came I was sure I could convince them I was no thug. I had my Volvo 740 parked in the driveway to prove it. Mint condition. I had to give up the Caprice Bubble when I moved to the hills. Hopefully my new image would pay off and they didn't run ID checks on gentlemen sipping scotch and soda in this neck of the woods. As I added some soda to the Chivas I realized I had another problem. My point was that I had nothing to hide. Moving the body didn't fit in with that image. I ran down the hall to the bathroom, opened the door and yanked on her left leg. She slid out into the hallway. I was holding a coldish foot, trying not to look at her face. I closed my eyes and wrapped the blanket around her again. Her once-firm breasts flopped like a pair of socks with golf balls inside.

She ended up next to the pool under the blanket. I folded her hands on her stomach. She was resting in peace. I vacuumed again. I probably should have just left her in the pool.

The sirens had stopped. False alarm. Probably just the EMT rescuing some old man from a heart attack. I hosed down the pool deck one more time just to make sure. Suddenly I realized I needed to call 911, at least get a call on record.

I poured another shot of Chivas as I dialed.

"Emergency services, how may I help you?"

"I want to report a drowning at 12 Lancaster Road, Carltonville."

"Is the person breathing, sir?"

"I said it was a drowning. Do drowned people breathe?"

"Have you tried CPR?"

"What?"

"Artificial respiration."

"I banged on her heart and breathed in her mouth quite a few times. I held her nose while I did it."

"And she didn't respond?"

"No. I just found her in the pool when I came home. She can't swim. She's my wife."

"Keep trying CPR, our team is on the way. Your name, sir?"

"Calvin Winter, like the season."

"Thank you, Mr. Winter. Have a great . . . I mean thank you."

In the flatlands of Oakland where I grew up there was a fifty-fifty chance an ambulance would come if you called them. If they did arrive, it took at least half an hour. The opulent hills were different. Within five minutes the siren was whining in my driveway. I thought about giving the cops a different name. I had a Colorado license in the name of Edgar Winter. I could tell them my brother Calvin had just left. Probably not a good idea.

The doorbell chimed "Oh give me a home . . ." I don't know why in hell I chose that tune.

I put away the whiskey bottle. As I let them in I realized I couldn't remember how to spell Prudence's maiden name. Something long starting with an "m." But of course her passport said "Deirdre Lewis." And she was Deirdre on our marriage certificate. I'd stick with that.

Three medic uniforms filled the doorway with navy blue. The two in front held pieces of equipment—a resuscitator, a medical bag, a fold-up gurney. A huge flashlight dangled from the belt of the freckle-faced linebacker body who looked the like the team leader. At least they weren't cops.

"She's over there," I said, pointing to the lumpy green blanket by the pool. "I think you're too late. So was I."

Freckle Face charged across the room and out onto the patio. They unraveled the blanket, felt the neck for a pulse, then lifted the eyelids.

"No pulse," Freckle Face told the others. "Try the jump start."

His much taller Hispanic partner with "Guerrero" stitched on his shirt lined the resuscitator up. A few feet away the third team member, a young Asian woman, was unfolding the gurney.

Within a few seconds Prudence sprung into arcs like a flopping fish. I couldn't watch. Then Freckle Face tried breathing into her mouth like I'd done, only he did it a lot longer. Finally Guerrero disconnected the machine and laid the blanket back over her Prudence.

"I'm sorry, sir," said Freckle Face, "there's nothing we can do." He touched me lightly on the shoulder but avoided eye contact.

I could never relax with this many uniforms in my presence, especially at a time like this. These people were the gentle, human side of officialdom. Still, they were too clean, too soulless. I worked hard to keep such people out of my life. I always had something to hide. Even when I didn't, I felt like I did.

I thought of offering them a cup of coffee. Is that what a suburban husband in grief would do? I had no idea.

"Put her on the gurney," said Freckle Face, "and load her in."

He looked at me for a second.

"I'm sure she died before you arrived, sir. There's nothing you could have done. I'm so sorry."

The truth was I was glad I hadn't arrived too much earlier. The killer could have just wasted me too.

"What about the police?" asked Guerrero. "They might want to look around."

"What about them?" said Freckle Face. "They're welcome to do what they gotta do. The woman drowned. No sign of a struggle. The gentleman doesn't need her body here any longer. My call."

"Sir," Freckle Face added turning to me, "the police will come to question you. It's routine."

"Okay," I replied. I wasn't accustomed to polite explanations from authorities. I guess this was how they did it in the hills.

"I just came home and found her floating in the pool," I said. "She can't swim."

"How were you acquainted with the victim?" asked Freckle Face.

"She's my wife."

He went silent.

"I'm so sorry," he said, pausing for the appropriate few seconds until the next question. Well-trained, sensitive, but still an alien uniform.

"Your name, sir."

"Calvin Winter."

"Like the season?"

"Exactly."

Freckle Face had some kind of computer with a pen attached. I guess the thing could read his writing. I saw him recording my name and address, the time of day. Computers were almost as foreign to me as uniforms in my living room. I'd used e-mail, visited some porn sites, and tracked down a few women seeking husbands. That was about it. The truth was, I hadn't moved much beyond programming my old VCR and sometimes I still had to read the manual to do that.

I told him her maiden name was Lewis, that she rarely used Winter. I decided not to tell him that "Lewis" was made up, just like almost everything else about Prudence's life.

His last question had something to do with "grief counseling." Freckle Face told me he knew the bereavement process could be "difficult, especially when it involved a spouse."

I declined the offer. The only help I'd need was a case of Wild Turkey. That and a bit of weed. Red Eye would take care of all that.

I thanked them politely as their little caravan retraced its tracks and removed Prudence's physical presence from my life forever. They left me with the phone number and the website of the morgue to deal with funeral matters. I had no idea what a website had to do with a funeral.

As soon as they were out the door I reconnected to the Wild Turkey, then got Red Eye at Philly Joe's. The noise from the gymnastics competition on one of the TVs was too loud to explain what happened.

Red Eye promised to get to my place within an hour. He was waiting for the results of his favorite event, the parallel bars, or the "ball crunchers" as he called them.

The police got there before Red Eye. By that time I was almost catatonic from the Wild Turkey. The pair of them rattled and jingled their way across my living room. They didn't even take off their hats before they planted their black-uniformed butts on my sofa, a place Prudence and I had occasionally enjoyed an evening together. She liked to watch old tearjerkers like *Terms of Endearment* and *Love Story.*

The talker was Officer Carter, a stout-bellied veteran who no doubt felt more comfortable on a barstool than in my elegantly furnished living room. Offer him a Bud, a Big Mac, and a few porn videos and he'd figure he'd died and gone to heaven.

His partner, McGee, was the sniffer, a hyperactive weasel who looked here, there, and everywhere for clues of something. He walked around the pool, pulled out some type of high-powered chalking device and drew an outline of where I told him Prudence's body laid.

"Why did you drag her inside?" he asked. Apparently I hadn't hosed down the deck as well as I thought.

"She was my wife," I said, "I couldn't stand seeing her outside in plain sight of God and everybody."

"Then you dragged her back outside?"

"Yeah, I just wasn't thinking too clearly. She was my wife." He didn't seem satisfied but cops rarely do.

As the Weasel got down on his hands and knees to peak under the sofa, Carter let loose a gigantic sneeze. His effort to get his elbow in front of his nose was a second too late. The spray arched out across my carpet.

Once he'd finished dragging his sleeve across his nostrils, Carter told me they needed a picture of "the deceased." He said it was standard operating procedure.

I knew that was a lie but I cooperated as politely as I could manage. Anything to keep them from running my ID. The latest photo of Prudence I had came from her thirtieth birthday party. She'd worn a skintight black number with a neckline that finished at her jewel-studded belly button.

"Nice tits," Carter whispered to McGee as his finger ran down Prudence's body. He looked back at me.

"She was a beautiful woman," he said, "if you don't mind me saying so."

I did mind but I had too much to hide to let him know how I felt. They'd have to start pulling up the rugs and the floorboards to find my stash but it hadn't stopped them before. Back in the eighties they'd knocked holes in my bedroom wall after the dogs went crazy next to my dresser. Luckily for me I'd taken out all the dope they day before. I didn't mess with that stuff anymore. But the dogs still might find something.

They asked me a few more questions and the Weasel suggested they'd come back if they had any more concerns. I told them they were always welcome, but they just didn't look all that interested.

Carter managed a departure handshake.

"I know this must be hard on you," he added. "Contact us if you think of anything else we should know."

As soon as they left I went to the cupboard under the kitchen sink and found my can of Re-Nu, a "miracle cleaner" for sofas, chairs and carpets. The late-night purveyors of the product boasted that you could pour a glass of red wine on a white couch, spray on Re-Nu, wait for five minutes and scrub the stain away like "a few loose grains of sand." I'd called the 800 number the first time I saw the commercial. The three cans of Re-Nu plus a set of steak knives were on my doorstep the next morning. I gave the steak knives to Luisa, my Salvadoran house girl who came every Tuesday. Without Luisa I'd be living in chaos.

I sprayed half the can on the spots where the cops sat, then waited the required five minutes. A few strokes with a scrub brush wiped away their aura but I still felt defiled. No aerosol could erase the day. I was drunk, wanted to cry or scream. I couldn't figure out which. But then I didn't really know how to cry. If someone had murdered Prudence, and they probably had, I had to be next in line.

Red Eye rang the bell just as I'd popped a new bottle of Wild Turkey. Good timing is one thing we have in common.

"What's up, boss?" he asked with a cheery smile. His boy must have scored big on the parallels. Probably wearing red tights. Red Eye had on his usual Adidas tracksuit with a Chicago Bears cap. Although Red Eye and I were Raider Nation diehards, he had a thing about the Bears. He could talk all day about Walter Payton, Gale Sayers, Dick Butkus. Then there was Willie Galimore, Red Eye's favorite Bear. Red Eye said Galimore would have been the greatest running back of all time if he hadn't died in a car crash. The Bears were a perfect fit for Red Eye. He was truly a bear of a man. Even though he shaved all the way down to the neckline of his T-shirt, he couldn't totally suppress the jungle of brown hair that covered him front and back. He was just a little taller than me but had a body like a grizzly—pumped up from years of bar work and pushing iron on various prison yards. Of course his muscles had softened a little, especially since he'd started this competitive eating thing. Two years before he'd won the Greeley, the West Coast's most prestigious hot dog–eating contest.

"You want a drink?" I asked.

"Not until you tell me what's going on."

"Prudence drowned in the pool this morning."

"I'll serve myself," he said walking toward the bottle of Wild Turkey. "Sorry, bro."

He poured me another, then went back to the bar, squatted down and opened the half fridge.

"I need ice," he said. He broke open a tray and dropped three cubes in his glass. I heard them crack.

"Sorry, bro," he repeated. "What happened?"

"I came home and found her floating face up in the water," I said. "She couldn't swim."

"Then how did she get in the pool?"

"You tell me."

"What did the police say?"

"Not much. I told them she drowned, that she couldn't swim and they left. One of them looked at her picture and said she had nice tits."

"The piece of shit," he said, mimicking the sidearm motion of sliding a knife under someone's ribs.

He kept drinking and pouring for both of us. Whiskey flowed easier for Red Eye than words of condolence.

"Prudence didn't jump into that pool by herself," I said. "She had help."

"She have enemies?" he asked. "Was she using?"

"We went our separate ways. That was the arrangement. But a woman like that always has enemies. Probably left a trail of jealous bastards from here to London."

"She ever mention any?"

"We didn't talk about her men. I knew she had them. That's all. I can't believe this shit. I'm like the heroin dealer hooked on his product. I just couldn't let her go."

"She was a beauty," he said. "Never met a black girl like her. Or any girl for that matter."

He went back to the whiskey bottle. I could count on Red Eye. He had nondescript talents, just like me. I'd often used him to transport my various commercial goods, human and otherwise. He was totally reliable and with the aid of a few tablets he could drive thirty-six hours without a rest. The jury was still out on how he'd perform as a bereavement counselor.

"You've got to find out who did this," he said, "for your own peace of mind. Our property is our manhood, bro. If we let people get away with this shit, we're nothing." He knocked back the whiskey and let out a monumental belch. "I'm ready when you need me," he said.

"Thanks, bro. It means a lot." I was telling the truth. I had no one else but revenge wasn't really on my mind. I was trying to live the square life. I'd even gone to a couple of anger management classes.

"Maybe you need to chill for a few days," said Red Eye. "Go away. Get your mind off this. Then we start."

Getting away was a good idea but I couldn't think of any place to go. I'd never really gone on a vacation and it felt like the wrong time to start thinking of holiday packages.

"How about Reno?" he said. "Or Chumash?"

"Nah. I'll stay here. A few bottles of Wild Turkey and some videos and I'll be good to go."

"Careful, Cal. You don't know who you're dealing with. There's some straight jay-cats out there these days."

We left it like that. Red Eye promised to come back the next day. A couple minutes after he left, the cops came back. Two cars this time. They got out with their hats on and guns drawn. So much for my reputation with the neighbors.

"On your belly, hands behind your back," Carter shouted. "You know the drill." He was right. I did know the drill. Just like something kicked off in the yard at Leavenworth.

I moved half a step to the left so I wouldn't have to lie on the grass. Cashmere and mud were a bad combination. Carter and the Weasel crept up on me slowly.

"Don't fuckin' move," the Weasel shouted when they were about ten feet away. "We know all about you." Two Godzilla types were coming out of the other squad car. They were going to have a party.

"I'm just a respectable citizen trying to live my life in peace and quiet," I said.

"You're a fuckin' ex-con scumbag," said Carter, "getting our kids hooked on drugs."

"I gave all that up. I'm as square as a pile of blocks," I said. "If your kids are on drugs, it's because you drove 'em to it."

Carter kicked me a couple times in the ribs while the Weasel put on the plastic cuffs and pulled them nice and tight. My hands started to tingle. They left me on my belly for two hours while they searched the house. A small crowd of neighbors stood in the street. After a while it started to sprinkle and they all went back in their houses. I'd be the fuel for gossip sessions for the next ten years. A cat caught in a tree was big news in this neck of the woods. The stench of wet cashmere was really pissing me off.

Finally the Weasel came and lifted me up by the by the handcuffs.

"We should take you in on GP," he said.

Suddenly Carter was right in my face while the Weasel pulled my arms back by the cuffs.

"This woman didn't live here, Winter," Carter said a little bit of saliva clinging to his lower lip. "What kinda game were you playing with her? Was she turnin' tricks for you? Pushin' a little heroin? Better to spill your guts now because we'll find out anyway. Once an ex-con scumbag, always an ex-con scumbag."

"I haven't done anything and I got nothing to say," I replied looking Carter right in the eyes.

"We'll be on you like ten flies on shit," said Carter. "And don't leave town."

"You can't tell me where I can go," I said, "you need a court order."

"We've got one," said Carter patting the 9 mm on his hip, "didn't you get the memo?"

The Weasel giggled as he snipped the cuffs and pushed me toward the front door.

"Have a wonderful day," said Carter.

They hadn't torn the place up that bad, no holes in the walls or pulled up kitchen tiles. They hadn't even gotten near my stash. They did rip open all my dry cleaning packets and throw my yellow and white Arrow shirts into a pile on the bed. Luisa could iron them back into something wearable. What pissed me off, though, was that they squeezed the toothpaste out of the tube onto my pillow. I'd told them I didn't mess with drugs any more. To tell the truth I was a little insulted they had me as a penny-ante pusher—the kind who stuffed a thimble full of coke in a toothpaste tube. Back in the day, I moved weight or I didn't move at all.

The biggest pain was all the dirty boot prints on the carpet. I had some spray for that as well. Never Stain, they called it. Took a whole can to restore the cream-colored elegance to my thick-pile broadloom.

After about six hours of cleaning and Re-Nu spraying I collapsed in a stupor on the bed. I woke up at two in the morning with my shoes still on and my wrists feeling like they'd been squeezed with piano wire. As I rolled over I thought I heard someone in the living room. I got up to have a look but it was nothing. Probably just the wind or the neighbor's cat, Toodles. She was always up to something.

I had a look in Prudence's room but didn't really want to go in there. Maybe the following morning I'd get up the nerve. As I pulled the door to her room shut, I heard the lock click. I'd have to look for the key. We had an understanding that I didn't go into her space. But given the circumstances, I figured it would be okay if I broke that agreement.

CHAPTER 2

The first thing I needed to find out was Prudence's real name. I knew Deirdre Lewis was an alias because I'd gotten her that passport through a connection. The photos on the Internet only said, "Prudence, a lovely Londoner, can cook, clean, and love you to death." She cost me $5,000 plus a few grand more along the way. That's not how I told the story though. I always said I was doing her a favor, that she was paying me to be her husband so she could get that precious green card.

Whatever the arrangements, when Prudence came along, I was ready for a change. I'd been through three marriages and had nothing to show for any of them except a scar on my neck, lawyers' fees, and restless nights. A black Brit was definitely going to be something new.

She turned out to be even more beautiful in person than in the pictures, the first black woman I ever met who spoke with an accent like the Queen of England's. Not that I'd ever met that many black women. They waited on me at McDonald's, took my money on the Bay Bridge. There was a CO named Washington at Santa Rita County Jail when I passed through there. She used to talk to me about the Raiders. She was Raider Nation all the way.

But to sit down and talk to a black woman in my house, that just had never happened. The closest I ever got was my Luisa. Not very close at all but life is strange. After a while I got used to Prudence being five inches taller than me. Her love for life and sense of humor brought us to the same level.

"I don't know a soul in this flippin' city," she'd say. "It's quite perturbing." That's how she talked.

When we went out for drinks, she kept saying "cheers" and touching my glass before each round. She told me she was "infatuated with America" and was so grateful to be here.

I'd always succumbed to the quest for excitement. I started as a con man. Bad checks, three-card monte on the street, petty flim-flam. No one ever thought a scrawny little harelip could outsmart them. Then I went to the next level: running drugs and people from Mexico to California for more than a decade. I made enough in the first two years to retire. The dope was where the big money was but I liked being a coyote better. I was actually giving people something they wanted, something that would improve their life—a ticket to America. I wasn't like these *polleros* today. I fed my people, gave them blankets to sleep under. We usually traveled in a mobile home, with bicycles tied to the back like the family gone camping. I could pack twenty-five people into that RV. As long as they laid low, they were comfortable.

Today these guys rape and beat up their charges, leave them to bake inside a trailer for fifteen hours. The worst I did was squeeze some four-year-olds in the trunk of a car in the middle of a desert. That wasn't really my fault. These people knew better than to bring little kids. Kids could make noise at the wrong time. Get you into all kinds of unnecessary trouble with the INS.

I was actually lucky when I got caught in 1989. I had less than half a gram of coke on me and my house was clean. The federal prosecutors in Frisco promised to let me go if I just told them where I got the dope. I was buying from some big boys. I took the two years—did a few college courses in the joint, read a lot of books, played a little handball. I stayed out of the prison politics. Then I got out and started living the square life, sort of. Back in those days the Feds didn't search high and low for your ill-gotten gains like they do now. In various accounts from Idaho to Virginia I'd stashed more than half a million. I'd used at least half a dozen aliases, all the names of former Raider players: James Otto, David Casper, even the black stars like Clifford Branch and Eugene Upshaw. With my nest egg I bought a four-bedroom house in Carltonville, a drab suburb in the Oakland hills. I was "out of the mix," ready to live the quiet life like my doctor and accountant neighbors.

As it turned out, I couldn't quite keep my hand out of the action. I still trafficked in women. I hooked up desperate blondes, brunettes, and redheads of all ethnicities with the paper they needed to stay in the United States. Through one of Red Eye's amigos, I provided social security cards for Belarusians, drivers' licenses for Filipinas, passports for Guatemalans. With modern computers and color printers, a skilled artist could forge anything. When I felt ambitious I hooked these women up with husbands. That's how I stumbled onto Prudence.

Before she arrived, the cream of my customer crop received more personal service, often passing through my home for several days to celebrate their newly established legal status in this country with an extended session in my bed. Fringe benefits, I called it.

Prudence followed a different path. Before we'd even consummated the marriage, she'd moved into my second bedroom. I bought her a queen-sized Sealy Posturepedic. She said she had "woman problems" and didn't want to give me any diseases. I bought it or maybe I just hoped as we got to know each other things would change.

To compensate for the lack of sexual action, she cooked curries and baked those biscuits the Brits call "scones." I loved having her around. She sunbathed topless and let me take pictures, not that she really needed a tan. She joked, flirted, and drank up my whiskey. When she changed the lock on the bedroom door, I didn't complain. I don't know how but all this seemed totally normal to me. She ruled the roost. After a while she started disappearing for days at a time and I accepted that I had no right to ask where she'd gone. She always came back with that bubbly smile.

On that rare occasion when she agreed to pretend to the world she was my wife, I waltzed like a king. Men don't age that gracefully. As a five-foot-four harelip, I was no Stacy Keach. Nothing restores masculine self-esteem like the jealous glances of other men lusting after your paramour. I lived for those moments.

The highlight of our public life was Dr. Robson's fiftieth birthday party. Robson lived three doors down and wore his half century well. He was a gym regular and had forsaken the evils of fast food, alcohol, and caffeine. On a typical Saturday morning, I'd see him standing on his front lawn after his run pouring water out of a plastic bottle over his sweat-soaked, graying hair.

The good doctor invited the whole neighborhood to his affair, including the reclusive Calvin Winter and "guest." This was to be my debut in mucky-muckville. Up to then the only friend I'd made in the neighborhood was Toodles, that cat from next door. Sometimes I left her an open can of tuna on the back porch.

The setting was a hotel garden in the exclusive village of Montclair, just a few miles down the road from us. Robson went the whole nine yards. He hired a sixties band, put up marquees, and covered dozens of linen tablecloths with vegetable dips, bowls of fresh fruit salad, and meatless pizzas. He added a few bottles of appropriate red wine, since, as he told me, "medical research has proven its efficacy in reducing cardiac disorders."

Prudence wore a strapless white satin gown with a slit up the leg just high enough to reveal the lace of her purple panties. It all cost me $923. She added purple stiletto heels and matching eye shadow for emphasis. While she pranced off with a string of admirers to do the twist, jerk, and mashed potatoes, frustrated men regaled me with tales of their moribund sex life. In the latter stages of the evening, a seriously lit-up Dr. Robson, toasted my "exquisite taste in female partners."

"Unlike most of us," he said gazing at my nether regions, "your sex life does not appear to be material for historians only."

I did nothing to dispel his assumptions about my relationship with Prudence. I let him go on assuming the tool of my marital trade resembled a gigantic gaffing hook.

I rode the good doctor's waves of praise, culminating my performance with a slow dance to the band's cover of "Michelle." My hand rested just a millimeter above the buttocks of "my belle" until the final note. While Robson and his friends fantasized, I went home to platonic small talk and futile hopes our relationship would change. I loved Prudence or Deirdre or whoever she was in my own little private way.

Despite my feelings I didn't know much about her at all. One night she arrived home very late after a three-day absence. She drunkenly implied that she wasn't British at all, that she was an "African Princess" named "Tarisai."

"That means 'look' in my language," she said. "I'm Princess Tarisai." Then she told me her last name, that long one that began with "m." I asked her to repeat it three times but I still couldn't pronounce it.

The next morning she denied it all, again telling tales of growing up in the south of London.

"My name is Deirdre Lamming," she said. "Mum always called me Prudence. She came from Jamaica, said that was the name of an auntie who looked like me."

Then Prudence told me she had a conviction for possession of marijuana in Britain, that's why she needed a passport in another name.

"The Americans don't let in drug users," she said.

When I asked her if she was a drug user she laughed and said she got caught holding a bag of weed for a friend. I never knew what to believe. As a con woman, she was flawless, except for that one mistake that landed her in my pool.

CHAPTER 3

Try as I might, I couldn't find a key to Prudence's room anywhere. Red Eye came over the next morning with his lock picks. After thirty seconds the doorknob turned.

"Easy as opening a Top Ramen," he said.

There wasn't much to see inside the room. The bed was made, covered with a bright blue comforter. Three matching blue pillows were lined up precisely against the wall at the head of the bed.

The closet held just two pairs of jeans and a brown skirt. Prudence had a vast wardrobe. I had the receipts to prove it. Did she have another husband somewhere? I ruffled through the nightstand: a bottle of lotion, some cheap perfume, and a scrap of paper with the words, "Mandisa, Tuesday at 2." The dot over the *i* was a huge circle. Strange. Prudence once mentioned a friend named "Mandy," said she was a night manager at one of those chain restaurants—Denny's, IHOP. I couldn't remember which one.

A purse under the bed had a red wallet inside. I pulled open the Velcro and found an Iowa drivers' license for Deirdre Lewis. I doubt Prudence had ever been to Iowa but the picture was her. The address was an apartment somewhere in Davenport. Not exactly a hot lead.

Red Eye searched the five dresser drawers and found a green thong and an empty black leather shoulder bag. The bathroom yielded lots of bottles, tubes, and bars of sweet-smelling soap. Nothing of use. Prudence hadn't planned to live with her legal husband much longer.

I lifted up the mattress to find two photos underneath. One showed a much younger Prudence standing in front of a brown wall wearing flip-flops and a blue cloth dress. Her short-cropped hair was coated with a layer of dust. Next to her was an old woman in a yellow headscarf—either her mother or grandmother. The old woman's face was wrinkled and shiny like she was healing from a burn. Her smile revealed three missing front teeth. At their feet lay what looked like a short-handled hoe with a wide blade. It resembled an adze. I'd once seen a movie where they shaped timber with an adze back in the 1850s. I couldn't imagine Prudence as a wood chopper.

The other photo was a studio portrait of a girl about five years old. The white lace of her collar set a stark contrast to the color of her skin, the same deep black of Prudence's and the older woman's. The girl's hair was plaited, white ribbons dangling from each side. None of the photos had dates. No one had written anything on the back. How could I piece together her life from this? The photo of Prudence could have been taken anywhere you could find an adze. Maybe they had them all over London. I'd never been there. For all I knew vast sections of London were full of brown walls and black women in headscarves.

"Where was she living?" asked Red Eye.

"I don't know," I replied, "but she was pretty well moved out of here. She never said a thing to me."

Red Eye lifted the plastic liner out of the waste basket.

"There's a card in here," he said, reaching down to pick it off the bottom.

Sam "Pearly" Gates, the card read. "Owner and proprietor" of the King and Queens. I knew the place—a not-so-sparkling club with dancing girls and topless waitresses in the little podunk town of Sunnyvale, near San Jose. Except for San Francisco, most cities in the Bay Area had banned adult clubs. Not Sunnyvale. It was the only reason anyone went there.

"I knew this cat Pearly back in the day," said Red Eye. "Dude looked like Sean Connery, hairy chest and all. Someone told me he was Connery's backup in one of those James Bond movies. *Goldfinger*, I think."

"I wonder if she was working there," I replied. "Do they do lap dancing?"

"Let's find out," said Red Eye. He dialed the number on the card. "Pearly" Gates was gone for the day. They were coy when he asked about the lap dancing.

"We can go by there with her picture," said Red Eye. "In the meantime there's this Mandy or Mandisa. Strange name, eh?"

I'd tried talking to managers at twenty-four-hour restaurants on more than one occasion. They liked to put lots of barriers between themselves and disgruntled customers. A complaint about a fly in the soup or a search for a job as a cook wasn't going to work. We needed a more elaborate scheme. But then elaborate schemes were our specialty. With a couple of bottles of Wild Turkey, Red Eye and I could hatch a scheme to sell boat tickets to Mars.

As we parted, Red Eye reached into his jacket pocket and pulled out something wrapped in a brown paper bag.

"You better keep this with you from now on," he said, handing me the parcel.

I could feel the automatic inside. I peeked. Walther 9 mm.

"Whoever got Prudence might be after you next," he said.

"Could be," I said, "just wish I knew why."

It had been almost a decade since I'd touched a gun. For an ex-con, just having this thing could get you five years. Any self-respecting square would have handed the piece back to Red Eye.

"Better to be caught with it than caught without it," he said. He was always full of convict wisdom, but he had a point. What was I supposed to do, count on Dr. Robson to come jogging to my rescue if Prudence's killer showed up?

I fingered the Walther and released the clip. He'd only put five rounds inside.

"You got any more ammo?" I asked. Though I didn't care for Walthers, it felt comfortable in my hand.

Red Eye brought out a box of hollow points and slid it into my jacket pocket. As soon as he left I decided to stash the Walther. I rolled back the rug at the foot of my bed, took off the piece of molding at the bottom of the wall, lifted out the floorboards, then groped for the bent coat hanger I used to lift the metal box that held a slough of fake papers and IDs and a little bit of dope. I might be living the square life but the underground wasn't that far away. Just as I hooked the box I realized what a stupid idea this was. What good would the Walther be hidden under the floor? I put everything back into place and opted for sleeping with it under my pillow—safety on, round in the chamber. The next morning I'd practice sighting on a target. Even in my shell-shocked state, I suspected my hand was still pretty steady. I always liked to think I was a good shot even though I'd never really fired a gun at anyone. It felt like my first chance was just around the corner.

CHAPTER 4

Zimbabwe, November 1985

Tarisai Mukombachoto had only one kilometer left to walk. It was still morning; that hot African sun hadn't started the sweat percolating through her skin. She walked alone today. Her twin brother, Garikai, was sick with some kind of stomach flu. She thought he was faking. He didn't want to go to school because the results from the grade seven exams had arrived from the Ministry of Education in the provincial capital of Mutare. That's why the walk felt so long for Tarisai, even though the sun wasn't yet burning bright. If she'd failed those exams, all chances of going to high school were gone.

Her bare feet slapped along the dirt path just as they had for seven years. She was confident she'd done well. After all, she'd been number one in her class since grade two. No one could top her, not even the teacher's nephew, who had the benefit of extra help from an educated uncle.

Tarisai's parents had only gone as far as grade three. Since they rarely used English, they'd forgotten most of what they'd learned. Occasionally when someone came from town with a newspaper she would see her father reading some of the articles. Sometimes he asked her the meaning of a word. He would always say what a clever daughter he had when she would tell him that "rapid" was the same as "fast" or that a "general anesthetic" was something the doctor used to knock you out when they removed parts from your body. Like almost everyone else at Kudzai School, Tarisai's parents were farmers. They worked the land day in, day out, just as their family had done for generations. When money ran short, they contracted to work for Mr. McGuinn, a white farmer who lived nearby. McGuinn was stingy but at least he paid in cash. Some farmers still paid workers with bags of mielie meal and packets of rotten meat.

The hope of Tarisai's parents, though, was that their two children would excel in school and eventually end up with good-paying jobs in town, jobs that would provide their parents with enough money so they wouldn't be plowing and weeding until the day they died.

As Tarisai came down the grass-covered hill toward the school, she wasn't thinking of her family's future. The only thing on her mind was that group of her classmates she could see gathered around the notice board outside the headmaster's office. They were waiting for the results to be pinned up.

As she walked past one of the goalposts on the grassless soccer field, she saw the headmaster come out of his office with a piece of paper in his hand. The students crowded around him, as excited as if he were handing out free ice cream cones.

"Boys and girls," she heard the headmaster say in his refined English, "please allow me space to pass so I can pin up your results." He repeated the words in the local Shona language, to make sure everyone understood.

The eager students moved back a step or two. They all wanted to be the first to see.

Tarisai started to run. She hated the thought that someone else would see her marks before she did. The headmaster stepped away from the board and caught sight of Tarisai striding full speed past the grade four classroom, her feet leaving a faint trail of dusty prints on the bright red cement walkway.

"Slow down, Tarisai," said the headmaster. "You know running is not allowed."

It took all the will power Tarisai possessed to reduce herself to a walk.

"And well done, Tarisai," he said. "You are the only pupil to score a 1 in both English and maths."

The buzz of the students went silent as they turned to look at Tarisai. Gladys, her best friend, galloped toward her and gave her a joyous hug. The headmaster smiled. The two girls skipped toward the board.

Tarisai's eyes ran down the list. First she saw Garikai Mukombachoto.

Her brother had gotten a 3 in maths and a 4 in English. Better than he expected. Tarisai had told him he must study harder.

Her results were there under her Christian name, Prudence Mukombachoto: 1 in English, 1 in maths, just like the headmaster said. She jumped up and down, clapping her hands. She never expected perfection.

Suddenly the headmaster was at her side.

"Congratulations, Tarisai," he said, adding a "makorokoto" the Shona word for such occasions. "With a mind like yours, you will go far in life. You may end up in the UK or America at one of their famous universities."

Tarisai had never traveled farther than Mutare, a little more than an hour's bus journey away. And she'd only gone there twice, to help her mother do some shopping.

The UK, America, these were places she'd never dreamt of going. She'd seen some photos of London once in a very tattered magazine. The buildings were old. Someone once told her it was also very cold there.

Tarisai stayed and chatted with her friends for a while. Everyone was excited for her.

"We always knew you would succeed," Gladys told her. "You got what you deserved."

After an hour Tarisai set off for home to give her parents the news. They would be so proud. No one from their village had ever gotten a 1 before.

CHAPTER 5

here were three Denny's and five IHOPs in the East Bay. I didn't want to think about the possibility that Mandisa worked farther away. These days some people travel a hundred miles to jobs. It's crazy. My first thought was to phone all the stores but it seemed awkward asking if the manager was a woman named Mandisa. If I did get her on the line, what would I say?

Instead, Red Eye and I prepared my paperwork as an official Denny's shopper, one of those fake customers employed by the company to go around and check up on the restaurant's service and smiles. I left the house just after midnight with a stack of business cards, evaluation forms, a handheld stopwatch, a clipboard and a letter from headquarters verifying the credentials of one Peter Clark, my new alias. I doubted if anyone used handheld stopwatches any more but it felt real official.

I started with Fruitvale Denny's, out near the freeway. I wasn't the least bit hungry but I ordered a stack of silver dollar pancakes. The waitress, a young, blonde collegiate type was tweaking. Even though only three tables were occupied, she couldn't stop wiping surfaces and putting coffee packs and sugar bowls in precise little rows. The pancakes weren't hot enough and were only about the size of a quarter. I felt short-changed. After I'd mopped up the last of the blueberry syrup, I motioned the waitress to the table. She slid the bill under my coffee saucer and started to move away.

"Excuse me," I said, "is there a night manager I could speak to?"

"Was there something wrong, sir?" she asked. "I can bring more pancakes if you want. No charge. Just don't say anything to him. I've already had a warning."

"No, nothing wrong at all. I'm actually a shopper employed by head office. I just reviewed your performance and I wanted to tell the manager how excellent everything was."

I showed her my stopwatch and the evaluation form attached to the clipboard. Not a computer but she looked impressed. I invited her to glance at the all the check marks in the "excellent" column.

"You only faltered in not removing all the extra side plates," I told her. "Minor, but something to work on."

"That's great," she said reaching over to wipe the table one more time. "I need something to go right in my life. I flunked my geology midterm today. All I need now is to lose my job."

She sped off to the kitchen and came back with a middle-aged white guy in a cheap white shirt and an even cheaper blue tie. His tie clasp had a "D" inside a pancake, an icon for Denny's I guess.

I stood up as he approached.

"Hello, sir," I said. "I'm Peter Clark with Quali-Serv Associates. I'm a shopper contracted by your company. I wanted to inform you that everything was excellent. I'm not supposed to reveal my work, but when performance is outstanding, I believe it merits recognition, instant recognition."

I paused to scrutinize my stopwatch.

"Your waitress was here within forty-five seconds of my sitting down. The food arrived three minutes and thirty-seven seconds after order completion. And your waitress," I added, stealing a glance at her name tag, "Charlene, never stopped cleaning and prepping. She's fabulous."

"Thank you, Mr. Clark," he replied. Two decades ago he might have been a high school football star. Lots of pancakes and more than a few beers had intervened since then. He blushed a little with my praise, as if I was a cheerleader admiring his biceps.

"Are you the regular night manager?" I asked

"Yes, sir, five nights a week. Sometimes six. I'm Dave Johnston. That's with a 't,' not Johnson."

"Another night manger works on your off days?"

"The other guy works two days a week but I have to fill in when he's sick. He gets migraines, at least that's what he says. I don't know. Doesn't exactly love to work, if you know what I mean."

"Got you. People are different these days."

The fast food business must be vicious. After talking to this guy for three minutes he was already backstabbing another manager. Johnston-with-a-t wouldn't last five minutes in prison. But then to me, working all night at Denny's five shifts a week was a form of self-incarceration. I flipped through some sheets on my clipboard.

"My brief says there was a woman manager here." I looked both ways. "A colored girl, if I'm not mistaken. One of those affirmative action things."

"We've never had a black manager here," he said, "at least not during my five years."

"What about the other Denny's in the East Bay?" I asked. "The company insisted I review her performance. Apparently there were some problems. Top priority. I can't get anyone at the office at this hour to verify which store she's at."

If Johnston-with-a-t would bad-mouth his relief manager, I figured he'd love to help me grind down a black female competitor. I can smell a hater. After Prudence, all that racial stuff seemed more twisted. For the sake of solving her murder, though, I'd play on Johnston-with-a-t's prejudice. No harm in that.

"I don't know about the other stores," he said. "I've never been there."

"Do you think you could do me a favor and call a couple of them? I don't want to look like a fool."

"Sure, I can phone around and find out," he replied. "Come on back to my office."

His office was slightly larger than a broom closet. There wasn't a single piece of paper in his "in" or "out" tray. His desk was so small he had to keep the white computer tower on the floor. The screen and keyboard took up all the space on top.

He leaned back in his typing chair, lacing his hands behind his head, looking up like he was a CEO with a corner office. Feeding frustrated egos is a con man's bread and butter.

He dialed the phone ceremoniously, then asked for the night manager. His voice had dropped a few notches. He forgot to identify himself. He gave me a wink as he waited for the call to go through. I could hear Springsteen's "I'm on Fire" playing out of the receiver. At least Denny's didn't make people wait while listening to Barry Manilow.

After three minutes someone came on the line and told him the night manager was busy.

"By the way," added Johnston-with-a-t, "could you tell me his name?"

"Oh, I'm sorry," he said, "I didn't mean it like that. Is she, uh, dark in complexion?" he asked giving me another wink.

"I'm sorry, ma'am," he said, "I meant no offense. I just met a manager from Denny's at one of our management training sessions. She was, uh, Afro-American. I wanted to see if it was the same person."

Johnston-with-a-t listened to half a minute's sermon on racial terminology. At the end he rolled his eyes, thanked the woman on the other end and hung up.

"J-e-e-sus," he said, "touchy, touchy, fuckin' touchy. Always think there's a plot against them. Get over it, honey."

"Thanks very much for your trouble," I said. "I gather the manager there wasn't a black woman."

"No trouble at all. I can phone a couple of other stores if you want. I'm on a roll."

If this was a "roll" for him, I'd hate to see what a bad day looked like.

"If it wouldn't be too much inconvenience," I said. "I know you're a busy man."

Johnston picked up the phone and went through the same routine three more times. Though he managed to say "Afro-American" instead of "dark in complexion," none of the stores had a black woman night manger. Time to try IHOP.

I thanked Johnston for his assistance and shook his hand. He prolonged our grip, as if we'd traveled a long journey together.

"I'll be sure you get an excellent recommendation," I said, "five stars not only for food and service but for the night manager's helpful attitude."

"It comes with the territory," he said, loosening his hold on my hand and regearing for another all-nighter of order forms and sales reports.

All my paperwork said I was a shopper for Denny's. I'd have to redo everything for IHOP. I didn't want to stagger in cold and take a chance. Besides, it was nearly 3:00 a.m. and the nearest IHOP was eight miles of the Oakland flatlands away. When you're an ex-felon nothing good can come from driving late at night in those neighborhoods. The police may pull you over for the slightest infraction. Then they run your license and they're all over you like maple on syrup. I headed for the cop-free hills where I could sleep without sirens and gunfire. The noble residents of the hills viewed ex-felons as the invading enemy, not part of the natural landscape. As long as I didn't run into Carter or the Weasel, I could keep to my blending in act.

At least my sojourn with Johnston and his t had taken my mind off my problems for a few minutes. There's always excitement in running an effective con, no matter how small. And now, for the first time in my life, I was doing it for a good cause. I'd be off to IHOP the following night. In the meantime, Red Eye and I would pay a visit to Pearly Gates.

CHAPTER 6

Redeye and I showed up at the King and Queens just after lunch. They were holding tryouts for pole dancers. About a dozen parking meter thin blondes and a couple of Mexicans were eagerly lined up in skimpy outfits preparing to show their stuff. Normally I would have enjoyed the display but we were there on business.

The bartender was a big huge Samoan-looking guy whose King and Queens golf shirt had "Fetu" embroidered on it. He said everyone called him Fast Freddy.

"I'm looking for Prudence," I said, putting on my best English accent. I pulled out the picture from Robson's party and showed it to him.

"We grew up together in East London," I added. "She told me she was working here and that I should pop in sometime."

"She's one of our favorites," Fast Freddy said. "I'll find out if she's in."

"She said a guy named Pearly would knew where she was," I told him.

Fast Freddy got on the phone and said something in a language I didn't recognize. A few seconds later an offensive-tackle-sized Samoan wearing sunglasses and a Raider Nation T-shirt came out from what looked like the kitchen.

"G here will show you back to Pearly's office," Fast Freddy told us. "Just follow him."

G didn't say a word, just shook our hands and led us back through a dark hallway into a windowless office decorated with three oil paintings of someone who I assumed to be Pearly Gates about twenty years earlier. The man liked mustaches and gold jewelry.

"Just wait here," G said, "Pearly will be with you in a minute." G closed the door behind him, then I heard a key turn to lock us in.

"I should have packed some heat," said Red Eye.

I nodded as I weighed up our chances against G and Fast Freddy. About the same as mine against George Foreman in his prime. I looked around for a way out. Unless there were secret panels or tunnels behind those portraits of Pearly Gates, we weren't going anywhere.

"Just let me do the talking," I said.

"Wish I had a cell phone," Red Eye replied.

"You'd need a hotline to God to get us out of this one."

The key turned in the door. Sure enough G had returned with Fast Freddy. Before I could get a word in edgewise, G had me by the shirt collar and up against the wall, my feet about three inches off the ground. Fast Freddy had an automatic pointed at Red Eye's head.

"Okay, who the hell are you guys?" G asked.

"Just a couple of ex-cons trying to solve a murder," said Red Eye.

Fast Freddy was sizing up the ink on Red Eye's arms.

"This motherfucker has an NLR tattoo," said Freddy, "Nazi Low Rider punk bitch. I oughta do him now."

"Stands for 'no longer racist,'" said Red Eye. "I got the whole thing written out on my back."

"You better not be bullshitting me," said Fast Freddy.

I was keeping my mouth shut, trying to figure out if it was time to ditch the English accent. I knew Red Eye had the Harley Davidson logo and a bunch of naked women on his back. I wasn't sure about the "no longer racist" stuff.

Suddenly a guy I figured was Pearly Gates stood in the doorway, sniffling like he'd just hit about three lines of coke. He hadn't held onto much of the movie star good looks in the portraits. Dope and aging aren't kind to lowlifes. Still, a pinstriped suit, white straw hat, and a blazing diamond ring on each hand kept up a bit of the façade. Something close to the truth in an American accent was looking like our only way out.

"We're friends of Prudence's," I said. "She's dead. No one came to claim the body and she left your business card in her room. We're trying to find her family to notify them."

"Slow down there, Bud," said Pearly, "what happened to her?"

"Not sure," I said, "she just turned up dead."

"So you come stumbling into my place like I had something to do with it," said Pearly, "disturbing my business. You think we go around killing young girls?"

"If we did, we wouldn't have come in here asking politely," said Red Eye.

"We supposed to be grateful?" said Pearly. Freddy pulled the hammer back on the automatic.

"Let me do him, boss," said Freddy. G pulled a little tighter on my collar. I gagged a couple times then managed to catch my breath.

"Hold on, hold on," said Pearly, "let's back up here. I got no idea who these fools are but a young girl we all knew may be dead. We need to respect that, hear them out. They seem like they're doing the right thing by her, though it feels all wrong."

Pearly stepped toward me and put his nose about three inches from my face.

"Talk to us like you're trying to save your life," he told me.

"Can you get this gentleman to ease off?" I asked Pearly. G let me slide down the wall and moved his hand down to the middle of my chest. I couldn't move but the breathing was getting easier.

I quickly weighed up what version of the story would save our ass. I always figured I could talk my way out of anything, Red Eye had other specialties. None of it looked like it was going to give us the upper hand, especially if any of these guys actually had something to do with Prudence's death. If they did, our warrants of execution were already signed.

"Okay, okay. Here's the whole story," I said, the sweat starting to pour down my cheeks. "Prudence was my wife. Arranged marriage. I came home found her face up in the swimming pool. She couldn't swim. I figure someone pushed her in, maybe drugged her first. I don't like people disrespecting my property like that. And she was a nice girl. Well, maybe not exactly nice but special. Whoever did this is scum." I could feel that gigantic hand on my chest sag.

"That girl was a real queen," G whispered. A solitary tear trailed out from behind his sunglasses and down his cheek.

"That bit about no one coming to claim the body and us trying to find her family is true," said Red Eye.

"You got a swimming pool?" asked Pearly.

"Yeah, kidney-shaped," I said.

Pearly waved Freddy and G off and went back to standing in the doorway.

"No one could make up a story that crazy," he said, "and no one but a couple of ex-cons could do something as stupid as show up here asking questions. What'd you guys do, get out of the pen last week? Not even a dumbass cop would do that shit."

Freddy laughed and put away the automatic. G took his hand off my chest and wiped the tear away on the sleeve of his T-shirt.

"You guys take the fuckin' cake," said Pearly. He adjusted his hat, as if the perfect angle would make him look like a high-steppin' twenty-year-old again.

"Bring me a bottle of Jameson and three glasses," Pearly said to Freddy. The two gigantic Samoans lumbered out the door. Suddenly there was room to breathe.

"I'm sorry to hear about Prudence," said Pearly in a tone that gave away nothing. His wheels were still turning but at least we'd live to see another day.

"She worked here for a few months," he added, "then she just disappeared. It happens in this business."

He parked himself in a high-back leather chair behind a dark wooden desk. "She was what we call 'Queen for the Day,' a hostess really. Showed people to their seats, encouraged them to buy drinks. We called her Deirdre sometimes. She said that was her official name. Everyone loved her accent."

Freddy showed up with the Jameson and poured us each a double. Red Eye and I downed ours in one hit. Pearly swirled his around in the glass.

"Is that all she did?" I asked.

"One night we got to talking, just the two of us. She told me she did some accounting work in England. I could tell she knew her stuff. Smart and beautiful. What a combination. I told her we might give her a shot in the office. She seemed real excited. Too bad she never got the chance."

Pearly wasn't the kind of man who gave a young woman a chance for nothing. I didn't want to think about it. His hands were a mass of wrinkles and bumps.

"Were there any men she met at the clubs that she saw, you know, socially?" asked Red Eye.

"You mean was she bangin' any of the customers?" asked Pearly.

"Yeah, that," said Red Eye. He gave me a pitying look. Someone had to ask that question and it wasn't going to be me.

"Not that I know of," said Pearly, "but these girls make their own arrangements. I don't want to know. I'm not a pimp. I'm a club owner. Legit entrepreneur." He smiled. His teeth were a disaster area, even the gold front tooth didn't gleam.

"We respect that," I said.

"So I apologize for the not-so-cordial welcome," said Pearly. "These days you don't know who to trust."

"No problem," said Red Eye gazing longingly at the Jameson. Pearly picked up the bottle and handed it over.

"Maybe you should talk to some of the girls. They'd know more than me," said Pearly. "A lot of pervs come through this place."

He got up and headed for the door.

"I'll bring a couple of them here," he said, "but let me bow out." He looked at his watch. "The girls might not want to say certain things if I hang around and I want to see you get whoever did this. I ain't no saint but I draw the line at killing young girls."

"We appreciate that," said Red Eye.

Two tall, thin white women arrived about five minutes and two more shots of whiskey later. Linda was bleached blonde with extraordinary pink false fingernails, doused with silver glitter. She wore a shiny blue vinyl coat and looked like she spent a lot of hours in tanning parlors, maybe as much time as she spent chasing after crank. The drug hadn't started its full assault on her good looks yet, but it wouldn't be long. Darlene by contrast was wood glue white. She was top-heavy and showed it off with a bare midriff and a see-through blouse with no bra. I wasn't sure if this was part of her performing clothes or if she dared to dress like that on the street. I'd already lived in the hills too long to judge. Her nipples were bigger around than Denny's silver dollar pancakes.

I didn't know what Pearly had told them so I just said Prudence drowned in the pool at my house and we didn't think she fell in.

"I don't let things like that happen on my property without a reply."

To my surprise, Darlene wept solemnly when she heard the news. She dabbed her eyes with a crumpled-up Kleenex.

"You call the cops?" asked Linda.

"Yeah, but they're not interested," said Red Eye. "Besides, we don't care much for the man."

"We never heard a black girl talk like that," Linda said, "that English accent, always saying 'bloody' this, 'flippin' that. Kept callin' 7-Up lemonade. She was a peach."

"She was," said Red Eye.

I couldn't bring myself to speak. Darlene's pained sighs had me reeling, fighting to keep my own eyes dry. I don't let go in public.

"Did either of you know any of Prudence's friends?" Red Eye asked.

"You mean friends or the pond scum types from the club?" asked Linda.

"Either one."

"There was this one African girl who picked her up a couple of times. Can't remember her name. Real square."

"Mandy," said Darlene, "her name was Mandy."

"I thought maybe they had something going on," said Linda, "if you get what I mean. It's not for me but some of the girls, you know. Who am I to judge?"

"It wasn't like that," said Darlene. "They were just friends, came from the same place."

"Where was that?" I asked.

"England," said Linda. "She never talked much about her past but she was from London. You could tell by the accent."

"Uh-uh," Darlene interjected. "She came from Africa. She once told me the whole English thing was an act. She said something to me in African. Sounded funny."

"That's all she told you?" asked Red Eye.

"Said her family had a lot of problems, that life was hard in her country, that Americans wouldn't understand."

"My life ain't been no picnic," said Linda, "my Daddy was slammin' it to me when I was in junior high."

"Please," said Darlene, "the girl is dead."

"You ever see her with any men?" asked Red Eye.

"I saw her drive away with this white guy once. Business type. Drove a Lexus or a Beamer. I'm not good on cars," said Linda.

"Ever see him again?" asked Red Eye.

"I can't remember," said Linda with a not so subtle grin. Her business sense had taken over from her grief. She'd already given up too much for free. I opened my wallet and laid fifty dollars on the table.

"Maybe this will lubricate your memories," I said.

Linda looked at Darlene, then picked up the Grant and stuffed it inside her bra.

"It was a Beamer, E36," said Linda. "You know, the one with the six-speed tranny."

"Those are badass," said Red Eye. He offered Linda a shot of Jameson but she declined, claiming she was a Glenlivet girl.

"Prudence told me she was pulling some white guy's chain," said Darlene. "He had big bucks. A banker or something. Handsome guy with a wife and kids. The usual."

She tossed the crumpled up tissue in the waste basket.

"Any other girls who work here know anything?" Red Eye asked.

"Don't think so," said Linda. "Darlene talked to her the most. Darlene's got two black babies. Different fathers."

"Oh yeah," said Darlene, "I think she was married. One of those arranged deals. Said her husband was a lowlife but had a big house in Oakland with a swimming pool." She paused for a second. I could hear the wheels turning.

"You must be the husband," Linda said. "Goddamned Darlene can't keep her mouth shut for nothing."

Darlene added a blushing apology while I tried to laugh it off.

"Don't worry about it," I said. "This isn't about love. Some lame has disrespected my property. The rest doesn't matter."

Red Eye and I stood up to leave. I thanked the two girls. Linda grabbed the bottle of Jameson and tucked it into the inside pocket of her jacket.

"You gonna have a funeral or something?" asked Darlene.

"Don't know yet. We'll get ahold of you if we do," I said.

"I'd appreciate that," said Darlene. She pulled another Kleenex from

38

her purse and dabbed at eyes that were now very dry. To them, we were looking more and more like just another pair of tricks.

We shook their hands and waited for Pearly to come back. A couple minutes later Fast Freddy came in and told us Pearly had to tend to some business.

"He said he'd let you know if he heard anything else. Me and G are down for whatever. We loved that girl. Everyone here did."

"Thank Pearly for us," I said. "We'll be in touch."

"I saw her drivin' away one night with a guy in a white car," he said.

"You get a look at him?" asked Red Eye.

"I did but . . ." Fred's face went blank, "it was dark."

I'd already forked out fifty bucks for one set of two-bit memories. I didn't feel like a repeat performance.

"Let's get out of here," I said. Red Eye and I headed for the front door.

We got outside and just stood on the sidewalk contemplating the next step. We hadn't realized just how stuffy that little office of Pearly Gates's was. Freddy came out the door.

"Jeffcoat," he said, "the guy's name was Jeffcoat. Prudence called him 'Mr. Moneybags' but warned me away from him. Said he had a 'dark side.' That's all I know. Hell, we all got dark sides."

I pulled out a twenty.

"Keep it," he said, "just send me an invite to Jeffcoat's funeral."

"Will do," said Red Eye.

"And one more thing," Freddy said to me.

"What's that?"

"Lose that English accent of yours. Sounds like shit."

"Appreciate the feedback," I said.

Red Eye and I got in the car.

"Okay, level with me," I said. "You got 'no longer racist' tattooed on your back?"

He turned his back toward me and started to pull up his shirt, then stopped.

"Hell no, but I thought about doin' it once. This one white dude at Folsom had it done. The Skinheads kicked his ass."

"You're a dumb motherfucker."

"It worked, didn't it? Nobody wants to look at my hairy-ass back."

I started the Volvo and we headed back to Oakland only a little worse for the wear. I'd probably end up having a nightmare or two that involved a big Samoan guy's hands around my throat, but for the moment, my mind drifted back to Prudence.

I'd never dreamed she was running around with the likes of Pearly Gates, Fast Freddy, and big-breasted Darlene. Only a surgeon could have produced boobs like that.

My wife must have been desperate for money or cheap thrills or both. I imagined Pearly had skinny little legs with no hair left. Probably kept his suit coat on in bed. I didn't want to think about it. Maybe she was knockin' boots with G too. The thing I couldn't really understand though was how she could have called me a lowlife when I lived in Carltonville? If she hadn't been killed on my property I wouldn't even have bothered to keep this thing going. But Red Eye was right, this was about respect. I had to get to the bottom of this, for my own peace of mind as a man.

CHAPTER 7

he IHOP was on what I knew as E. Fourteenth Street when I was growing up. Sometime in the 1990s they'd changed the name to International Boulevard since so many different people had moved in—Mexicans, Asians, Islanders. Arabs owned most of the stores. In my day, blacks and whites ran the show. Some blacks were still around but there weren't many whites left. They'd fled to Hayward, Dublin, and suburban points beyond. As I cruised past E. Twentieth Avenue, I realized a white guy in a Volvo would stick out like ten sore thumbs. I should have rented a Taurus, something that would blend in. International wasn't the spot for a refined Swedish sedan, even if it did have dual exhaust. Plus, I was carrying a full set of fake IDs. At least I decided to be careful this time and stash the papers for Peter Clark inside the driver's side door panel. Peter was now a fully accredited shopper for the International House of Pancakes.

The usual selection of drug dealers, streetwalkers, and thrill seekers was going about their business. About two blocks from the IHOP a balding white man in a shiny new Buick was negotiating with a young black person in high heels and a fake fur coat. Some things never change. Not that I gave a shit, but I hoped he didn't think he was buying a woman.

The IHOP parking lot was sparsely populated which suited me just fine. I wasn't looking for a crowd or scratches in my fenders.

All three waitresses on duty fit my image of Mandisa. I figured she was a large, dark-skinned woman even though no one had ever described her to me. African women were either starving like the famine in Ethiopia or plump and spry. Prudence fit neither of those types though. If she was African, she was special.

The three women were talking at the register as I entered. Though

I'd dressed casually, my golf shirt and slacks didn't blend in with the more bling-oriented clientele. I caught two nametags as I walked past the waitresses: Ginger and Fontella. I eavesdropped on their conversation, hoping to catch a hint of their accent. These women sounded as American as Queen Latifah.

I found an empty booth and ordered silver dollar pancakes. If I was going to be a shopper, might as well compare them with Denny's. The IHOP had a slightly larger concept of the size of a silver dollar. I appreciated the selection of syrups. I spread the pancakes in a circle, placing a smidgen of syrup of a different flavor on each one. I liked the raspberry the best. I liked it so much I asked Fontella if I could buy a bottle to take home. She promised to bring it with the bill.

"It'll be $2.95," she said.

As Fontella ran my bill through the register a short, plain-looking woman walked over to where the waitresses gathered. She was light-skinned with her hair pulled back into some kind of ponytail. I guessed black women called them ponytails too. I didn't know. She wore a brown suit. Had to be the manager. Except for a little red streak in her hair, she definitely fit Darlene's idea of a square.

I tried to catch her voice but I always had a hard time hearing clearly if I wasn't looking at the person speaking. I knew enough about after-hours race dynamics not to stare at these women too long. White man accused of gawking at black women was troubled territory where I didn't want to venture.

My manager lady was talking to Ginger about her shifts for the rest of the week. I heard her say schedule just like Prudence used to do—without the "k" sound—"shed-yule." I had my woman. Now I had to find a way to talk to her. I could go through my Peter Clark routine but maybe there was a shortcut. Fontella was busy wrapping up my bottle of raspberry syrup. I'd probably end up giving it to Luisa. These things never tasted as good when I got them home.

The manager abandoned Ginger and started walking my way. I stood up as she got near my booth. Ginger did a double take as if my standing up had an ulterior motive. Her eyes homed in on me. She was ready to pounce if I turned out to be some kind of predator. Too many of them around these days.

The manager stopped a couple of steps away.

"I hope you're enjoying your food, sir," she said. The accent was different from Prudence's, neither American or English. Her nametag said, "Ms. Jack, Manager." Jack didn't sound African, didn't sound like a last name at all. Could it be short for Jackson?

"I'm fine," I said, sitting back down, "but could I ask you a question?"

If she was a manager, she couldn't say no. The customer is always right.

"Certainly, sir," she replied, lacing her fingers together at her waist like a dutiful daughter.

"I hope it doesn't sound like I'm prying," I said, "but is your first name by any chance Mandy?"

Her eyes darted left, then right. She looked confused.

"As you can see, my name is Ms. Jack," she said, pointing to the white tag on her suit coat, "but why are you so curious about my name, sir?"

"A lady friend of mine named Prudence said she knew someone named Mandy who was a manager at IHOP. It's important that I talk to her."

Fontella was approaching with my bill and the bright blue bag containing my syrup. She looked annoyed.

"Is everything all right, sir?" Fontella asked.

"The gentleman is doing fine, Fontella," Ms. Jack said. "He's complimenting your service. Please bring us a comment card. There aren't any in the booth."

A smiling Fontella walked back to the register to find the comment cards.

"How is Prudence?" Ms. Jack asked. "I haven't seen her for some time. She used to come by often. I was a little bit worried."

"I'm afraid she's not too well," I said, not knowing the next step. If I told her the truth, she might turn hysterical, even attack the messenger. If I tried to make an arrangement to see her later, she might doubt my motives. Predators come up with all kinds of funny stories.

"Please visit me in my office when you've finished eating," she said. "I want to hear the news. I'll ask Fontella to take you back there."

"Thank you," I said. The woman was a mind reader.

I stared at the three remaining pancakes: blueberry, banana, and peach. None of the flavors would solve the problem of how to break the news.

I put the three pancakes into a stack and attacked them in one gigantic bite. Blending three syrups together doesn't create a new, exciting flavor. I was glad I bought the raspberry.

As I chewed I visualized the scenario in Ms. Jack's office. How much did she know about Prudence? Maybe they weren't even good friends. It might not even bother this Ms. Jack that my wife was dead. I washed down my apprehension with another cup of coffee. I wouldn't sleep a wink with all that caffeine, but then ever since Prudence died, I wasn't sleeping anyway. Every time I closed my eyes, I saw that hollowed-out corpse from the bathroom staring at me. Wild Turkey helped blur the image but didn't make it go away. I was thinking of sleeping pills but I didn't want to get hooked. My Wild Turkey addiction was enough.

Ms. Jack's office was more substantial than Johnston-with-a-t's. She even had a small green sofa opposite her desk. I sat on one end. She got up from her desk and parked on the arm at the other end.

"I'm Mandisa Jack," she said, extending a hand over the cushions. She paid lots of attention to her silver nails, not so much to her hastily arranged straight hair.

"Calvin Winter," I replied. "I'm sorry to be the bearer of bad news." She looked away but didn't respond.

"I'm not sure how well you know Prudence," I said, carefully avoiding the past tense, "but she speaks of you often." A small but necessary lie. She'd only mentioned "Mandy" to me once. I tried to think of more positive things to say to soften the coming blow. I drew a blank.

"Prudence drowned in my swimming pool last Thursday," I said. "I found her lying in the pool face up. I tried to revive her but it was too late. She was my wife."

"So she's gone?"

"Yes."

"Nkosi yam. My God." Her hands went over her face. I heard her whispering a short prayer. I couldn't tell if it was English or not. After a minute she took her hands down, kissed her fingers and made the sign of the cross.

"How did she end up in the pool?" asked Mandisa. "She couldn't swim. We once went shopping for swimming costumes and we laughed as we tried them on. Neither of us could swim."

"Still trying to find out. The police came by but they didn't do much. No autopsy or anything. I have my suspicions. Like you said, she couldn't swim."

Mandisa went quiet. It was a lot to take in.

"Has there been a funeral?" she asked. "What about the body?"

"We're planning a small service."

"I would like to be there."

"Definitely. As to the body, I'm not sure. Cremation I guess."

"Oh no," said Mandisa, "we don't do that in Africa."

"She told me she was from London."

Her hands slipped back over her face. Now she was crying. I needed more information from her but sometimes silence is the only way to communicate. I didn't know her well enough to offer a hug. Maybe Africans don't hug. Prudence didn't, at least not much. But then I still wasn't exactly sure where she came from.

Someone knocked on the window. Fontella's face pressed against the glass as she tried to see inside. She was chewing a big wad of gum.

"Just a minute," said Mandisa, "we're almost finished here."

"I brought the comment cards," said Fontella, sliding a stack of about five under the door. "I've got a party of four on 5B. Drunken assholes."

"Thank you," Mandisa replied.

"I must get back to work," she told me, wiping her cheeks with her hands. "I need to clean up a little."

"Do you know anything about her family," I asked, "like how we can contact them?"

"We met here in Oakland. Single African women are few here. I will miss her. She had problems though."

"So she wasn't from London?"

"Never. She was from Zimbabwe. Have you heard of it?"

"Not really."

"It's a small country just next to South Africa, where I come from."

"Can you inform the family?" I asked.

"I don't know them at all." She stood up, trying to resume her composure. Even with her face soaked in tears, she looked much more the manager than Johnston-with-a-t.

"Ring me when you know about the funeral," she said. "We can talk more then. Thank you for informing me. I'm sorry, sir. But please, no cremation."

"I'll think about that," I said. I thanked her and we shook hands again. The moment was gone.

The room filled with the smell of pancakes and bacon as she opened the door. I put the blue bag in my pocket and walked out. I was home in twenty minutes. The next day, I'd go to a bookstore and buy a world atlas. I had to find out where the hell this Zimbabwe was.

CHAPTER 8

We had a small service for Prudence at the Medley Funeral Home in North Oakland. I paid for everything, not that the Medley was the Hyatt Regency of the funeral world. They did spruce up their dismal little storefront chapel with Easter Lilies, Chrysanthemums, and a few roses, all on my nickel. I opted for a closed casket, gray with black trim, a dignified departure. Though a cemetery burial would cost an extra $200, I followed Mandisa's advice. If Prudence was an African, I didn't want evil spirits chasing after me because I opted for cremation.

Red Eye came for the service, along with Pearly, G, Linda, Darlene, and several other girls from the King and Queens. Mandisa wore the appropriate black, including a broad-brimmed hat with a veil. Darlene and Linda made vain attempts at propriety. Darlene's black jacket strategically covered her white chiffon blouse. She'd even included a bra in her outfit. Only the stiletto platform sandals and the three gold toe rings gave her away. Linda also managed some black, a tight-fitting fake mohair sweater with an enormous gold cross pendant hanging down in front. Her mother probably gave that cross to her twenty years ago.

The Reverend P. Stokes led the service. He came with Medley's "Deluxe Burial Package." "The Reverend always has the right words to honor your loved one," the brochure said.

"Everything happens for a reason," the Reverend told us. "One day we will all be together with Mrs. Winter and our maker."

I'd never heard anyone call Prudence "Mrs. Winter." I wasn't sure what to make of it. I doubt that's how Prudence would have wanted to be remembered.

The Reverend continued. His hands had a little tremor, either early Parkinson's or he needed a drink. I bet on the latter.

He reminded us that eternal happiness awaited if we stayed on the "path of righteousness." I heard a snicker from one of the girls. The Reverend took off his glasses and surveyed the group. He couldn't detect the guilty party. The multiple layers of grease on his hair did nothing to slicken the remainder of his eulogy. I decided to try to avoid him once it was over. I knew he'd have a funny smell.

As he turned over the last page of his yellowed script, he peeked at his watch.

"Does anyone want to say anything on behalf of the deceased?" the Reverend asked.

I had lots to say but standing in front of people and baring my soul wasn't my style. Besides, after three sleepless nights in a row I wasn't sure I could make sense. I'd just talk to Red Eye later, when there wasn't a game on the TV.

"We'd like to sing a song," said Linda. She and Darlene scooted past Pearly and took their place in front of the coffin. Now I could see Linda's micro miniskirt. At least she'd worn dark tights. Neither had spared the mascara or eyeliner to rise to the occasion.

Darlene snapped her fingers to warm them up.

"Prudence told me once that this was her favorite song by the Beatles," said Linda. "We dedicate it to her memory."

Linda counted the first beats under her breath, then started her attempt at singing lead. She had the volume but Darlene's harmony overwhelmed her. Their version of "Let It Be" wasn't John and Paul or even Ray Charles, but it brought tears from my eyes for the first time in eleven years. That's how long ago Blanda, my prize bulldog, got run over by some drunken 49er fan. I thought I saw Red Eye rubbing his nose during the girls' final chorus. I hoped Prudence would find her Mother Mary, whoever she may be.

After the service I saw Mandisa shaking Darlene's hand.

"You have a lovely voice," Mandisa told the suddenly gangly-looking Darlene. Linda moved in to take over the conversation. I beat a retreat for some solitude. I didn't want anyone asking me about the redness in my eyes and I definitely didn't want Reverend Stokes to corner me. If he wasn't preaching to me about the glory of God, I had a feeling he'd be asking me to line him up with Darlene or Linda.

As I walked toward my car, Mandisa called me back.

"Thanks for inviting me," she said. "We had to do something for her. Dying so far from home is difficult."

"I guess so," I said. I'd never given the location of my death much thought. My string of foster parents and my counselors at juvie never talked to me about old age. When you're "state-raised," you take it as it comes. As long as I didn't die in prison, anywhere was all right with me.

"At home hundreds of people would come to bury someone like Prudence," Mandisa told me, "so young, so clever, so beautiful."

"We did the best we could, and no cremation."

"You are to be commended. I'd love to see the tombstone." I didn't bother to tell her we hadn't ordered a stone. The funeral was as far as a lowlife husband could go.

Mandisa paused for a second, gazing at the passing traffic. No one's death stopped the street life of Oakland. I should have done more for Prudence than the Medley and that pathetic excuse for a preacher. A funeral isn't something where you can promise to do better next time. You only get one shot.

"I have some things of Prudence's," said Mandisa. "Maybe you need to see them. After all, legally you are her husband. I don't think she had a will."

"If they can help me get an idea of how this happened, I'd like to come and take a look."

"Come by tomorrow morning," she said. "I won't touch a thing until you get there. I'll do what I can to help. Like I said, single African women here are few."

She reached into her black leather handbag and found a tiny spiral notebook. She wrote her address on one of the pages, tore it out, and passed it to me.

"You can come about ten, if that's convenient," she said.

"I'll be there," I promised.

Red Eye was waiting for me in the Volvo. I asked him to drive. I wasn't in the mood.

"They're cremating the body now," he said. "I couldn't stay for that part."

"What? I told them no cremation. That it wasn't African."

"Maybe I got it wrong," said Red Eye, "but that Minister told me they'd already slid the body into the whaddyacallit, the oven I guess."

I tore out of the car and ran back to the storefront. As I got to the door, I stopped. I couldn't face it. I'd already had to play around with her body once. I couldn't do it again. What if they pulled it out half-baked? Then what? I turned around and headed back to the car.

"Let's go to my place for a drink," I said. Red Eye pulled the car out into the traffic. He didn't ask me at all about the cremation. He needed that drink as bad as I did.

Why hadn't I done better for Prudence? She was the only one of my wives who left me with at least a few fond memories, a lot better than Jenny, my number two. She left a three-inch gash in my neck when she stabbed me with a kitchen knife. We had a few irreconcilable differences. Marriage and Calvin Winter just didn't mix. I was beginning to think seriously about that tombstone.

CHAPTER 9

andisa's apartment was in Alameda, a quiet town just North of Berkeley. She lived in one of those areas where apartment buildings seemed to clone themselves, then sprout variations in paint, landscaping, and shingle color. Her building was three stories in yellow stucco, sheltered by a few trees. She lived on the third floor, in the front.

Her kitchen looked like a closeout sale at Circuit City. Two microwaves, three food processors, rows of blenders and juicers. The sandy-colored carpet in the living room supported enough sofas and chairs to accommodate at least twenty people if they could squeeze between the furniture to reach their seats. Maybe her church held Sunday services there. More welcoming ones than the Medley.

"Prudence used the second bedroom," she told me. "She paid me $200 a month."

"You've got a lot of furniture," I said.

"Some of it belonged to her. I don't know what to do with it."

"Just keep it," I said. "But where the hell did it all come from?"

"Prudence had a lot of funny connections. I think one of them owned a furniture store. I never asked."

It was mostly dralon stuff. Not my cup of tea. Some men have funny ways of expressing their affection.

"Do you want to look around the bedroom?" she asked. "I still haven't been in there."

"Let's go," I replied, though I had mixed emotions about finding out more of Prudence's "other life."

Mandisa went straight to the clothes closet, which she opened with a key. Episodes of my times with Prudence dangled from the hangers.

Every slinky top, her black leather jacket, and the white Fila hi-tops with the red laces were all there. Why had she left my house without saying a word? How did I miss it? I was supposed to be the con man. I opened the drawer of the nightstand. The biggest object was a cube, which held more pictures of the old woman and the girl whose photos I'd found under the mattress at my house. There was also a wedding party picture, taken somewhere in a park. A slightly younger, slightly less shapely Prudence was a bridesmaid in passionate pink. Her smile was innocent, a look I'd never seen.

"Who are these people?" I asked as I moved toward the closet with the cube in my hand. Mandisa was loading the clothes into black garbage bags. I handed her the cube.

"That's her mother," said Mandisa, pointing to the older woman. "The young girl is Prudence's daughter. It's her sister's wedding."

I never knew Prudence had a daughter. If truth be told, I didn't know much about her at all. But then some real husbands and wives don't know much about each other either. I never knew wife number two could slice someone in the neck while they slept. I was lucky to live through that one, though the memory didn't help me sleep soundly.

"Where does the daughter live?"

"Somewhere at home with relatives. Prudence was going to send for her, plus the sister's two children. I think the sister is late."

"Late?"

"She passed away."

"Sounds complicated," I said.

"African families are complicated, my friend. We don't just live by ourselves with our big screen TVs like Americans."

I went back to the nightstand. I hoped to find a lead somewhere, maybe a store of letters. Prudence seemed to live in a dark hole. She had no cell phone, no computer, not even an address book. Underneath a couple of *People* magazines I found two letters from Zimbabwe written by G. Mukombachoto. They weren't in envelopes but were "air letters," a curious thin blue paper that folded neatly into a rectangle and got glued shut for mailing.

G. Mukombachoto wrote in a language I couldn't understand beyond the greeting: "Dear Tarisai." I went back to the closet to show the letters to Mandisa. She was on her fourth garbage bag. The clothing rails were almost empty. She hadn't started on the shoes.

"Prudence used to go to church rummage sales for clothes," said Mandisa. She held up a bright blue suit with matching hat and showed me the masking tape price tag. Two dollars.

"It's a Donna Vinci," she added, "pure silk. Probably cost two hundred new. Worth a lot more in Africa. She and I were thinking of doing an import-export thing. Even with the kitchen appliances. It's big money back home." Mandisa wasn't such a square after all. She was already calculating the profits from Prudence's little estate and hoping I wasn't interested. I wasn't. Legally it all belonged to the husband but my years of easy money were behind me. Something about selling off the property of dead friends pricked what conscience I had left.

"I found some letters from some G. something or other that starts with an "M." I said, "Can you read them?"

"Let me see." She took the letters.

"That's Mukombachoto," she said, "Prudence's real last name."

She unfolded the blue papers and stared for a few seconds.

"Was she a princess?" I asked. "She once told me she was Princess Tarisai. That's the name on the letter."

"It's probably Shona," said Mandisa. "That's what most Zimbabweans speak. I don't understand a word."

"What do you speak?" I asked.

"English."

"What else?"

"A few vernac languages."

"What's vernac? Never heard of it."

"Vernacular. Local African languages. Zulu, Sotho, Tswana, Venda, Xhosa."

"You speak all of those?"

"Only about four, plus Afrikaans."

"You speak six languages?" I asked.

"Something like that."

"That's impossible," I said. "What was that last one again?"

"Xhosa," she said pronouncing it with a click like you use to get a horse going.

"How did you learn them all?"

"It just happens. I don't know. Americans only know English. Shame."

I thought maybe Mandisa would help me. Now I knew I couldn't trust her. No one could speak six languages. She was just like the guys in prison who tell you how many millions they made on the street and then bum a cigarette. If she could speak six languages, why couldn't she understand these letters?

"Do you know someone who can translate these things?" I asked.

"I don't know any Zimbabweans. Maybe there are some around. I keep to myself."

"It has to be a Zimbabwean?"

"I could try writing to Mr. Mukombachoto in English. He probably understands. If not he can find someone who does." She looked at the address on the air letter.

"He's in Harare," she said. "That's the capital. Everyone can speak English there."

"Maybe we can find the name in directory assistance and give him a call," I said. "There can't be that many people there with this long name. Or he could be on the Internet."

"You can try the phone," she replied, "but I doubt you'll find anything. Please keep it short. A call to Africa costs a fortune."

I picked up the receiver and dialed "0." I guess "0" still meant something in phone language because I got a recording with some options. After hopping through several sets of choices, I got a woman with an Asian accent.

"How do I get directory assistance for Zimbabwe?" I asked.

"I'll put you through."

The ring of the phone was different—two rings, then a pause. It rang about two dozen times. No one picked it up, no electronic voice came on to tell me which button to push.

"They don't answer before three rings like here," said Mandisa. "Sometimes they don't answer at all. It's a different way of living. Phones don't rule our lives."

I went back through the same series of digital Janes. This time I asked for the number so I could direct dial.

"The international code is 011," said another Asian woman. "The country code is 263, then 4."

"Are there 263 countries in the world?" I asked the operator.

"Have a wonderful day," she said and hung up.

I tried directory assistance four more times. The first three times it just kept going: two rings and a pause, two rings and a pause. On the fourth call the rhythm changed. I let Mandisa listen.

"It's engaged," she said, "I mean busy."

I picked up the letters to Prudence again. The second one had a PS written in English that ran up the edge of the page.

"We look forward to seeing you," it said. The postmark showed the letter had been sent a month before Prudence's death.

"What do you think this means?" I asked, pointing to the PS. Mandy's silver fingernail followed the writing up the page.

"Who knows?" she said. "Maybe Prudence was planning a trip home. She never mentioned it to me though."

"What the hell was going on here?" I asked. "Why were all of Prudence's things at your place?"

"She wanted to move out but was afraid to tell you," she said. "She was looking for an apartment. Half of this furniture belongs to her and most of the kitchen things."

"I see."

Mandisa had filled five garbage bags with Prudence's clothes. The closet was empty except for a pair of silver lamé flip-flops.

"What are you going to do with all this stuff?" I asked. Mandisa was about six inches shorter than Prudence and much rounder. No alterations would have made those dresses look good on her.

"I don't know," she said, "sell them I guess. Have a yard sale. Isn't that what they do here? I don't know anyone her size, at least not someone who wears these kinds of things."

"Let me have one last look through them before you let them go," I said.

"No problem," she replied, but she looked annoyed.

She started tying the tops of the bags together and promised to leave them there in the closet until I was ready. There was no garage sale in Mandisa's plans. I was sure she knew places in Africa where people would pay big bucks for these high-class threads of Prudence's. An arranged-marriage husband could only get in the way.

Mandisa went into the kitchen for a couple of minutes. I looked under the mattress. No photos, only an old newspaper with an article about Zimbabwe. A picture showed some soldiers escorting an old white man, a Mr. McGuinn, and his wife out the front door of a farm-house. The date was July 22, 2002.

"Evicted white farmers flee Zimbabwe," read the headline, "Mugabe tightens the screws."

As I read on I figured out that this Mugabe was the president of the country and he was taking farms away from whites. Crazy business, but what did it have to do with Prudence? I stuffed the article in my jacket pocket. Maybe if I read it later it would make more sense.

I smelled coffee and cinnamon. I peeked out into the kitchen.

"Come and have a coffee," she said. "There's an apple tart there." Sounded even better than silver dollar pancakes.

Mandisa had laid out her small kitchen table with two white cups and saucers, a matching little milk pitcher and a blue sugar bowl. The coffee plunger stood in the middle. She'd sliced the apple tart into eight precisely equal pieces and fanned them around on a yellow serving tray.

"How do you take your coffee?" she asked.

"A Cadillac. Two sugars."

"What?"

"Cream and two sugars."

She pushed the plunger down, picked up my cup and saucer and poured slowly. She added my sugar, shaking off the excess each time to give me a level teaspoon.

"It's Italian blend," she said. "I hope it's all right."

"As long as it's black and hot," I told her, "I'm happy." I took a sip, then realized she might think I was referring to something other than coffee when I said "black and hot."

"It tastes fine," I said. She didn't look offended.

She reached over and scooped a piece of apple tart onto my plate and set it down next to my saucer.

"Have more if you like," she said. "I'll never eat all that."

The apple tart, as she called it, was really a pie with a laced crust top. The apples were too sour, the bottom crust thick and soggy. I didn't ask if she made it. I heard my lips smack as I calculated how to break the silence.

"Prudence liked you a lot," said Mandisa, "but she had so many things going on. She didn't want to cause trouble for you."

"I can handle trouble," I said.

"I was just trying to explain how her things got here, why she was moving out."

"I understand. I appreciate that."

I reached for a second piece of pie, just to make her feel better. I lifted it carefully off the serving dish but a few crumbs fell onto the table, prompting Mandisa to jump up and get a cloth from the counter to wipe them away. There was no place for crumbs in her world. I was meticulous like that in prison, mopped my cell floor every day, swept in the morning, afternoon, and night. On the streets I didn't worry about such things. I had Luisa. We didn't have Luisas in prison, none that interested me anyway.

I sprinkled a little sugar on the tart.

"Suit yourself," she said. "I know how you Americans love your sugar."

"Did Prudence have any enemies?" I asked.

Mandisa didn't flinch or answer. She went back to the sink, got a dishrag and wiped away a few phantom crumbs from the table.

"Why do you ask?" she said.

"I don't know. I just don't think Prudence jumped into that pool by herself."

"What do the police think?" she asked. "You said there was no autopsy."

"Filled in a few forms and left. It didn't hint of foul play to them."

"Didn't you tell them you suspected something?"

"Not really. I was still in a state of shock."

I didn't actually feel like going into it all. I sure wasn't going to mention the part with me on my belly for two hours. Besides, how could I explain to someone that even if a friend was murdered, my duty was to keep quiet, to "hold my mud," as we say?

"To be honest," I said, "I don't trust police. I don't like having them in my life. Whatever they do, they can't bring Prudence back."

"I can appreciate that," she said. "Police are never on the side of black women. Not here. Not in South Africa."

"I don't know about all that," I said. "I just don't trust them. I'm not trying to make a racial thing out of it. Cops are just haters."

"So are you a jealous husband seeking revenge?" she asked.

"No. Why would I be jealous over someone who was moving out, who wasn't really my wife?"

"You tell me," she said. She looked straight into my eyes. I tried not to blink. There was more than a little bit of jealous husband in me, but when you're state-raised you learn how to hide these things. Survival depends on it.

"Someone violated my space, my territory," I said reverting to my prison voice. I hadn't talked like that in a long time. You don't need threatening undertones in Carltonville.

"I want to know who it was," I added. "I think you can help."

"I'm not so sure," she said. "Let me think about it."

The apple tart was much better with the sugar on it. I went for a third piece. Mandisa looked pleased.

"I found this in one of her pockets," said Mandisa. She handed me a business card. Johnny's Camera Shop.

"I'll phone them," I said, taking my cell out of my pocket.

"What are you going to say?"

"I'll figure something out," I said. "I'm a con man. We have an answer to everything."

"Wait," she said, "it's better to plan." English might have been her fifth language but she was no fool. I cut the phone.

"I know the place," I said. "It's on College Avenue. Small shop. Upmarket. For the university crowd. If Prudence had any dealings with them, they'd remember her. No one else who looked or sounded like her would go there."

"Stick to the truth," she said. "You're a bereaved husband. That means something. Maybe you think she left some items to be printed there, films of your last night together."

I liked the way she pronounced "film," as in "fill 'em up."

"You said I should tell the truth," I reminded her.

"It's close enough."

I laughed and phoned the camera shop. Johnny answered.

"I'm so sorry, sir," he said. "I remember the young woman. Charming thing. She bought a video camera from us. Old-style VHS. Don't sell many of those any more. Said she hadn't figured out this new technology yet. Wanted it for shooting her honeymoon in Yosemite. It was a couple of months ago. Let me bring it up on the system. Here it is. Mrs. D. Winter. That was her name. I remember it now. A Panasonic. Lovely woman. Elegant. I'm so sorry."

I thanked him for his condolences and the information. I asked Mandisa about it. She'd never seen Prudence with a video camera. Neither had I. I'd check with Darlene. At least I had something to follow up on.

Mandisa promised to write to G. Mukombachoto and go through Prudence's clothes one more time.

"There may be a scrap of paper with a phone number or something," she said. "If I find anything or think of anything, I'll call you."

I gave her my number but I doubted I'd hear from her again. Mandisa was almost as mysterious as Prudence. She didn't need me poking around in her life.

CHAPTER 10

The next morning Officer Carter showed up at my door. This time his partner was a short, stocky woman who looked like a possible candidate for the Olympic team in the shot put. Lovely creature. Their timing could have been better. It was Luisa's day to clean and I was on my way to a meeting with a young woman from Belarus. Red Eye told me she was tall, blonde, horny, and looking for a husband. With Prudence gone, I could call myself "available." My heart wasn't really in it but at least I'd be thinking about something besides that look in Prudence's eyes when her head popped out of that rolled-up rug. Maybe poking a blonde would cure my insomnia. Something had to work.

"We have a couple more questions for you about the girl who drowned in your pool," said Carter. As the two of them parked on my couch again without an invitation, I heard the bedroom window sliding open slowly. Luisa was making her escape. I coughed to cover up the noise. Though I never asked, I figured her chances of having a green card were about as good as those for me becoming lifelong friends with Officer Carter.

"What else do you need to know?" I asked. I could feel a noose tightening around my neck. I was about two questions from calling my lawyer. Maybe we could file a civil action to recover the costs of the Re-Nu.

"Do you have a marriage license?" he asked. "We want to verify the name of your so-called wife."

"I'll get it for you," I said. I went into my bedroom. Carter followed. A cool breeze wafted in through the open window.

"I'm a bit of a fresh air freak," I told Carter. He didn't pay any attention, just headed straight for my bed. I slid open the top drawer of my dresser. My marriage license had been there since the day Prudence moved in but I wasn't even thinking about the license. The top drawer of my nightstand contained my Walther—an automatic five years if Carter found it.

"The license is right here," I said, "you can come and see for yourself."

Carter didn't respond. He was too busy pulling the blankets and sheets off the bed. As I turned to take the license to him, he bent over the bed and took a deep breath.

"That's the smell of African pussy," he said, "wet and wild. She must have been more than you could handle, Winter."

I threw the license on the bed, right under his nose.

"She was my wife," I reminded him, "for better or worse."

He ignored the license, sat down on the bed and slid open the nightstand drawer. I thought about diving out the window but even as fat and slow as Carter was, he could probably get a bullet through me before I got away. I was already starting to taste that watery corn meal mush they doled out in the Feds' chow hall.

He scooped out a bunch of condoms and dropped them on the bed.

"You must have been planning to have a lot of fun with your Chocolate drop bride," he said, "but you didn't want any jungle bunny babies running around, did you?"

He picked up one of the condoms and studied the packet.

"My mistake," he added, "I got you all wrong, Winter. These things say 'extra large'. Couldn't be yours. What'd you do, take pictures while someone else bonked your wife?"

I directed him again toward the marriage license on the bed. I wasn't going for his bait. I was just trying to figure out where the hell that Walther was. I knew I'd put it in that drawer but maybe I'd changed it up in one of my drunken stupors. Wild Turkey could do that to you.

Carter tossed the condom on the floor and examined the marriage certificate carefully, running his finger over the seal. Strange feeling to be handing a cop a document that was legit. Too bad Prudence wasn't.

"One of your buddies make this up for you?" he asked. "We've looked at your jacket. Forgery, fraud, trafficking. You're a fuckin' jack of all trades."

"I've given all that up. I'm what they call rehabilitated."

He stood up and hollered to his partner that it was time to go. "There's nothing here," Carter shouted. "Besides, Winter's just told me he's rehabilitated."

The woman waddled through the bedroom door.

"Yeah and I'm Meryl Streep, expecting another Oscar this year," she replied. Carter led the way as the two headed for the front door, their keys bouncing against those pudgy hips as they moved away. He stopped halfway to the door to look at my collection of videos. He crouched down and pulled a copy of *Cool Hand Luke* off the shelf, popped the case open and looked at the cassette.

"I figure a guy like you's got a collection of kiddie porn sandwiched in with the Paul Newman."

"Just Paul Newman plus all the Disney favorites. You wanna watch *Bambi*?"

He put *Cool Hand Luke* back, then rummaged through a few more videos. I just wanted him to get the hell out.

"I was hopin' for some ebony porn in your collection, Winter, like your wife fuckin' the dog."

"I'd appreciate it if you left now," I said.

"We'll be back," Carter assured me.

"I'll look forward to that. I'll bake chocolate chip cookies for the occasion."

"Don't be a smartass, Winter. We could strike you out in a heartbeat."

"While we wait for that heartbeat to finish, kindly make your exit."

I stood in the front door and watched until they pulled away, then circled around to the backyard to hunt for Luisa. When I called out her name, I heard some bushes rustle in the corner of the yard and out she came, a bit of topsoil clinging to her uniform. She held the Walther in her right hand, pointing toward the sky.

"I thought maybe they shouldn't see this," she said.

"You're a star," I said, "a real *estrella*."

"You are a crazy man, Mr. Winter. Very loco."

She gave me a hug. That had never happened before. When she pulled away, her sweaty hair left a stain on my shirt. Hopefully the spot remover would take it out. Re-Nu wasn't recommended for clothing.

"I wish I could help you more," said Luisa. "Prudence was a very nice woman. She was always laughing, but inside I could see that she was sad. She never told me why. Her life was her secret. That's how it is with us *inmigrantes*."

"We all have our secrets," I reminded her. She went quiet and started to weep. I gave her the rest of the day off and headed for Olga, the Belarus girl. I really needed a stress reliever. Hopefully she would fill the bill.

～

Olga was waiting for me in the Lighthouse, a dive in downtown San Leandro with lots of pictures of ships on the wall. She could have passed for Anna Kournikova and her bright blue mini skirt wasn't much longer than Anna's tennis togs. I battled to keep my eyes off those deep-tanned legs. We had a few drinks. She wasn't looking for a husband. She had one of those, though I suspected he didn't see much of her.

"My husband paid me $3,000 and I got a green card," she said, "but our marriage isn't working out." She opened her purse to show me her little plastic card with "Permanent Resident" printed across the top.

"I can do massage," she said and proceeded to gently run her hand along the inside of my thigh under the table.

"I need a drivers' license in another name just in case. They tell me you've helped a lot of girls."

"Who told you that?"

"A girlfriend."

"I've helped a few get on their feet," I said, "but I'm semiretired now."

"I can do other things also," she said as the massage relocated itself a little bit higher up my leg. Maybe Red Eye had told her I needed some cheering up.

After six drinks I'd agreed to get her a drivers' license and landed her in my bedroom. She did know how to do other things. I thought of Kournikova sliding across the clay courts in Paris to chase down a backhand as Olga's athleticism delivered me momentarily from the evil complexities of a dead wife, paranoid fears, and perverted cops. She insisted on a trip to Nordstrom the next morning, her way of collecting a fee for services. I spent $763, which got Olga some enticing perfume, and two shiny, slinky blue dresses with no backs. The blue matched her Kournikova eyes.

I drove her to an apartment building in San Leandro where she said she was staying with several friends. Obviously none of them was hubby. She offered to meet me again in a few days, to get an update on job possibilities. I suppose Pearly was looking for a Queen for the Day, but I didn't offer. I said I'd let her know if anything came up. Then for some reason I told her my wife had just died. "Me and Red Eye are investigating what happened."

"A husband in sorrow needs to lift his spirits," she said. "Don't forget about Olga. I am there for you."

"We had a nice time," I said.

She kissed me on the cheek, then licked the inside of my ear for a long time, leaving me with my flag flying high to remember her by. Any other time in my life I'd have dropped everything to get my fill of Olga. She actually seemed to like me. Not every girl can get used to a cleft lip. They say we kiss funny.

As I approached my house an odd feeling came over me, one I hadn't experienced in a long time—guilt. I couldn't feel comfortable with another woman until I solved Prudence's murder. When she was alive and out of the house for days on end, I had no problem hooking up with whatever the wind blew my way. Now that she was gone, I was getting attacks of conscience. Go figure. A couple of shots of Wild Turkey succeeded in bringing me back toward level ground. Guilt never kept Calvin Winter down for long. If I could just score a good night's sleep, I'd be ready for real action.

CHAPTER 11

Mandisa phoned at seven the next morning. I'd just nodded off. The Wild Turkey wasn't doing its job. She said she wanted to meet me at Denny's in Alameda in half an hour.

"I might as well check out the competition's menu," she said, "while we discuss our business." I didn't know she had a sense of humor.

I got there five minutes late and resisted ordering the dollar size. All I needed was a bottomless cup of coffee. She ordered a root beer float.

"I've only discovered them recently," she said. "They're terrible for the waistline but so delicious."

Her outfit surprised me—ordinary blue jeans, a Nike T-shirt and matching cap. Totally casual and the red streak was gone. Wraparound sunglasses hid her greenish eyes.

She swirled the ice cream in the root beer with a long silver soda spoon.

"I found the names and phone numbers of a couple of men in one of her bags," she said. "I remember her mentioning them before."

"Business associates?" I asked.

"Social, but there may have been some sort of business as well. There was an element of desperation in Prudence's life."

"So it seems."

"She used men as sugar daddies," Mandisa said, "got what she could from them."

"Including me?"

"I wouldn't know about that."

"Or wouldn't tell me if you did."

"I suppose not but I don't know."

She poked around in the float trying to break up a big lump of ice cream at the bottom.

"I think she had quite a few, uh, gentleman companions. She was clever and beautiful."

"It didn't help her much in the end."

"She was desperate because of problems at home. Life is different in Zimbabwe. So hard."

"I read something about this, what's his name?"

"Mugabe?"

"Yes. Kicking all the whites off their farms. Sounds like a real bastard."

"It's a little more complicated than that," she said.

She was probably right but the last thing I needed was a discussion about complications in a far-off land. I didn't even keep up with Sacramento, let alone Washington, D.C. My conversation had raised one burning question for me though—one apparently without an answer: did Prudence ever call me a sugar daddy?

Mandisa handed me a piece of binder paper with two names and phone numbers printed in careful, feminine lettering.

"Be careful," she said, "these are important people. They're married, respectable. They're not interested in being connected to a murdered African seductress."

"You're sure she wasn't English, with that accent?"

"Zimbabwe used to be a British colony. Also South Africa. They taught us Africans how to speak like them. If the Americans had colonized us, we'd be saying 'French fries' and playing this funny football of yours instead of soccer."

I read the names: Alfred Jeffcoat and Carlton Newman. Fast Freddy wasn't lying to me. Jeffcoat was the name he'd given to us outside the King and Queens. At least someone believed in us.

"Do you know anything about them," I asked, "like where they live or work?"

"Prudence told me if I ever needed money, they could help but that I should be careful. She said they had houses, boats, planes. They're loaded."

"Did they ever threaten her?"

"Not that I know of. She just said they were rich. Newman is black."

"Did you just remember all this now?"

"Some of it came to me earlier but I didn't know the names."

"Anything else come to you?"

She slurped at the bottom of her float until every drop was gone.

"No, but if I think of something, I'll call you." She moved the empty glass to the edge of the table.

"She said if you ever had trouble with Jeffcoat, just mention the name Peter Margolis."

"Who the hell is that?" I asked.

"No idea," Mandisa replied. She wrote down the name on the napkin and handed it to me.

"Did you talk to the police?" I asked.

"No. Never."

"You're sure?" I asked.

"The police shot my neighbor Billy Mzimane when he was coming back from the shops with a loaf of bread. He was running, pretending he was playing soccer. He was eleven years old. It was like that for us then."

"For who?"

"Blacks, blacks in South Africa."

"Is that why you left?"

"Something like that," she said. "I have to go. I must catch a cab and get to work."

"I'll give you a ride."

She adjusted her cap and got up to leave.

"No thanks, I'm fine."

"By the way," I said, "where is it?"

"What?"

"This place where you grew up."

"You've never heard of it."

"Try me."

"Katlehong. Near Johannesburg."

"I know Johannesburg," I replied. It was the biggest dot on the map when I was looking for Zimbabwe. Almost as big as Philadelphia.

"Good for you," she said and headed outside to look for her cab.

CHAPTER 12

After paying for my coffee and Mandisa's float I powered the Volvo straight to Chumash casino, about a four-hour drive from Oakland. I made it in three. I got $1,000 from the ATM in the casino. My stake. I needed an escape and since my escapade with Olga had only left me with a guilty conscience, I opted for a gambling binge. I couldn't think of any other alternative.

I have two rules about gambling. I never do it for more than ten hours at a stretch and I go home when I lose all my stake. I've never broken either rule.

After ten hours and lots of blackjack hands, my $1,000 had grown to fifteen grand. I headed home with my $14,000 in profit stuffed in a Ziploc bag, not feeling one bit better as I pulled out of the parking lot. I had a few more hours on the road to contemplate the investigation. I hoped I wouldn't fall asleep.

A mile outside the little tourist trap of Solvang with all its fake Danish houses, an Indian guy and his woman stood by the side of the road. The man held up a crude sign lettered in magic marker: "Broke. Need Job. Kids 2 Feed. Do Anything."

I pulled over about a hundred yards in front of them. The man came running to the car.

"Thanks, boss. I'm a carpenter. I can fix anything for you." He wore a tattered carpenter's belt. A hammer and screwdriver dangled from two of the loops.

"I'm ready to work, sir," he added. "Just give me the word."

A little boy appeared and grabbed onto the man's leg. He looked about three years old. The bottle of milk in his hand held about one more sip. His shirt had a rip in the shoulder.

I reached into the glove compartment and grabbed the Ziploc bag. "Come here," I said to the boy, "I've got a present for you."

He looked up at his father, not sure what to do.

"It's okay," said the father.

The little boy let loose of his father's leg and took two steps toward the door. I held out my arm and gave him the Ziploc.

"Don't spend it all in one place," I warned the man, "and make sure that kid gets some more milk and a good steak in his belly."

I drove off, feeling a little better anyway. I looked in the rearview mirror long enough to see the man jumping up and down and throwing me kisses. A different breed altogether from the "associates" of Prudence I'd soon have to face. They were corporate tycoons. About as close as I ever got to those types was Dr. Robson's fiftieth birthday party. I didn't even know how to dress for a meeting with them.

Somewhere south of San Jose I decided to do the logical thing, just drop the whole affair. It was all driving me crazy and nothing could bring Prudence back. Even if it could, she was on the verge of moving out. If she didn't care enough about me to even let me know of her plans, why should I be taking risks to solve the mystery of her death? I could go on for the rest of my life happily believing she just got drunk, slipped and fell in the pool. I didn't owe her a thing.

A few miles later, my mental pendulum swung back in the other direction. It was the violation thing. Once you open yourself up to that kind of abuse, it never ends. If prison taught me anything, that was it. I'm small and not all that strong but no one ever punked me. No one. If they'd tried, they knew I'd fight back. I'd catch them when they were asleep or sitting on the can and slice open their liver. It kills every time. I never had to do it but people thought that I could and I did too. That's all that mattered. Now someone had invaded my territory. Life threw you tests and this was one of mine. I couldn't let those Oakland hills get in my blood. I had to fight back for me, not for Prudence or her family. My manhood was on the line. Pure and simple.

As soon as I got back to Carltonville, I called Red Eye for a strategy session. We finished off a bottle of Wild Turkey trying to figure out how to tackle these millionaires. Red Eye didn't go down well in a suit.

His tattoos and prison-built bulges would make him look like a bull wrapped in silk. I would have to be the one to talk to these guys.

"Why don't you go through your house for clues?" he asked. "You know, DNA and all that stuff."

"We need a crime lab for that, a CSI operation," I said.

"I've got a hookup," he replied. "Billy Trout works for some crime lab company. He owes me."

"Won't work, bro," I said. "I swept and hosed down the pool area. Luisa scoured the house with disinfectant. Bless her little heart."

"Maybe she knows something about Prudence and her men."

"I already asked. She told me Prudence's life was all a secret. Not wrong there."

"So you want me to forget about Billy Trout?"

"For now, yeah."

All roads kept leading back to me interviewing Jeffcoat and Newman. The problem was that if one of them killed her, they'd know me. They might even have killed her over jealousy because I was married to her. If I was the next target, doing an interview could be walking into the lion's mouth. We racked our brains trying to think of anyone else who could do it.

"Back in the day," said Red Eye, "we were convicts. Today you can't trust anyone."

"If they're not a rat," I said, "they're so high on crank they blab to everyone anyway. Same difference."

After we finished whining about the demise of the convict code, we accepted the inevitable. My best pinstripe suit would have to go to the dry cleaners.

"I've got an idea," said Red Eye. "We'll tell them Prudence left a will and that they were the beneficiaries."

"She had nothing," I said. "These guys are millionaires. She was hitting on them for money."

"She won the lottery, Cal."

"Then what?"

"You found the winning ticket in her purse."

"I don't get it," I said. "This is as crazy as the scheme with the Super Bowl tickets." Red Eye had bought fifty tickets from a scalper for the

Super Bowl the year the 49ers made it. He figured he could double his money. The tickets turned out to be fake and a bunch of Niner fans got arrested trying to get into the stadium. Some of them came looking for Red Eye. Eventually, the charges were dropped and it all calmed down but Red Eye still never goes near a Niner game. You don't anyway if you're Raider Nation.

"This is way different," he said. "Just listen. She won the lottery. And you, being an honorable man, did the right thing with the ticket. Collected the seventeen million and put it in an account to be distributed to those mentioned in her will."

"Then what?"

"You read them her will. Each beneficiary gets a third. Jeffcoat, Newman, whoever."

"I don't get it."

"You want to convince a man of anything, start off by telling him he's got the biggest dick in town."

"And they'll think they got the money because they were bonkin' her the best," I said.

"Now you got it. Just got to iron out the details. They'll be drooling at your feet over that money."

We spent the better part of a second bottle of Wild Turkey on those details. Red Eye had an ex-con friend who was a paralegal. He was ready to write up the will and dress it in all the right jargon.

"Then you'll go and meet these guys individually," Red Eye added, "read the will and test their response. Use that English butler accent of yours."

"I'm through with the Prince Charlie act," I said, "but I will buy some new ties. Brown, gray. Whatever. Do these guys wear hats?"

"I don't know," he said, "you're the one who lives in Carltonville."

"I try not to look at them."

We discussed how to read their expressions, how I'd know if I'd stumbled into the office of the killer.

"You'll get a gut feeling," he said. "These guys aren't pros. Their nerves will crack if you push the right button."

"I don't know," I said, "rich dudes know how to cover their tracks. That's why they don't pay taxes."

"Trust me," said Red Eye. "You'll know."

"Maybe they used a hired killer."

"Too sloppy," he replied. "A pro doesn't take a chance with drowning. Too slow. Too risky. And there was no sign of a struggle. She probably knew the guy. Otherwise there'd have been pushing and shoving."

"You're right," I said, "Prudence would have fought back."

"It'd be a trip bustin' a fuckin' millionaire. I'm just lookin' forward to seein' him squirm."

"We should cut the prize down to four or five million. Seventeen is a little hard to believe."

"Whatever works," said Red Eye.

I phoned the numbers Mandisa had given me for Jeffcoat and Newman. Both were business lines. I got the street addresses from their receptionists. In the meantime, Red Eye's paralegal friend completed a will plus a cover letter from a lawyer explaining the lottery ticket. The lawyer wrote that the executor of the will, Mr. C. Winter, would be contacting them to "discuss the matter." Using my real name took a little edge off the hustle but we agreed if the thing unraveled or one of them knew me, a false identity would dig us into a deeper hole.

Red Eye and I financed a couple of throwaway cell phones, one for the lawyer, another for me as the executor. If I could just keep them straight, we'd be in business.

I started with the white guy, Jeffcoat. He ran some kind of financial services company from the fourteenth floor of the Oaks Building, not far from Jack London Square in downtown Oakland. I phoned his secretary and made an appointment to talk about some investment opportunities.

The elevator got to the fourteenth floor in about three seconds. The office could have been a set for one of those soapies about tycoons. A thirty-foot-wide floor-to-ceiling window looked out over miles and miles of the central region of the city. From the fourteenth floor even Oakland looked spectacular. I always thought of my city as somewhat like myself, not much to look at but loaded with character. Jeffcoat had a different perspective, I'm sure.

He had the body of a marathon runner, topped by a micromanaged wave of brown hair with dignified streaks of gray. His charcoal suit no doubt came from some tailor in an exotic land. He'd have preferred jumping out of an airplane at thirty thousand feet without a parachute to being caught in an off-the-rack.

"Mr. Winter," he said after a chilly handshake across his desk. "This is a highly unusual situation. Can you please fill me in on the details? As briefly as possible please. I've got clients waiting." At least he didn't seem to recognize me. He straightened a pile of papers on his massive desk, then straightened them again while I made him wait for my reply. The guy was straight OCD. All the edges of those papers had to be perfectly even or the sky would fall.

I'd already explained Prudence's death over the phone, providing the exact amount of detail I wanted him to have. I could hear his voice tense when I said the sum he stood to inherit was likely to go "well into seven figures."

"Apparently you were a friend or associate of one Deirdre Lewis," I told him to kick off the interview. "She also seems to have gone by the name Prudence."

"That's correct."

"In what capacity were you acquainted with the deceased?"

"To expedite matters, let's say we had a business relationship. She was a client, albeit on an informal basis."

"So there's no official record of your transactions?"

"I do everything above board, Mr. Winter, though I fail to see how that's relevant here."

"I'm not in any way trying to impugn your character, Mr. Jeffcoat. It's just unusual for a somewhat distant associate to be named a beneficiary. We have to be careful." I had his attention for the moment. I'd always wanted to use the word "impugn" in a sentence. Jeffcoat looked impressed. The bait was bouncing against his lips. He'd be opening wide in a minute.

"I assisted her with some financial matters," he replied. "Investment advice. I assume she's returning the favor. Her investments did well."

"Perhaps she didn't expect to be leaving you such a substantial sum. No one calls buying a lottery ticket an investment strategy."

"A lottery ticket?"

"That's right," I said as I reached down to get my briefcase. The will was at the bottom of a pile of papers bearing forged letterheads.

"According to the figures here," I said, "the payout is $4,523,000 and some change. You will receive about one third of this, a little over $1.5 million."

"We are all saddened by the death of this woman of great potential," he replied sounding as if he was talking to a press conference. "I'm deeply touched by this gesture she has made of remembering me and our time together. In this day and age, gratitude is a rare commodity."

"Yes, it is," I said. "It's remarkable. You must have made quite an impression on the young woman."

Jeffcoat fiddled with his tie for a moment before he let loose with his next words of wisdom: "In the course life one never knows who is touched by your actions. It's what makes it all worthwhile."

"I couldn't agree more," I said. I should have brought a mirror to give Jeffcoat a better chance to admire himself. As it was, his reflection in that thirty-foot window would just have to do. Running this con was a new test of my power to endure the arrogance of the mucky-mucks. I was nearing the vomit threshold, but knowing I'd have the last laugh helped settle my stomach.

"I have only one more question for you, sir," I said. "Do you know anything about her family? We haven't been able to contact them."

"She never spoke about that to me," he said.

"Didn't she even tell you where they lived?"

"I assumed they were in London, where Miss Lewis grew up."

"I see. Thank you, sir. I don't want to take up any more of your time. Once I've spoken to all the beneficiaries, we will have to meet again."

"If it's necessary," he said. "I'm a busy man." He stood up to facilitate my departure.

"Surely the amount of money involved would make it worth your while."

"Of course, but I loathe unnecessary meetings, they consume our most precious resource—human capital. Where possible I prefer electronic communication. Clean and quick, with a clear trail. Superfluous meetings are a hallmark of ineffective business practice."

"I can appreciate that," I said, standing up to shake his hand. I suspected he had a series of prepared speeches on ineffective business practice ready to unleash at any time. Lecture one was enough for me.

As I neared the door, I stopped to look at a picture on the wall. Jeffcoat's high school football team. There he was in the back row, number fourteen.

"I played quarterback," he said, "all-conference for three years." Next to him was number seventy-four, a towering kid with a tomato nose and an old school harelip like mine. Tore halfway up to his nose. You don't see 'em like that any more. Modern surgery has made us into dinosaurs.

"Oh, there's one more thing," I said, "just so you can be forewarned. This case may attract a little publicity. There's a lot of human interest here: dying woman wins lottery, leaves millions to relative stranger. It will prick the paparazzi."

"I hope we can avoid that, Mr. Winter," he replied. "I cherish my privacy and that of my family. The less said to anyone, the better. No rational man advertises when he's won a million dollars. The parasites come out of the woodwork. I hope we agree on that."

"I'll do what I can," I replied, "but I can't give you any guarantees. There's always someone willing to come forward with a story if there's a little money on offer."

As he sat back down in his chair, for the first time I felt some nervousness from this eminent creature of the fourteenth floor. I don't think he wanted me to leave just yet but he couldn't figure out how to get me to stay and extract the information he wanted. I paused for a moment to enjoy watching his butt fidget in that big leather chair of his before I left the office. He'd spend the next twenty minutes straightening those papers trying to figure out what this little harelip dude pretending to be Santa Claus was actually up to. There was always the chance that he was onto my scam but I didn't think so. I can read a mark. I grew up playing the monte, moving the red card and the black card faster than the eye could see. I've done my share of pool hustling as well. Never lost much, only got beat up once. That was all before I learned how to convince immigration cops that I didn't have anything in the trunk of my car or the back of the mobile home. I can read people. That was what made the con so much fun. Marks always know something is a little bit off, but when they smell that money and power they can't help themselves. When Jeffcoat got done straightening those papers, he'd probably start patting his dick and praising its powers. I bet that useless pecker of his couldn't last thirty seconds. I almost wished he had committed this crime. I enjoy watching the well-oiled take a fall. A young woman left him a million dollars and he was worrying about wasting twenty minutes of his precious human capital in a meeting. What bigger problems did the world face than the "ineffective business practice" that seemingly tormented this undeserving heir to a million bucks?

Despite finding him a despicable character, I wasn't sure Jeffcoat had the balls to kill Prudence or even order the hit. I hadn't encountered many inhabitants of fourteenth-floor offices so maybe I misjudged his character. I just didn't think he could pull it all off that smoothly. They say the wealthy are capable of almost anything when it comes to protecting their money, so maybe I underestimated his capacity for deceit. All I could do was hope that Newman seemed like more of a killer.

CHAPTER 13

When I arrived back at my place after seeing Jeffcoat, I found a note from Carter under the door, one of those little old school forms that come in a tablet. He'd checked the "stopped by" box and the one that said "please call back." On principle I didn't return messages from the police. No cop ever stopped by my house with good news.

Carter had also left two messages on my machine. On the second one he said if I didn't phone him by the end of the day, he'd have me "down at the station for questioning." I drank a shot of Wild Turkey. I'd think about calling him the next morning. I had to get my papers in order and rush off to visit Newman. First things first.

As it turned out, the muscle-bound Newman operated on a different level from Jeffcoat. He ran a trucking company out of the converted garage of his five-bedroom house in North Berkeley. A gold Jaguar sat in the driveway, late seventies, with tinted windows in mint condition. Almost as cherry as my Volvo.

He'd tiled the garage floor and added a couple of windows and a skylight but it was no Oaks Building. The man himself projected a youthful, sporty image—state of the art hi-top basketball shoes and Levi 501s. His shaved head held a high gloss. Looked like he touched up that thin moustache to hide the gray.

He'd loaded his office with Oakland Raider souvenirs and memorabilia, including a four-by-six-foot silver and black "Raider Nation" flag on one wall. The Raiders were a little rough around the edges for Jeffcoat. Probably a 49er fan if he followed football at all. Golf was more his speed, Freddy Couples or Bernhard Langer.

A picture on the wall behind Newman's desk showed him smiling in front of a fleet of thirty cabs with the logo "serving all of the West Coast" written on the doors. Not that catchy but those trucks were more than enough capital to finance a nice little blackmail payment to a desperate African girl.

Before I got the papers out of my briefcase he insisted I have a look at what he called his "gadgets," that it was part of the tour of his headquarters.

"I'm sort of an amateur spy," he boasted. He had some device rigged up to a computer that recorded all the police calls and transferred them to a map on the screen.

"You see," he said pointing to a moving white dot on the map, "that car's heading for E. Seventy-Eighth, probably a drug bust." He bought most of his stuff online from a site called AmateurSpy.com. He had some little gizmo hanging off his left ear, said he could listen in on "whatever." I didn't ask him what that "whatever" of his included but I had some not-so-nice ideas. We went back and sat down and I read him the will.

Once I finished the document, his chatty show-and-tell mood evaporated.

"I can't quite believe this," he told me. "She's gone and then she left me this money. I really don't understand."

He asked me to read the will a second time and to "go slow." When I reached the part about the lottery ticket, he shook his head, then went silent. I waited. I'd read a lot of interrogation manuals, always trying to stay one step ahead. Most of them advised that when a suspect goes quiet, you either pounce or wait them out. Never help them fill in the blanks.

I got pretty tired of watching Newman stare at that Raider flag while he tried to sort all this out. He tapped his finger gently against his upper lip and looked more and more uncomfortable.

He attempted a power pose—adjusting himself in the chair so he was leaning over the desk, looking me right in the eye.

"Let me be honest with you, Mr. Winter," he said in a subdued but deadly serious voice. "This situation presents me with a helluva problem. A helluva problem."

He rubbed his hands along his forehead as if he was slicking down some hair.

"Only a fool can refuse a million dollars, and I'm not a fool. Not when it comes to money. Prudence and I got together a few times, Mr. Winter. I'm not proud of it. The only time I've ever messed around on my wife."

He perched his hands on top of his head and looked up through the skylight. I thought he might cry. Life's so goddamned hard for the rich in America.

"I shouldn't have, but the flesh is weak," he said. "That girl was so fine. How do I explain $1.5 million to my wife? My kids? I'm sorry the girl died. Very sorry. What do I do next?"

He was Raider Nation. I should have had more sympathy, but my heartstrings had gone limp.

"I can't advise you how to handle this, Mr. Newman. I'm only here to inform and facilitate the execution of the will. If you want to donate the money to charity anonymously, you can do so. I could probably find someone to assist you in this regard."

The sweat made the shine on his head even brighter. He asked me to hand him the will so he could read it to himself, as if he could find a way out of his mess between the lines.

"I'm sorry, sir, I can't do that," I told him. "You will receive a copy when the formal reading takes place. I'm only here because of the unusual circumstances in this case. It's preventative medicine. Sometimes inheritances can spark ugly events among families and friends."

"I need some time to think," he said.

"Mr. Newman, did the deceased ever speak to you about her family? We've been unable to locate them."

"She told me the family had a lot of financial problems, that she tried to help them out as best she could."

"Did she ever ask you for money?"

"That's a little personal."

"I'm sorry. I'm just trying to locate the family. Sometimes families want to find out about assets, beneficiaries, etc."

"I gave her some money to help out. Three or four times. Not a lot of money. A few hundred or so."

"Apparently enough to make her remember you in her will."

"I like to think she remembered me for other reasons."

I smiled, amazed that one of Red Eye's schemes was actually working. For once, he had it right. This scam brought out all the vanities of Jeffcoat and Newman. If I wasn't Prudence's husband I would have admired how she had these two men drooling all over themselves to get at her. But at least they'd gotten to touch her. She'd given them some grounds to think they were the world's greatest lovers. I had nothing but doubts and unfulfilled desires.

"Please don't repeat the things I've told you about my relationship with Prudence," he said. "My family means the world to me. Everyone makes a mistake now and then."

"Not every mistake makes you a millionaire," I said. "It could be worse, Mr. Newman, way worse."

I stood up to go. His whining was starting to get to me.

"What about the money?" he asked.

"I'll call you when I've spoken to the other beneficiaries. We'll have a meeting."

"When?"

"Soon, very soon."

I spared him the warning about publicity. He was already scared enough. The problem was, he didn't look any more like a killer than Jeffcoat. But it had to be one of the two.

As I left him in his office with his hands once again atop his shiny head, I wondered what I'd gotten myself into. There is a famous section in the Oakland Coliseum known as the "black hole." During games the diehard members of the Raider Nation gather there. Anything goes. People come dressed as pirates, wild bulls, gorillas, their faces painted in the wildest combinations an artist can create with silver and black. The citizens of Raider Nation drink in the black hole, they smoke weed, shoot crank, fight, probably even make love every now and then when the Raiders score a spectacular TD. To outsiders the black hole is entertaining, yet enticing. And a little scary. Who knows what a crazed pirate can do when defeat looms?

This investigation was becoming my personal black hole, filled with sexual predators dressed up as investment bankers, trucking magnates, maybe even cops. Where were their boundaries? Like the citizens of the Raider Nation, Jeffcoat and Newman might be capable of desperate things if all of a sudden the tide turned against them. Yet the danger of my black hole was alluring. I delighted in watching these deep-pocketed men fret like a Bronco defense facing Kenny Stabler and Clifford Branch.

We were entering the exciting part of the game. Crunch time. We'd had the marching band and the baton twirlers at half time. My opponents were heading into the locker room to recalculate their strategy. I was definitely the underdog, even with my muscle-bound Red Eye defense. If I wasn't careful I could get swallowed up like a lonesome, drunken Charger fan who staggered into the black hole wearing the blue, gold, and white of San Diego. Common sense told me to rush for the exit. But once a Raider Nation diehard enters the black hole, common sense never prevails.

CHAPTER 14

When I got back from Newman's, Carter was reading a magazine in an unmarked car in front of my house. He opened the door and got out as I walked past. His blazer was a definite blue light special from K Mart. The sunglasses were still there to hide the hangover or whatever else those eyes might reveal.

"We need to talk," he said. I avoided his gaze and glanced down at the magazine on the passenger seat of his car—the latest issue of *Barely Legal*. The editors promised that their cover girl, Hot Coffee, would bare all inside.

"Shoot," I said, "I've got nothing but time. I'd invite you in but the house is a mess. Maid's day off." Actually I could see Luisa peeking through the blinds. She'd be heading out that bedroom window in a few seconds.

"Some privacy would be better," he said.

"Fine," I said, "let's go to the station. That is, if I'm under arrest. Otherwise, unless you've got a warrant, let's talk here."

"Listen up, Winter," he said, "I'm trying to be reasonable here. Don't play that smartass shit. You'll end up second best."

I stared at his sunglasses. Even though I couldn't see into his eyes, I knew he'd blink first.

"I don't want to be in your business," he said, "but you seem to be making rounds saying something about this girl's will."

"I don't know what the hell you're talking about."

"You know a Jeffcoat?"

"The name doesn't ring a bell, Let me check my phone numbers." I pulled my cell from my pocket and pretended to be going through my directory.

"Okay, you want to play games," he said, "fine. But let me tell you. I don't want this case coming back to bite me in the butt. I'm in line for promotion. I don't want you fucking it up. This case is closed. Let's keep it that way and not start talking about wills, lotteries, and all sorts of other silly shit. Close the book or I'll have to start going through your business operations with a fine-tooth comb."

"Do what you gotta do, boss," I said. "I'm clean."

"Don't tempt me," he said, reaching toward his shoulder holster, "just don't tempt me." He pulled his empty hand out and pointed his forefinger between my eyes. "Bang," he said, mimicking a trigger pull, "bang, bang you're dead. Shot fleeing police. Found with an unregistered firearm on his person. I'd enjoy writing that report."

He turned around and walked back to his car.

At least I didn't have to waste more of my Re-Nu to get rid of the aftertaste of this visit. I had to admit, though, he was giving me sound advice. My business activities couldn't stand the scrutiny of an investigation. I wasn't deep in the mix like the old days, but squeaky clean was too boring for me, especially living up in the hills where they didn't even have a pool hall.

What I couldn't figure out was how he found out about my visit to Jeffcoat so quickly. Maybe I should have mentioned this Peter Margolis to Carter to test the waters but I wasn't sure how that would have helped. To tell the truth, I felt a little out of my depth and common sense kept kicking me in the head and telling me to back off. The problem was, I just didn't feel in the mood.

CHAPTER 15

Mutare, Zimbabwe
October 15, 1991

Parents and relatives of the pupils filled the lush green hockey fields of Mutare Girls' High. Many of them had traveled a great distance to attend the year-end prize-giving. Tarisai Mukombachoto's parents sat in the front row. They'd never been to such an event. The two rarely left their rural village. They'd definitely never set foot on the grounds of a place as auspicious as Mutare Girls' High. Opened in 1959, Mutare Girls' High, or MG as they called it, was constructed along the lines of its sister school, Wolverhampton Girls' in England. The founders named the buildings at Mutare after famous British settlers who came to Zimbabwe in the late 1800s and early 1900s: Alfred Beit, David Livingstone, Allan Wilson. The student residences took the names of famous English cities: Manchester, Liverpool, and the one where Tarisai lived: Cornwall Hall.

During colonial days only white girls attended MG. But when Zimbabwe became independent in 1980, schools opened up to all students. A flood of talented young black girls rushed to enroll at MG. Most of them came from the newly emerging elite. Their parents were lawyers, certified accountants, medical doctors. Many worked in the higher echelons of the government bureaucracy—positions previously reserved for whites. The children of the elite arrived at MG in their parents' Peugeots, Audis, and Mercedes Benzes, sporting portable stereos and a collection of the latest cassettes from America: Lionel Richie, Atlantic Starr, Michael Jackson.

But the school offered a few scholarships to girls who otherwise could not afford the levy and the uniforms MG required. In 1987 Tarisai Mukombachoto earned one of those scholarships by submitting an essay explaining why attending this prestigious institution would be the first step toward lifting her and her family out of the "misery of crushing rural poverty."

For the next six years, while her classmates fretted about the boys at the high school just up the road and strove to master the latest dance steps to their music, Tarisai lived for her academic work. In her first two years at the high school she struggled. Many of her classmates had lived overseas before 1980. They spoke English better than the local languages of Shona and Ndebele. They had educated parents who'd spent hours assisting them with their homework during primary school days. Since all of the classes at MG were done in English, they had an advantage over Tarisai. But none of them loved to read and solve mathematical problems as much as Tarisai. She'd spend her Saturday nights reading Charles Dickens or practicing how to bisect an angle with a compass while the other girls hunted for potential boyfriends.

By her third year she was the number one student in the entire class. She even surpassed Sheila Chikomba, who'd grown up in the UK and whose father, Dr. Phineas Chikomba, was a former professor of chemistry at Cambridge University.

In her final year the teachers and principal selected Tarisai to be head girl. She was the first black to fill this position in the history of MG. One of the head girl's many responsibilities was to give an address to the crowd that gathered at the prize-giving ceremony. On this occasion not only were the family and friends of students in attendance; the British high commissioner had come all the way from Harare to be the guest of honor.

The day started with some songs by the school choir, then a speech by the principal. Finally Tarisai's turn came. She walked to the podium fully mindful of the erect posture her teachers had encouraged throughout her time at MG. By now Tarisai had blossomed into a beautiful young woman, though in her red school skirt, white blouse, pink blazer, and straw bowler hat, she still looked like a girl. Other pupils envied her long-legged, rounded figure, her flawless mocha skin. Tarisai was oblivious to such issues. She wore no perfume and kept her hair in a short Afro, just like when she first arrived at MG. For her, only schoolwork mattered.

Tarisai surveyed the faces of the hundreds of people seated in folding chairs across the well-manicured grass. Though her parents had worn the best clothes they could find in the village, they were no match for the sea of stylish suits, silk ties, and imported dresses donned by most of the crowd. Tarisai didn't care. Her parents were happy and proud of their daughter. One day she would earn enough money to buy them outfits even finer than those of the high commissioner and his wife.

Tarisai had never used a microphone before. As she began her speech by acknowledging the presence of the high commissioner, the power of her English almost frightened her. She no longer spoke like a rural schoolgirl but had picked up the intonation of the many white teachers at MG. She spoke, as the local people described it, "through the nose."

Her mother couldn't understand a word her daughter said. The father managed to grab bits and pieces. Still, both beamed with pride, confident that their child would one day bring great wealth and happiness to their family. When Tarisai and her brother were young, her parents expected that Garikai, being the boy, would be the one on whom the family's future would depend. Now they counted on Tarisai. No one else. When they were too old to plow or weed their fields, Tarisai would provide.

"My fellow students," said Tarisai, "we have an obligation. As successful students in our newly independent country, we must use our wisdom and our knowledge to build up this great land of ours. In the past, doors were closed to African girls. Today they are all wide open. We must burst through those doors and show the world that a Zimbabwean girl can achieve anything that any man or woman anywhere can achieve. If we apply our minds we can become doctors, lawyers, accountants, scientists, even astronauts. Let us set our sights very high and never give up our goals. That is the message and the challenge I put to you today. Rise to greatness, my fellow students. Opportunity is in your hands."

Tarisai's parents led the clapping. They applauded so long and hard that it almost bruised their field-hardened hands. Their daughter had done them so proud. She was destined for great things in life, of that there was no doubt.

CHAPTER 16

The morning after the encounter with Carter in front of my house I woke up with what Red Eye called an "anvil" hangover—one where your head feels like someone reshaped it on an anvil with a ball peen hammer. At least I slept through the night. That hadn't happened since the day I found Prudence in the pool.

I tried vodka and tomato juice, the hair of the dog. It got me drunk right away. The second one worked even better. As I poured the third, Red Eye rang the bell. He'd won $1,500 betting on Thai kickboxing the night before. He wanted to celebrate.

"I'm not quite ready," I said. "I need another vodka and TJ."

"Add some Worcestershire," he said, "to clear the head."

"Carter was here again yesterday," I told him while I tracked down the Worcestershire. Luisa had reorganized the kitchen cupboards the day before. When she did that, I couldn't find anything. She had a system, I just kept forgetting what it was. My method was to just line everything up in neat rows of the same size, spices, tuna, evaporated milk. She said my approach made no sense. *Estúpido*, she called it.

"Carter knows about my meeting with Jeffcoat," I told Red Eye. "Our little financial wizard must have called the cops."

"Or maybe they're best buddies?" Red Eye suggested.

"Yeah, right. Cops and tycoons always hang together." Red Eye was my homie but sometimes he just connected the wrong dots.

I kept looking for the Worcestershire, finally found it hiding behind a bottle of vinegar. The brown paper wrapper was still intact but the liquid at the bottom had dried out.

"How much did that broad mean to you?" he asked.

"I'm not sure," I said. "Anyway, it's not about her, it's about me."

He took the Worcestershire bottle and added a little hot water to the dregs at the bottom.

"It'll give you a taste anyway," he said.

"Carter's a lame," I said.

"He's a cop. What's new, homeboy?"

When Red Eye started using that "homeboy" stuff on me, things were getting serious. Prison slang was almost as hard for him to give up as his tattoos. He could try for a while but the minute the pressure came, Red Eye's convict self resurfaced. That's what made him a very special human being.

"I want to try one more thing," I said. "Can you still pick locks?"

"Can priests still stick it to little boys?"

"I think Mandisa's hiding something. We need to get into her place."

"Okay, but this is my sayonara, the swan song of Red Eye, the house breaker. I'm retiring. Let me stick to my gambling. There's more money in it and it's less risky."

"So you're quitting the day job? Then you better learn something about those weird little sports of yours instead of just betting on red."

"Red is the best," he said. "You can't go wrong with red."

Who could argue with Red Eye? He'd never stop betting or picking locks. He thrived on the excitement, the buzz. Maybe when he hit sixty he'd slow down. But then I doubted he'd ever hit sixty. Guys like Red Eye weren't built for the long haul. Neither was I.

He took less than a minute to open Mandisa's door.

"Apartments are candy," he said.

The place looked different. The extra furniture was gone, there was only one lonely blender on the kitchen counter. Mandisa had been wheeling and dealing, but she'd kept her word about the clothes. The bags were still tied up in the closet. I guess she expected me to look through them under slightly different circumstances. Maybe I should have just asked.

"Let's dump this shit out and go through it," I said.

"Whatever."

Red Eye pulled out a massive black-handled hunting knife to slash open the plastic bags.

"Hold on," I said, "we've got to leave this place like we found it."

"We can find more bags."

By that time I'd undone the knot in the plastic. Red Eye tucked his knife back into his belt. The first bag was blouses and skirts, nothing solid. Most of the blouses didn't even have pockets where something could be hidden.

"What do you expect to find?" he asked.

"Don't know. You said to rely on gut feelings. My gut tells me there's something here."

"I need a smoke," he said.

Red Eye liked the breaking in part of the job but he didn't have the patience to sort through piles of clothes.

"If you're getting bored," I said, "go and watch TV. Probably a beach volleyball tournament or something on now."

"Lumberjack contest from Idaho," he said. "Got to see 'em chainsaw the big ones."

"Just keep the volume low."

"Makes me nervous," he grumbled. "I like to get in and get out."

The second bag was all underwear. I skipped that one. Feeling my way around her bras and undies was a little too twisted.

The third bag held shoes, some still in their boxes. I dumped them out on the carpet. Two of the boxes were closed with rubber bands.

Red Eye had decided against the lumberjacks. He grabbed the two boxes with the rubber bands on them. The first held five videotapes, the other contained four. Maxell C-120s. No one used these things any more but I still wanted to have a look.

"Probably the family picnic," I told Red Eye, "Little Johnny's birthday party."

"Just leave it," he said, "let's went, amigo."

"A quick look, maybe Johnny had a stripper in the birthday cake."

The tapes had date labels in Prudence's writing. The most recent was two months old. The first two cassettes were blank.

"I told you," he said, "let's get out of here."

The beginning of the third tape had an episode of *The Bold and the Beautiful*, Prudence's favorite.

"I'll go ahead and fast forward real quick," I said, "if there's nothing . . ."

"Whatever, homeboy," he said, "I'm gonna put on some coffee so the cops have something to keep them warm when they get here. Should I throw in a pizza? Domino's can get here in ten minutes. Pepperoni okay?"

The shot of the naked Prudence mounting Jeffcoat halted the flow of Red Eye's pizza jokes. The film was shot in the bedroom where we found the tapes. No wonder Prudence was moving out of my house. She had a business going on here.

"Jesus," was all Red Eye could manage. The pepperoni could wait.

I tried to play the detached detective, fast-forwarding deeper into the tape as if it was a talking head of a police investigator explaining the details of crime scene findings.

The next tape was a virtual carbon copy only this time Newman was the costar. Things didn't get better as we moved through tapes three, four, and five. There was licking, sucking and thrusting, punctuated by cries of ecstasy from all cast members. I hoped Prudence's were fake.

"Do you know these guys?" he asked.

"It's the two I interviewed. The white guy with the hairy back is Jeffcoat. His office is something out of Donald Trump. He said he and Prudence were 'business associates,' that he loaned her money."

"If those two distinguished gentlemen didn't know they were porn stars," said Red Eye, "these films could have kept money flowing into Prudence's pockets forever, especially if these guys are married."

"They are," I said. "Very respectably."

Tapes six, seven, and eight were different sessions with the same players. I ran through them as quickly as possible. Prudence's beauty was lost on me.

I'd spent all that time and money on her and never touched her boobs or even her lips until I tried to save her life by the pool. How did I let a girl from Africa outfox me? I deserved better. Here I was risking my ass trying to find out who killed her. What did I owe her? Not a goddamn thing. I could end up back in prison behind this. The only people lower than her were the assholes she was humping. I just didn't think I could forgive her, as if forgiveness mattered to a dead woman.

The ninth and final video of this excruciating series held a change of pace. Something was wrong with the film. The lighting was dim.

By now I could recognize Prudence in any lighting at all, but the man was a new partner. Could have been black or white, but too rotund to be Jeffcoat or Newman. Maybe this was the infamous Peter Margolis. As I emptied the VCR, Red Eye summoned me into the closet. "Come here, Cal," he said. I went and stood next to him. Just above the closet door someone had sloppily patched and painted over a hole in the wall. "That's where the camera was mounted," he said.

We stepped inside the closet from where we could see screw holes and the outline of a metal bracket on the other side of the patched spot. We now had a motive and three suspects. My gut feeling was right. There was something in this apartment. A lot more than I bargained for.

"What does this other African chick know?" Red Eye asked.

"Mandisa?"

"Yeah, the broad who lives here."

"I don't know but we're going to find out."

"If I was her I'd be scared shitless right now," he said, "unless she was in on the murder."

"Or doesn't know a thing," I said.

"Anyway," he said, "we can use these tapes to flush out the killer."

I didn't want to contemplate what Red Eye meant by "flush out," but he was right. Those tapes gave us some leverage to get some answers.

I took the tapes home and put them in my stash under the bedroom floorboards. Now the investigation would get interesting. Red Eye said he might be able to hang on for one or two more break-in jobs just to solve the case.

"A personal favor for my homeboy," he said. "These guys are dirt," he added. "The respectable types always turn out the slimiest of all. Probably in church every Sunday, pumping the pastor's hand and congratulating him for a wonderful sermon on the evils of lust."

"All right," I said, "I got the point."

I didn't need Red Eye's philosophy. I wanted to indulge my desire to waste the two men I'd just watched fucking the hell out of my wife. I was debating whether to use a chainsaw or a machete. I'd had such urges before but they always passed. This I time I wasn't so sure they would.

CHAPTER 17

I gave up on the lottery scheme. We hadn't really figured out where we were going with it anyway and now it was time to take it all to a higher level. I had everything I needed on Jeffcoat and Newman. I just had to figure out how to use the tapes.

"We can put them on the Internet," said Red Eye. "People will pay. Interracial is big."

"What the hell are you thinking, homeboy?" I asked.

"It'd be big bucks," he said, "and we can watch those fat cats sweat."

Red Eye assumed the tapes had shattered all my illusions and fantasies about Prudence. I wanted to hate her permanently but it wouldn't come. My own hang-up. Putting her naked body out there for all the world to see? Never.

Anyway, before I did anything with those tapes, I needed another round with Olga. Guilt-free this time.

We did our expensive little sex and shopping number. She made me feel better. I don't know why. Being a harelip I guess I've got issues with self-esteem. Kids used to tease me at school until I whacked Johnny Talbot with a baseball bat when he called me "hairy lips." That shut them up.

After I dropped Olga off with her bag of shopping from Nordstrom, I went back to Red Eye. He had this idea about tape number nine.

"My friend Stretch can bring it back to life," he said. "He's a computer guy, knows all about this shit."

I didn't understand what a computer had to do with a video but I could always count on Red Eye. I dug the tape out of my stash and handed it over. "I'm not saying he'll do it in a hurry," he said, "but he'll get it done."

At least so far there was no indication that whoever killed Prudence was after me. But if word got out that we had the tapes, we'd end up on someone's hit list. If they'd killed Prudence to protect their reputation and bank balance, they'd have no qualms about including me and Red Eye in the package. I wondered if Prudence had really sent these guys blackmail notes? Maybe she never got that far.

Mandisa had to know more about this. I phoned her and she actually seemed pleased to hear from me. Maybe the stress was getting to her. No matter how rough the place was where she grew up, I don't imagine she expected a friend of hers in Oakland to wind up dead. She and Prudence had survived all those wars and famines in Africa, now one of them gets killed in America. Doesn't make much sense.

I arranged to meet her at Lake Merritt, the centerpiece of Oakland's natural beauty. It was once a sewage dump, a real black hole. Even the beautiful things in my city have a shady history.

Mandisa was relaxed, once again in jeans. For a plump woman, she was actually attractive even though she had pockmarks on her cheeks and a few teenage pimples still hanging around on her forehead. I liked the shape of her hands and the way she hugged me when we met, even if she was a little hesitant. Prudence never hugged unless she'd had at least half a dozen drinks.

I could see Jeffcoat's office from the bench where we sat but we didn't stay there long. We walked and talked. I'd forgotten how a white man and a black woman walking together attracted all kinds of judgmental stares. People assume that you're doing something wrong.

"Since we met last time I've found out a lot of things," I said.

"Like what?"

"Prudence met Jeffcoat and Newman at your house and had sex with them. More than once."

"And . . . ?"

"It was taped and someone has copies of these sessions."

"That can't be right," she said. "It never happened like that."

"How did it happen then?"

"I don't know," she replied. "I can't imagine anyone making tapes. Prudence used my apartment a few times. I always worked nights. She was protecting you."

"Me?"

"She didn't want to bring men to your house."

"Mighty white of her," I said.

"Excuse me?"

"It's just an expression we use. I didn't mean anything by it."

"Right. Like when black people call each other niggers."

I wasn't going to put my foot in it again by responding to that one. We walked for a little while in silence. I hoped she'd realize it was just a slip of the tongue.

"There was a camera mounted somewhere in your apartment," I said. "These guys weren't trying to perform on film. They wanted to keep this all under the table."

"Like good white gentlemen?" she said.

"Luckily," I said, "that doesn't offend me. I'm not a gentleman."

I waited for a smartass reply but she just gazed off at some passing cars with what looked like a little smile on her face

"Prudence paid me rent for the room," she said. "I didn't go in there. I'm at work every night. Whatever she did was none of my business. As long as it wasn't illegal."

"So there's a porn studio in your extra bedroom and you don't want to know about it."

"I don't know what you're talking about. Whoever is feeding you information better get it right."

"What happened to the camera that was mounted above the closet door in that bedroom?" I asked.

"How would you know what was mounted above my closet door?"

"I saw it when we were going through her things."

She stopped in her tracks.

"You shit," she said. "You broke into my apartment. I thought there were footprints on the carpet. I should have called the police."

"Go ahead," I said, "call them. Your friend is dead and you want to worry about a little break-in."

"You don't understand any of this. You're just a pimp feeding off desperate young girls. And I'm not desperate. Too bad."

"At least I care enough to find out who murdered one of them," I said. "If that makes me a pimp, bring it on."

She started walking again, only much faster. She was trying to get away from me.

"Was she blackmailing these guys?" I asked. "Is that why she got killed?"

"I don't know if she was whitemailing them or not. I told you I don't know. I gave you the names—Jeffcoat, Newman, Margolis. Now just stay out of my life. I should have known better than to meet you here. Since when did I start hanging around with ex-convicts? America does weird things to you."

She looked angry enough to hit me but she kept walking.

"I'm leaving," she said. "If you follow me I'll phone the police and say you're a stalker. You're nothing but trouble. I told Prudence that but she wouldn't listen."

"I'm a good pimp," I said. "I look after my girls. A pimp with a heart."

She strode quickly, almost breaking into a run. I trailed behind.

"Slow down," I shouted.

"I've got nothing else to say to you," she said. "Nothing."

She kept up the pace for a while but after a couple hundred yards she was starting to wheeze. Apparently IHOP didn't pay for gym membership, but then I was no triathlon master either. My chest was heaving, my throat on fire.

"I'm not trying to bring misery into your life," I shouted in between pants. "Don't you realize whoever did this to Prudence can strike again? Who do you think are the likely next targets?"

She stopped.

"You think I haven't thought of that?" she said. "That's why I want you to back off. If you leave it alone . . ."

"As long as that person thinks those tapes are out there, we're in danger."

"She did come upon a lot of money about two weeks before she died. She sent it home. That's what she always did. For her daughter, her family."

"Work with me on this," I said. "It's not just for Prudence. It's for you, for our safety. Tell me what you know."

"I already have."

"I don't think so. Who was Prudence? What was her real name?"

"Tarisai Mukombachoto," Mandisa said. "She was a mother trying

95

to look after her child. The world is not kind to African mothers. Sometimes we end up ten thousand miles away from our children just so we can pay their school fees, buy them shoes."

"Is that your situation, too?"

"This isn't about me," she replied. "Prudence and I were different women from different countries. I have my problems. She had hers. Different from Americans who worry about what SUV to buy, where to fly for a vacation. That was my common point with Prudence. We never knew the details of each other's lives. We just understood."

The sunglasses only partially hid Mandisa's tears. She dug a tissue out of her pocket but kept talking as she wiped her cheeks.

"She didn't deserve to die for trying to help her child," she said. "She wasn't even buried at home."

"No one deserves that," I said. I was tempted to tell her that Prudence wasn't even buried, that her ashes sat somewhere in some urn. I decided this wasn't the time.

"I'm scared," she said. "Those two men are rich, powerful. If another African woman dies in Oakland the police won't care anymore than they did about Prudence. Do you know about Amadou Diallo?"

"Who?"

"This African guy the police in New York shot forty-one times. He was just walking down the street. They found the police innocent. We are nothing here. Completely nothing. They don't care about an African woman."

"Or about a pimp," I said.

We stood for a long time on a patch of grass by the lakeshore. A middle-aged white couple were rowing a blue boat across the water. The kind you could rent by the hour. The man dropped an oar. Their cackles carried across the lake as he tried to fish the thing out of the water. Each failure brought a new round of laughter. With every lunge the boat rocked. The woman shifted her weight to try and restore their balance. Finally the man got the oar, put it though the ring on the rim of the boat and they started off again. A pleasant respite from whatever might have been the slings and arrows of their lives. Maybe they'd bought the wrong SUV. Derogatory comments from the neighbors can be debilitating. Row your worries away. Life is but a dream.

Mandisa and I had lost both of our oars. I was trying to get mine back but she wasn't helping balance the boat. The problem was, if I fell in, she came with me. She couldn't swim and I couldn't do much better than a dog paddle. I'd meant to take swimming lessons when I bought a house with a pool but I never got around to it.

There were a hundred reasons for an African woman and a hare-lipped white pimp to quarrel. But the reality was that we needed each other. We had to find a way to get our oars through those rings. I hoped she'd stay on board long enough to get it done.

We walked back toward the park bench.

"I think Newman did this," she said. "He's a psycho."

"Now we're getting somewhere," I said.

An old man sauntered past with a little Cairn terrier tied to his walker. I felt sorry for the old guy. Probably took him three hours to get around the lake. Then came a loud bang, followed by a couple more. The dog made a little yelp and the old man keeled over on the grass. More bangs. Definitely gunfire. I dove under the bench and looked up to see Mandisa on her knees next to the old man starting to pump on his heart. I was more worried about the bullets than this geezer's cardiac arrest. Prudence's killer was nearby and either a little off-target or issuing us a very scary warning.

"Phone 9-1-1," Mandisa hollered at me in between pumps and breaths. I dialed, told them where we were. The gunshots stopped. I took off, leaving Mandisa with her lips on top of the old man's. I wasn't hanging around for the cops or Freckle Face and his crew.

I walked the half a block to my Volvo at a calm, orderly pace. I wanted to run but running always attracts attention and sometimes bullets as well. I heard someone shouting something about a drive-by, that a gangbanger got shot in the head. Too bad for him but I was relieved if this wasn't about Prudence or me or Mandisa or any of that. Life on the streets had its own rhythms and worries.

As I got near my car I looked back and saw the old man start to sit up. Mandisa gently eased him back into a prone position as the sirens drew near. She'd saved that old codger's life. That Katlehong where she came from must have been one helluva place.

97

CHAPTER 18

After the incident in the park, I couldn't sleep. Five hits of Wild Turkey didn't help. I got up in the middle of the night. For some strange reason, I wanted to watch those tapes again. I knew they'd heat me up enough to do something to make up for hiding under the park bench while Mandisa saved an old man's life. In prison, we'd call that a bitch move. I was lots of things but nobody's bitch.

I did the routine with the rugs and the floorboards and pulled the tapes out of the box.

I put in the first tape as I popped the seal on a fresh bottle of Wild Turkey I gritted my teeth and knocked back the whiskey. By tape number three the sun was coming up and I was ready. I put on my best suit, stuffed my Walther inside my belt and headed for Jeffcoat's office—ready to rock and roll. I didn't even take the time to put the tapes back in my stash.

When I came out of the elevator Jeffcoat's secretary's eyes were on me like a store detective. I'd popped two Wintergreen Lifesavers in the elevator to get rid of the Wild Turkey smell. Not everyone appreciated whiskey breath in the morning. When I got into her sights, I gave her my biggest smile.

"I'd like to see Mr. Jeffcoat," I told her. She looked at me for a long time before replying.

"I don't remember your name on today's appointments, Mr. Winter." I was surprised she remembered my name, even more shocked when she pulled a little Chinese paper fan out of her desk drawer and waved it in my direction. I guess the Life Savers didn't do the trick.

"I don't have an appointment," I said, "but I think if he reads this note, he'll make time for me." I handed her an envelope with a letter inside informing him I'd seen the tapes and would like to talk to him. She disappeared into his office and came back after a couple minutes.

"He'll see you when he's finished with this client," she said. "Can I get you some coffee?"

"Cream and two sugars," I replied. I was enjoying my momentary triumph over Jeffcoat's gatekeeper. She was a little past her physical prime but her hips were tastefully plentiful and the cleavage display extended a little beyond office protocol. She was more than enough to make plenty of wives jealous. But then Mrs. Jeffcoat had bigger jealousy concerns. The coffee was freshly brewed, just the jolt I needed to face the enemy.

"I didn't expect to see you again," he said as I strode through his office door.

"Some pests are harder to eradicate than others," I replied. I debated about pulling the Walther but left it in my belt.

"I'm an optimist," he said. "I always assume that little roaches die on the first spray. What's your price?"

"Information."

"I've got plenty," he said. "You want stock tips? Interested in a little foreign currency trading? I look for the value of the Euro to rise. I've got nothing but good advice."

"Prudence was blackmailing you," I said. "You paid her some money a couple weeks before she died."

"Interesting theory. Difficult to prove."

"I could always try. If I reported the matter to the police like what you did to me, they might launch an investigation. Videotapes linked to crimes play well on the evening news, especially when they're X-rated. Could make national, with some tasteful editing of course. Not to mention marketing the unedited versions to the porn sites. The whole world wants to know how the rich do it. They're hot and I haven't even seen them all."

"Perverted bastard," he said. "The girl's not even cold in her grave and you're already trying to squeeze money out of her corpse." He stood up and turned away, as if looking over the city would solve the problem. When someone sits on the fourteenth floor all day, the lives of everyone else begin to look small, insignificant. Tiny ants scurrying around the streets. Every once in a while, though, disgusting little insects like Calvin Winter manage to scale the walls.

I enjoyed his quiet suffering even though I could be provoking a murderer. I was coming back to reality, feeling more and more out of place with that 9 mm tucked in my belt. I wasn't a killer. Who was I trying to kid? That's part of why I kept Red Eye around. He'd earned his stripes. Had an SS tattoo on his leg to prove it. Luckily Fast Freddy hadn't seen that one. You only won the right to wear that ink in prison by completing a mission. Red Eye had done more than one. By contrast, I usually liked to think of myself as a coyote, living by my wiles. If I was going to pin Jeffcoat to the wall, it wouldn't be with a gun.

"I'll ask again," he said, "what's your price?"

"I'm trying to find out how Prudence died," I said. "I want information."

"She drowned," he said. "That's what you told me. That's what the police say. She died with the winning lottery ticket in her purse. Right, Winter?"

"That's part of the story. I think you know more."

If he was looking for an apology for the lottery scam, he could forget it. I'm no investor but I know there's no more underhanded game than playing around with other people's money. In other words, I know a hustle when I see one. He wasn't going to get away with sneering at a coyote.

"What information do you want?" he asked. "Yeah, I screwed her a few times. She made a film of it without my knowledge. I paid her $10,000 to destroy the film. I guess she didn't do it. Where's my crime in all this? I made a mistake. Everyone falls to temptation once in a while. She was a beautiful woman. And I wasn't the only one she fucked. "

"Would you care to name the others?"

"That's got nothing to do with this."

"And neither would all those other women you've been hitting over the years."

"My personal life is none of your business."

"It would definitely be the business of the court. If you've had a string of affairs that ended badly, expect a nice little parade of your conquests to stream up to the stand in your murder trial. Of course, since you've got the perfect marriage, the little lady will stand valiantly at your side like Hillary did for Bill. Then there's the issue of Peter Margolis."

I still had no idea who this Margolis was but I figured it was worth testing the waters. I was on a roll.

Jeffcoat glanced briefly at a gold-framed family photo on his desk. His wife had put on a few pounds after childbirth and hadn't lost them. And those gray roots were showing through big time. I guess she couldn't be bothered to keep up appearances. She didn't know what league she was playing in.

"Margolis's death was a boating accident," he said. "A great tragedy."

"I suspect there's a little more to it than that."

"You can surmise all you want, but you can't prove a thing. So if you don't want money and you're not going to give up the tapes, then get the hell out of my office."

"So you say she had other men?"

"I didn't worry about it. She was a good time for me. As long as I protected myself, what she did with the rest of her life was none of my business."

"So you always used a condom," I said. "That makes me feel better because she was my wife."

He laughed.

"I know that," he said. "I know everything about you." He stood up. He was losing his cool. Anger can do strange things to people.

"It's time we ended this meeting," he said.

"I know you hate unnecessary meetings. Something about ineffective business practice."

"Get the hell out of here or I'll call security."

"That's what you won't do," I told him with my first smirk of the day. "The Internet porn sites are just a mouse click away. And if you know so much about me, you know I'd love to put you out there naked for the world to see."

He calmed a little. He'd deployed nearly every weapon in his con man arsenal and I was still right in his face. Being a thorn in the side of a millionaire was better than shooting my wad with Olga any time. I had to find out about this boating accident.

"I'm just thinking that maybe you forgot to protect yourself one time and you caught something from her," I said. "She was, after all, an African. You knew that, didn't you? AIDS is rampant there. It could be a motive for revenge."

"You're way off the mark now," he said. "She was from London. Time to regroup your forces. This is going nowhere for either of us."

"But at least we're having a good time along the way." I gave him the broad smile I'd used on the secretary. My joy was not infectious.

"If I think of anything else, I'll call you," he said, moving toward the door.

"I'd appreciate that. I hope you don't mind if I drop in from time to time just to keep you informed. I'm sure you don't want to be out of the loop on this."

"Goodbye, Mr. Winter. If there has been foul play, I hope you uncover it. In the meantime, please call before you show up at my office again. I'd hate to miss you. If you continue to bother me, though, I will find an appropriate response."

"That almost sounds like a threat."

"Take it however you like," he said. "We in the business world don't issue threats. We make offers, prepare lists of negotiating issues, determine priorities. I'm quite skilled in all phases of my work."

"I'm sure you are," I said. "So am I. I've got a certificate from the Leavenworth College of Business. Perhaps you've heard of it."

He opened the door. I walked out, grabbing a quick glance at the harelip on his high school football team on the way. Poor kid was ugly as sin. I bet he was a reserve tackle. I paused for a second. The short kid next to him looked familiar, but I couldn't put a name to the face. Probably somebody I met in the joint.

I gave the secretary a replay of my greeting smile and headed for the stairs. Waiting for elevators doesn't make it when you're trying for a triumphant exit.

Jeffcoat was clearly a ruthless character. I was probably on over my head playing with him, but I couldn't stay away. This felt like my fifteen minutes of fame, wheeling and dealing on the fourteenth floor. If I was about to fall, let it be remembered that Calvin Winter successfully got under the skin of millionaires and cops in his quest to find justice for a wife he'd never kissed.

In the meantime, I had to find out about Peter Margolis.

CHAPTER 19

That night Red Eye and I went for a drive in the hills of Oakland. Life always looked different from up there. I'd had a taste of hills life in my house but I didn't have a view. A view would have cost me another $100,000. It didn't seem worth it at the time, but now I understood. My neighbors with those enormous tinted windows overlooking San Francisco Bay saw the same world as Jeffcoat from the fourteenth floor. I hadn't quite gotten over my encounter with him. Even with all my experience, I just wasn't sure I could out-con a millionaire on his own turf. I came from a different planet.

When I wasn't in juvie, I grew up in neighborhoods where the only view I had was peeping in on what the family next door was up to. What I couldn't see, I heard through open windows or thin walls. There was life in those streets, though, and on the playgrounds. Nowadays they'd probably call the families in my old neighborhoods "dysfunctional." Definitely two or three of the foster homes where I ended up fell in that category. Going to juvenile hall and then the penitentiary didn't help. Everyone knew your habits there. If you used an extra square of toilet paper, half a dozen guys would ask you if you had diarrhea. The hills had none of that openness. Everyone's life in Carltonville was a closed circle. Too much time to worry over nothing.

Red Eye halted the car in one of those places where you could see from San Francisco all the way down to San Jose. We wanted to get out of the car to take a fresh look. I waited while Red Eye put on a long-sleeve shirt. In this neck of the woods, he never showed off his montage of ink spider webs, dragon heads, prison bars, and the little graveyard with the RIPs for his fallen friends. If people in Carltonville saw all that, they might jump to dangerous conclusions.

"Just when I buy a house and get out of the ghetto," I complained, "a woman turns up dead in my pool. I wasn't meant to have any peace in life. The curse of the harelip."

"Trouble follows us," said Red Eye. "We can move up the hill but we'll always be foreigners here. Our past is only a few miles away. It can climb up here and find us any time."

"I've thought of moving to Hawaii," I said.

"We can't let go, don't know how to leave it alone. It's just like in the pen. Someone steps on your foot and doesn't say 'excuse me.' Another guy burns you for a few soups. Just a couple of bucks. But you have to retaliate. You know it's petty but you can't leave it alone."

"This isn't petty," I said. "It's a murder."

"One we should leave alone. It will only bring us more trouble."

"You're right, we should just forget about it, get on with our lives."

"But we won't, will we?"

"Hell, no. It's just not our nature," I replied, "just so we're on the same page."

"We're on the same paragraph," said Red Eye.

Before we'd left my house, Red Eye had rolled two joints and tucked them into his pack of Camels. Even with the weed I hadn't relaxed since Prudence's death, except for that one time with Olga. That really didn't count.

As we got back in the car, Red Eye put on the Eagles' "Lyin' Eyes."

The lyrics highlighted my situation. But whose eyes were lyin'? Was it Jeffcoat's or Newman's? Was it Prudence's? Her eyes were lying from day one. She didn't come from London. English wasn't even her first language. And she had a family she never talked about. Lots of lies. But they never bothered me that much. Some people had to lie to survive. All my years of bringing people across the border taught me that.

My worry was that the real lyin' eyes might be my own. I'd have to check the next time I looked in the mirror. Was I lying to myself thinking I could solve this? After all, I'd made so many bad decisions in my life, how could I be sure this wasn't just another one? But I knew one thing. Finding Prudence's killer was the right thing to do. I just had to stop thinking about all this other stuff and go and track down Peter Margolis. That's what would turn this case around.

CHAPTER 20

I Googled "Peter Margolis" and got 353,000 hits. I looked at the first hundred. There was a Dr. Peter Margolis in St. Petersburg, Florida, who did boob jobs. Another Peter Margolis in Lincoln, Nebraska, had won first prize in the county fair pork and beef grill-off. I stopped there. I'd have to find someone who understood this Internet stuff.

I got up to go and put the tapes back in my stash. I looked next to the Paul Newman classics where I'd left them the night before. Gone. *Cool Hand Luke* and *Harper* were missing as well. I couldn't believe it. I tiptoed around the house, checked all the windows and doors. No sign of a break-in. Nothing else disturbed. I'd violated a basic rule of survival: what belongs in the stash stays in the stash—always. A real professional doesn't think it's a waste of time rolling up rugs and prying off floor boards. It's always time well spent. Someone was invading my space. My first thought was Jeffcoat, though I wasn't sure why.

I phoned him but his secretary told me he was out of town for the week. When I told her who it was, she wouldn't give me his cell number or tell me where he'd gone or when he'd be back.

She did agree to take my message.

"Tell him if I don't hear from him by the end of the day, I'll Fed Ex the tapes to the webmaster of Zebralove.com."

"I'll give him the message."

He phoned me three minutes later. The secretary had grasped the urgency of the situation. I assumed he was poking her as well. Just a gut feeling. I figured we still had him by the balls but our grip was getting a little loose.

"What the hell do you think you're doing?" he said before I even had a chance to let him have it. "Whatever you have to say, say it straight to me. People can read between the lines. I don't need that."

"Call your thugs off and return what they stole," I said. "There's plenty of copies in other places. In Leavenworth we killed anyone who stole from us. Anyone."

"I don't have thugs," he said. "It's not my style. And I'm not a thief."

"So you have no idea who broke into my house last night?"

"I wish I did," he said. "I'd like to give 'em a medal."

"You're pushing me to where I don't want to go," I said, "but I've been there before. It's uncharted territory for you."

"You live in a fantasy world," he said. "Too bad you never investigate anything before you make wild allegations. You're a moron, Winter. Recognize who you're dealing with. I'm not from the world of break-ins and broken thumbs. I'm a businessman, but I'm no Scout Master. When I've had my fill, I fight back. You don't want to go there."

"You're nothing special just because you have an office on the fourteenth floor. We all come from the jungle."

"So you're stupid enough to think because I let my dick get the best of me now and then I'm a murderer?" he said. "Have a nice day, Mr. Winter." He cut the phone before I had a chance to tell him I wouldn't let him alone until he spilled his guts. He was just an arrogant bastard. I was beginning to think he might have killed Prudence after all.

The worst part of it all was that Jeffcoat was learning how to make me feel like a fool. Too quickly. This talking game was supposed to be my turf. I had to settle into my groove or Jeffcoat and his thugs, if he had any, would be dancing on my face.

Before I had time to pour another shot of Wild Turkey, Red Eye phoned.

"My buddy's through with tape number nine," he said. "He can't recover the audio and the video never came clear enough to ID anyone. All he knows is that the guy has a tattoo on his right arm and another one over his heart. Can't see what the tats say."

"How many guys we got in Oakland with tattoos?" I asked. "A hundred thousand? Two hundred thousand?" It wasn't my day. I asked him if his buddy could follow up Peter Margolis.

"I tried," I told him, "but there's about five thousand Peter Margolises around. I don't know where to start."

"No problem," Red Eye said, "homeboy is the bomb on computers." We arranged to meet later that night. I didn't even tell him the other tapes were gone. I was too wiped out to listen to his advice on how I should have put them back in the stash.

I filled in the afternoon with a business matter—matchmaking. Only for me it was usually more pleasure than business. If you got a perfect match it was like doing a good deed for the day. Even the Calvin Winters of the world like to do a good deed every once in a while.

As it turned out, I wasn't sure if this match qualified. I found a Filipina woman for Sunny Jim Fitzpatrick in Coeur D'Alene, Idaho. Sunny Jim looked like a geek. No teeth, no eyebrows. He'd pay $4,000 plus airfare. Corazon Pehau, his partner-to-be, said she was five foot four, 130 lb., aged thirty. She looked closer to 95 lb. and barely legal. Hard to tell in a photo, and I had to be careful in this business. Trafficking in minors was dangerous. Could get me plenty of federal time at 85 percent with no reduction for good behavior. Besides, I had some boundaries. I wasn't about selling some kid into sex slavery. If a grown woman wanted to put herself on the market, that was different. It was her affair. I was just a broker. Without the middleman, most trade would never happen.

I decided Corazon was over eighteen and e-mailed the photos to the prospective client. Like most Filipina women in my line of work, Corazon was ready to come at the drop of a hat, even if future hubby looked like the back end of a pit bull. I'd found out this modern world of ours had generated millions of desperately poor women in the far corners of our planet. Their flip side was the flood of lonely, socially misfit males in the United States. The women, the Prudences of the world, supplied companionship, sex, a little cooking and housecleaning, plus the image of a marriage—exactly what lames like my man from Idaho demanded. Of course Sunny Jim's demand was backed up by what made the whole process function—money.

Sunny Jim claimed to have a three-bedroom house on half an acre. He didn't post a photo of the place, either because it didn't exist or because the yard was strewn with old transmissions, broken down Lazy Boy recliners and piles of unrecyclable bottles. No guarantees in this matchmaking marketplace. Truth in advertising did not apply. The parties relied on that most elusive of commodities—trust. Hell, I didn't even know if I could trust myself. At this stage I might tell all kind of lies just to have another body next to me, a voice in the house to suppress that image of Prudence's eyes receding into her head next to my guest bathroom toilet.

At least, unlike my Sunny Jim, I had a presentable house. It would look good in photos but it was no longer the sanctuary I dreamed of. The house wasn't really the problem. It was the situation I'd backed myself into. I couldn't settle for a homely woman who worked at J.C. Penney's and made a terrific meatloaf. I had to show the world that a harelip could attract a sexy woman, the type everyone wanted to get their hands on. The world was full of Corazons—desperate, homely, hardworking. I wanted glamorous. But the glamorous types like Prudence only came to me when they hit rock bottom. Prudence still had dreams when I met her. A short little ex-con with a harelip was just a stepping-stone. Corazon might stay with that guy from Idaho for years. I couldn't hold Prudence for more than a few months.

Not long after I'd connected up Sunny Jim with his bride to be, Red Eye arrived for our meeting. He had information and a proposal. The information was that Margolis was a local businessman who died in a water skiing accident somewhere in northern California.

"My partner said something smelled fishy about it all," Red Eye said, "but he couldn't put his finger on it."

I had no idea. Maybe Jeffcoat was driving the boat, maybe Margolis was bangin' Mrs. J. Red Eye's friends didn't always paint in all the numbers, but if Prudence told Mandisa this would buy leverage over Jeffcoat, we had to pursue it.

After the tidbit about Margolis came Red Eye's proposal:

"Let me move in," he said. "I'll be your security. Say for a month or so, until things cool down. I'm sure my parole officer will agree. He's cool as hell. I'll tell him you're paying me a couple grand a month."

"You mean I have to pay for the privilege?" I asked.

"No, no. Just something to keep Mr. Roosevelt Johnson, my PO, happy," he said. "He doesn't trip. A closet Bears fan. Wanted to send me somewhere to get this SS tat taken off my leg. I told him I'd think about it."

"I think you're a little bit too late with this offer," I said.

"Whaddya mean?"

"Somebody broke in and stole the tapes."

"They got to your stash?"

"Not exactly."

"Shit happens, bro, that's why you need twenty-four security. Red Eye's five-star service."

It was an offer I couldn't refuse, even though I had my doubts. Red Eye slept at odd hours, liked weird horror movies, and obsessed on sports betting. Though I had no concrete proof, I bet he snored like a fat lady passed out after dollar-pitcher night. In prison you learn the power of a snore. A real snorter can keep dozens of men awake through the night. If you're unlucky enough to share a cell with one of those buzz saws, you're locked in your own private hell. If you don't move away you'll start dreaming of smothering him in midroar. I'm sure my Sunny Jim from Idaho made as much noise as twenty hungry warthogs. But Corazon would just put up with it to send a few dollars back to Manila every month.

Red Eye's offer left me in fits. I needed security but I needed solitude—my own space to plot my next move and completely recover from the death of my so-called wife. I didn't know how to handle such things other than alone.

I decided on a compromise. I moved all my business paraphernalia, desk and computer into my room. Red Eye could take the second bedroom and the living room for his all hours TV watching. He'd probably be betting on some bantamweight title fight in Indonesia at 3:00 a.m. Far be it from me to get in his way. Just so he kept the volume down. By that night he was camped out on the sofa in front of the TV with his *Daily Racing Form*s covering the coffee table. Somewhere in the middle of a special on the great Yankee home-run hitters of all time, I phoned Mandisa. I wasn't sure why.

"I'd like it if you'd just stay out of my life for a while," she said. "You bring nothing but trouble."

Before I could get her to rethink, she'd cut off the phone. Mel Allen, the voice of the Yankees sounded like he was jumping out of the press box over some home run that Mickey Mantle had hit fifty years ago. I had a feeling this arrangement with Red Eye might not work out.

CHAPTER 21

Harare, Zimbabwe
April 1994

The nurse gave Tarisai a small paper cup.

"Take this with you and fill it up with pee," she said. "Then we can run the test."

Tarisai did as she was told. She couldn't remember when she'd been this nervous. She hadn't eaten in two days. This morning when her stomach retched, nothing came out but bile. She could still feel it burning the inside of her nose. She should never have allowed Cephas to do it without a condom. He was a deputy minister, always used to having his way. He'd promised to leave his wife, Eternity, and marry Tarisai as soon as she graduated.

Tarisai had seen the wife on TV, giving a speech at the opening of a grinding mill in some village. Wives of deputy ministers were often called upon to do such things. Eternity looked like she was made for the rural areas. She had one of those workhorse bodies that not even perms and clothes from upmarket boutiques could disguise. Tarisai imagined that this woman called Eternity had those flat rural feet bulging with bunions as big as pumpkins.

Tarisai was proud of her soft feet—one of the marks of a sophisticated urban woman. Every night she covered them in Vaseline and slipped into some cotton socks before she went to bed. Cephas always commented about the smoothness of the skin on Tarisai's heels. In just a few months they'd be sleeping together every night. Tarisai would be going to diplomatic parties and accompanying her husband on overseas trips. Other girls at the university had been to Botswana or South Africa with their "sugar daddies" but those were just good-time jaunts. Cephas was no sugar daddy. This was for real. He'd already told her the name of the hotel in London where they'd stay during their honeymoon. The Princess's Arms.

Tarisai loved the fact that none of the other girls knew about her relationship with the deputy minister. Nearly every female student lusted after Cephas Kanyere. They all ran to the TV room in the hostel whenever he came on the screen.

"He may be forty-five but he looks ten years younger," said Tarisai's roommate Doris. "Unlike other cabinet ministers he's only got one chin and the tummy doesn't cover his belt buckle. That touch of gray makes him look distinguished."

Doris could speak with authority. She'd dated two cabinet ministers. One of them gave her a 67 cm Sony color TV and VCR, but his tummy looked like he'd swallowed three soccer balls.

Doris actually saw Cephas's wife on the news one day. She screamed with laughter.

"She's a country bumpkin," Doris said to Tarisai and the other girls who were watching. "SRB—strong rural background."

Tombizodwa, a girl who lived next door to Tarisai suggested that Cephas's wife would be at her best "helping a team of oxen plow the fields." The girls at university loved to belittle their rivals.

Luckily for Tarisai, the deputy minister was always cautious. He never came to collect his young girlfriend. He always sent a driver. Tarisai told her friends the driver worked for her "rich uncle" who owned a furniture factory in the industrial areas.

"Bought the business from a white man in 1980 for next to nothing," she told them. "He's rolling in money."

Tarisai played along with Cephas's game to the letter. She always packed her overnight bag when no one was around to see the scanty pink nightie or the diaphragm. The other girls thought Tarisai had no interest in men. Many male students had tried to approach her, telling her they loved her as Zimbabwean men often did when they first met a woman. She gave them all polite but firm refusals.

"Love can wait," she always told her girlfriends. "The only important thing in life is education."

When they teased her more intensely, she reminded them that her family was counting on her.

"I'm the only one from the Mukombachotos to ever finish high school, let alone attend university."

Now it could all be falling apart. She handed the nurse the urine-filled cup.

"We'll have the results in two days," the nurse told her.

Tarisai tried to distract herself with her studies. She spent hours in the chemistry lab monitoring the reactions of various lipids. Normally this work fascinated her. Lipids were essential in the formation of cell membranes. Few people recognized this. But while she waited for her pregnancy test results, the world of cell membranes didn't really matter.

Finally the moment of reckoning arrived. She jumped into the bus that drove from campus to town every hour. She got out at Fife Avenue, telling a friend who rode with her that she was going to the dentist for a checkup. It was the sort of lie the girl would believe. Few Zimbabweans went to the dentist—only the most responsible and most grounded in Western medicine. That's how everyone thought of Tarisai.

"I have good news for you," the nurse told her. "You're pregnant. Eight weeks. Congratulations."

Tarisai fainted. The nurse had to press smelling salts to her nose to bring her around.

"*Upenyu hwangu hwapera*," were Tarisai's first words when she woke up. "My life is over. I've let down my family. Everyone."

The university's policy was to expel pregnant students. After delivering a child, a female student could then reenroll at her own expense. That was fine for girls who came from wealthy families. Tarisai's parents could barely afford to buy her school uniforms when she was in grade five. The university cost thousands.

Some girls managed to hide their pregnancies. They tied belts around their waist and wore loose-fitting clothes. Tarisai couldn't do such a thing. "What a disgusting practice," she thought, "so demeaning." She would get Cephas to look after her and accelerate the plans for their marriage.

"If only I had refused that night," she thought. But Cephas was very drunk, claimed he wanted to feel the "real Tarisai" just once. Being a scientist Tarisai calculated the odds. They were in her favor. She could sense when she was ovulating. She was sure she was safe that night. She'd bet and now she'd lost.

She waited five days before meeting him. They rented a cottage at

Lake Chibero on a Saturday night. The lake was just a few miles out of town, a well-known getaway for illicit lovers.

Cephas told his wife he'd gone to Kadoma for a meeting. Fortunately, the phones in Zimbabwe were so irregular, his wife wouldn't think of phoning her husband when he was away. Besides, a deputy minister was always traveling. His wife had learned to live without knowing where her husband was or who he was with. Like every politician's wife, she knew important men had girlfriends. A wife ignored such things as long as the husband kept the money flowing into the household and didn't flaunt his affairs. The comfort of high society life outweighed the disadvantages of sharing a husband.

Tarisai decided to tell him before he started drinking. He was more reasonable when he was sober, more likely to understand. He took the news without flinching.

"What are you going to do?" he asked.

"What do you want me to do?"

"If you want to get rid of it, I can make arrangements."

"What about us?" she asked. "I'm about to graduate. Maybe we need to marry sooner."

"You must still graduate," he said, "then we'll go ahead with those plans."

Tarisai wanted to believe him but there was no emotion. He talked like he was discussing some office procedure with a secretary. Tarisai expected him to be happy. Proud. A man in Zimbabwe always took pride in fathering a child, even one that came at an awkward moment. Cephas left the cottage in the middle of the discussion, said he was going to the office to get wood for the fireplace.

He came back three hours later without the firewood. Instead he carried two quarts of Castle Lager and reeked of beer. By then Tarisai had fallen asleep in her clothes with a blanket pulled over her.

Cephas pulled off the blanket and tried to rub her belly.

"It will be all right, my dear," he said.

He tried to kiss her but she turned away.

"I'm tired," she said. "I don't feel well."

"I can make you feel better," he said, lying on top of her. She turned onto her side and he pulled her arm, pinning it to the bed.

"Stop," she said, "I don't want this."

He slapped her across the face, then got up and sat in the cane chair next to the fireplace.

Tarisai wept quietly on the bed. When she woke up, he was gone. She had to hitchhike the thirty-five kilometers back to town in her wrinkled dress and high-heeled shoes. A man in a Peugeot picked her up and drove her to the door of the university hostel. She offered him ten dollars for petrol but he refused the money.

"You look like you've had a hard night," he said. "A beautiful girl like you shouldn't have to be abused."

She thanked him and held a scarf to her cheek as if she had a toothache. Luckily it was Sunday afternoon and most of the girls in the hostel had gone out. She lay in her bed with the blanket pulled over her head. She'd never felt so low.

A month later Cephas sent his driver to fetch Tarisai from the hostel. She told him to go away. Tarisai had decided to face this on her own. She wrapped two belts around her waist to keep the baby from showing and was carrying on with her studies as if nothing had happened.

CHAPTER 22

Red Eye claimed he could only hear the television at volume 42. At that level the commentary on ESPN rocked the walls of my bedroom. Now that I lived in Carltonville, on those nights I did manage to sleep the only background noise was a few distant dog barks. I'd gotten used to the quiet. When Red Eye cranked up ESPN, I wouldn't have heard a pit bull growling in my ear.

While I lay on my bed trying to figure out how to track down this Margolis, Don Dunphy's stirring commentary on the Rumble in the Jungle filled the house.

"Foreman is down. His eyes are glazed. He doesn't know if he is on the streets of Houston or in the middle of Africa. Ali has pulled off another miracle."

While Dunphy got more and more excited, I pondered the nearest place to buy a set of earplugs. Then the phone rang. Red Eye'd already had about eight calls from punters that night, so I didn't think of picking it up. I got calls about as often as we had snow in the hills of Oakland. I liked it that way. Suddenly Dunphy receded. "That broad's on the line," Red Eye shouted. That didn't really narrow it down.

It was Mandisa. Newman had paid her a visit at work. Wanted to know if she knew some white guy who was going around talking about Prudence's will.

"I told him I had no idea," she said. "I thought you might want to know."

"How does he know where you work?" I asked wondering if Newman was standing right next to her as she spoke. Why should she trust a white harelip ex-con over a black millionaire with bulging muscles? She told me Prudence had brought him there once. I wasn't sure what that was all about. Mandisa had made out like she'd never met the guy.

She suggested we meet at the Berkeley Pier the following morning. I agreed but I wasn't exactly sure why all of a sudden she was being so friendly. I didn't have time to think about it. As soon as our conversation ended, Don Dunphy was pounding out his message again. Ali was dancing to his left. Foreman was looking bewildered. At the end of round three the doorbell rang. The volume sank again.

"Don't worry, Cal," said Red Eye, "it's for me."

A minute later he was standing in my bedroom door holding a jumbo pizza.

"What would life be without pepperoni?" he asked as he stuffed a piece into his mouth. A thin string of cheese floated down onto the carpet.

"Come and get it, homeboy, extra romano."

I got up and grabbed one slice, and Red Eye went back to Don Dunphy. As round five started, I got a wash rag from the bathroom and scrubbed the cheese off the carpet. I managed to doze off after stuffing some toilet paper in my ears. By that time Red Eye had left the Rumble in the Jungle and gone to Hagler-Hearns.

The empty pizza box was in the middle of the floor the next morning, along with a second one with two slices still inside. Must have been a midnight snack. I hadn't heard the doorbell ring. My light sleeping skills were fading away. But at least I was sleeping.

The Berkeley Pier was cold and foggy. Mandisa showed up half an hour late and I didn't have a jacket. I told her how much I enjoyed watching three old men fish off the pier and drink hot coffee from their Thermoses while I froze my butt off. She pulled her beanie a little farther down over her ears and shrugged her shoulders as if getting there late was out of her control. I figured maybe she was bonking Newman and they had to have one more round for good measure. The world is a strange place.

"I want to know about this business with the will," she said as we sat down on a wooden bench. I could feel the moisture seeping through my pants. The fog is the one thing I hate about Oakland.

"Why are you asking me?" I replied.

She only offered a damning stare as a reply.

"Okay, I'll level with you. We came up with this scheme about a will just to get a meeting with these guys. We didn't know how else to do it."

"Did you ever think of just asking them for an appointment, like telling Newman you wanted to hire some trucks?"

"We never do things the easy way."

"Well, you've got this weirdo Newman coming to my work, threatening me one minute, offering to satisfy my African urges the next. Just what I need in my life. I don't think he's a killer but he's a pain in the bum. Why don't you just give up all this private eye stuff before you have us all in hot soup. Leave well enough alone."

"Well enough alone has gotten at least one person killed so far."

"Let's make sure it stops at one," she said. "If I wanted to be killed by thugs I would have stayed in Katlehong."

"Do you know anything about this Peter Margolis?"

"You're not hearing me."

One of the old men fishing near us got a bite, a big one. His two friends ran over and drowned him with advice about letting out some slack and reeling it in. I'd never actually seen anyone catch a fish off this pier. Maybe I just came at the wrong times.

"I want to know about Peter Margolis."

She fumbled in her pocket and pulled out a folded up piece of paper.

"If you promise to drop this will thing, I'll let you have this."

"What is it?"

"You have to promise about the will thing first."

"The will thing is history. We've moved to a new stage."

She handed me the paper. It was a handwritten list of names, in Prudence's carefully spaced lettering. Margolis was at the top.

"Who the hell are these people?"

"I don't know."

I counted the names. Twenty-three in all.

"Prudence told me I could use this against Jeffcoat if something happened to her and I ever needed money."

"Doesn't make sense. Did all these other people die in boating accidents?"

"It's your puzzle to put together," she said, standing up. "It's been a pleasure." She held out her hand. She'd changed from silver to a deep red nail polish. It went nicely with her skin.

"Do you need any help keeping Newman away?"

"With friends like you, who needs enemies?" she said and walked quickly down the pier. I hoped Newman wasn't waiting for her in the same bed where he'd made those films.

When I got home, Red Eye was tucking into some jelly donuts. The living room carpet was speckled with the powdered sugar coating. The empty Winchell's bag was lying next to one of the pizza boxes from the night before. He'd told me he had to eat extra these days since the Greeley Hot Dog Eating Competition was drawing near.

"It's all about stretching the stomach," he reminded me.

Red Eye crumpled up the empty donut bag and picked up one of the pizza boxes to use as a notebook, jotting down the important points he was extracting from the *Daily Racing Form.*

"Can you throw that stuff away when you're done?" I said. "The garbage can is in the kitchen."

"Sure, homeboy. No problem. I'm just like you. I like to keep a place neat and tidy."

Before I made it to the bedroom, he'd hit the remote. Replays of the previous day's races from Santa Anita. Then the phone rang. I heard Red Eye say something about how the odds had fallen to 10 to 1. I was calculating that me and Red Eye lasting more than a week together was more like a 100 to 1. And those odds were growing with every empty pizza box.

CHAPTER 23

The next night Red Eye went out to the sports bar so I had some peace and quiet to chase down Peter Margolis. I'd never used an Internet phone directory before but after an hour or so, I'd located twelve Peter Margolises in the Bay Area. I posed as a reporter for the *Oakland Tribune* doing a story on boating accidents. After several voice mails, a grouchy old lady, and a Penny Margolis with screaming kids and barking dogs in the background, I found the widow.

"I'm so sorry about your loss," I told her, "but there's been a rash of boating accidents in Northern California over the last few months. I'm determined to get to the bottom of it."

"There's nothing too complicated about my husband's death," she said. "He ran his boat into a tree, the idiot."

My question about foul play or possible mechanical failure brought a long derisive giggle.

"The failure was Peter. He hadn't been sober behind the wheel of a boat since 1983. Or was it '73? Can't remember which. When it came to alcohol, he didn't know the meaning of the word 'enough.'"

I'd prepared myself for a delicate run up to any possible points about her husband's death that might lead us back to Jeffcoat. This Mrs. Margolis was an open book. Once in a while life deals you aces. "And that goddamned insurance guy was the icing on the cake," she said, "trying to claim Peter hadn't paid the premiums. What an asshole."

"So you eventually got the money?"

"After the bastard threatened to take us to court. Then I produced all the receipts and bank statements and shut him up. I had a lawyer on his butt. Ended up costing me fifty grand."

"And which insurance company were you dealing with?"

"We had an independent broker, some shithead out of Oakland named Albert Jeffcoat."

"Did you suspect him of being involved in your husband's death?"

"No. He just wasn't putting the premiums we paid into Peter's policy. I ended up suing. We settled out of court. The bastard belongs in jail."

I told her how sorry I was to hear all this and that perhaps I should be doing a story on insurance fraud rather than boating accidents.

"Absolutely," she said, "have a nice day."

Jeffcoat's list of sins extended well beyond humping other men's wives. He was a certifiable scumbag with a lot to lose. That list of twenty-three with Margolis at the top must have been other people he'd cheated out of payments. Or maybe it was just people who died in boating accidents. I searched for a few of the names and none of them came up dead at sea, or dead at all for that matter. But they weren't connected to insurance fraud either. Normal citizens, doing normal things I guess, deceived into thinking their life was secured by layers of insurance policies. Next to Jeffcoat's, the morals of a coyote and trafficker in willing wives looked pretty upright.

I decided to phone Mrs. Margolis back, to see if she knew any of these other people on the list. She picked up on the fifth ring. I figured I woke her up.

"So it's my reporter friend again," she said. "How's tricks, reporter friend?" Her voice told me that her husband wasn't the only one in the family who liked the hooch.

"Just fine," I said. "Did I catch you at a bad time?"

"No time like the present. You wanna talk about insurance or are you gonna talk dirty to me?"

"I'm all business, Mrs. Margolis. All business."

"Too bad because you know what the hottest thing on the planet is?"

"No idea."

"A horny widow." She cackled for a couple seconds until I heard something crash to the floor in the background. I hoped it wasn't Mrs. Margolis, but after a few seconds she was back on the line.

"You'll have to excuse me," she said. "I've got a situation here. I'll call you later."

She never phoned back. I decided to let her sleep it off.

A few minutes later, Red Eye came in with two young Chinese guys and three pizzas. Manchester United was playing, Red Eye's team.

"One of 'em's married to Posh Spice, homeboy," Red Eye reminded me as I headed for bed. "She's hot."

"Whatever," I said. I put the pieces of tissue in my ear. They drowned out the commentary but at exactly 1:47 Red Eye's celebratory screams let me know that Manchester had scored. I pulled the blankets over my head.

"Yes, yes, yes," said Red Eye, "Fulham motherfuckers are history."

A little while later I heard the Chinese guys leave. I pulled out one of the pieces of tissue from my ear thinking that the game was over but the English accent went back to volume 42 to let me know that Fulham was losing shape at the back. I replaced the tissue but after a few seconds Manchester struck again. Those balls of tissue were no match for Red Eye.

I imagined him standing on his feet, his fist pumping high in the air. Red was triumphing for him again. What the hell had I gotten myself into? Then I heard a shot and the shattering of glass. It sounded like my kitchen window.

CHAPTER 24

I hit the floor, waiting for more shots, hoping to hear Red Eye move. Even groans of agony would have been welcome.

The bedroom door was closed and I was in no hurry to open it. I crawled to the edge of the bed, reached up under my pillow and grabbed the Walther. The black steel felt good in my hand. There was movement in the living room—someone slithering across the floor.

"You all right?" asked Red Eye.

"Yeah, is it clear?"

I wiggled to the door like a fat dog sliding on its belly. I turned the knob, remaining below the line of sight for a sniper rifle. Those TV cops who barged into rooms with their guns drawn were sitting ducks. I believed in the power of crawling low to the ground.

I peeked through the crack in the door just above the bottom hinge. Red Eye stood in front of what used to be my kitchen window. The remains littered the counter. A foot-long glass wedge stuck up from the front burner on the stove.

"Someone jumped over the fence and threw a brick through the window," he said. "I'm not sure where the shot came from. Maybe there were two of them."

I felt brave now. If Red Eye could profile himself in the window frame, I could stand up and hug the wall.

I went into the living room, then to the sliding doors, my Walther at my side. As I stepped onto the patio, I grasped the 9 mm in both hands and pivoted in half circles around the yard, looking for anything suspicious. Maybe there was something to what those TV cops did after all, though I was pretty sure the intruders had gone. As I reached the corner of the house I did a quick 90-degree turn and pointed my pistol down the narrow alley between my house and the fence. Toodles, the cat from next door, jumped down from a window ledge. Luckily my shot missed her.

I ran along the fence toward the front of the house. I wondered if my neighbors had ever woken up to gunshots before. When I got to the front all I found was the cat squeezed under the Volvo in the driveway. I didn't fire a second shot.

I went as far as the sidewalk. No cars in the street. No lights on in the houses. I figure a gun goes off maybe once every ten years in this neighborhood. I also figure the well-healed are expert at diving under the blankets when a neighbor is under attack. My little trauma wasn't going to disturb their beauty sleep as long as the bullets and bricks didn't fly through their windows. Had Prudence screamed that day as she tried to fight off her attacker? Did those frantic cries fall on unresponsive ears tuned into HBO or blocked with space suit style headphones? She'd have had a better chance soliciting aid from the African wilderness.

Red Eye was busy sweeping up the glass. A strange moment to become fastidious about cleaning. He'd swept the big pieces off the counter onto the floor and started cruising over all surfaces with the dust buster. Then he showed me the brick that came through the window. The thrower had etched "Next time you die Winter" on its face in a black marker. This brick was definitely not a teenage prank.

Red Eye carried on sweeping the glass away, attacking the counter with a sponge.

"The little pieces can get into your food," he said, "they'll tear you up from the inside out."

"Who did this?" I asked.

"Don't know," he said, "they got away. But I did my job. If I wasn't here, homeboy, they'd have come through the front door."

I wasn't convinced by Red Eye's self-important evaluation, but he was right. I wanted him there, late-night soccer, pizza boxes, the whole nine yards.

I expected the police to arrive, but the quiet through the rest of the night was only punctuated by two more Manchester United goals and Red Eye's slightly repressed reaction. I heard him mumble something about winning $500 from "those motherfuckers."

The next morning a woman from the police phoned. They said they were following up a report of a "loud banging noise."

"Our call is part of the ongoing process of evaluating police services," she said.

"How did you find out about this incident?" I asked. "Did the pony express deliver the message?"

"I'm looking at a report," said a Miss Francona. "Someone called at 1:46 a.m. A squad car arrived three minutes later. They reported that it was all quiet. I'm just doing a follow up. Trying to maintain a high level of communication with our clients."

"Whatever," I said. "I never saw any police but maybe they spoke to someone else. Who phoned in the report?"

"I'm not at liberty to divulge that information," Miss Francona said.

"Have a nice day," I said and hung up. Even when they were trying to do the right thing the police pissed me off. I would have let them know it too, if I didn't have so much to lose. I had a shot of Wild Turkey and decided I'd give Miss Francona a piece of my mind after all. I hit the call back button on my phone. I got a recording saying that the number I had reached was out of service. Miss Francona lucked out. She wasn't going to like what I would have said.

But the more I thought about that brick, the more I realized police weren't really the problem. I had been violated again. I had to fight back with everything I had or just keep getting punked until one day I ended up lying on my living room floor just like Prudence. I needed a little more firepower than that Walther could provide.

CHAPTER 25

Mandisa phoned at seven the next morning. I slapped myself across the face to wake up before I picked up the phone. Said she wanted to talk, that she had some new information. The only information I wanted was where to get an AK-47. I told her to call back in a couple of days. Suddenly that Walther felt like a poor excuse for a weapon.

Once I'd downed a couple cups of coffee, my urge to feel that AK in my hands receded a little bit. I phoned Mandisa back and asked her if she could come over to my place that afternoon. She surprised me and agreed. I hoped Red Eye had cleaned up all the glass off the kitchen counter.

Before I could ask him about the cleanup or getting an AK, he told me he wanted to do a barbecue. He thought it might make me feel better.

"Being a bodyguard isn't just about security, homes," he said. "It means keeping the boss's spirits up."

I hadn't used my barbecue in months. Not many people grill steaks when they eat by themselves. While I drowned myself in more black coffee, Red Eye spent half an hour spraying oven cleaner on the bits of meat that were still stuck to the grid. Despite his determined efforts, flecks of black remained. I didn't want to think about how much residue from that oven cleaner I'd be swallowing with my dinner.

Red Eye bought three huge T-bone steaks and four pork chops. He made up his own marinade: ketchup, Worcestershire, Mrs. Butterworth's maple syrup and slices of those tiny green jalapenos— the extra hot ones.

"The hot will cook out," he promised, "don't worry, bro."

Red Eye didn't just buy meat. He felt the urge to be properly attired after he ran into a sale on aprons and chef's hats at Target. His sea of tattoos clashed with the Charlie Brown cartoon on his white apron. The one size-fits-all chef's hat didn't encompass his size. It sat like a shrunken derby atop his shaved head.

While I paced the yard looking for suspicious movement in the bushes and listening for cars driving past, Red Eye preached about the power of water and charcoal lighter to control the fire level.

"Can't just use any water," he said. "It needs the right mineral balance." He proudly set two quart bottles of Stream of the Gods next to the barbecue. Stream was the most expensive brand in the gourmet section at Safeway.

With the chops and steaks wallowing in the marinade on the kitchen counter, Red Eye focused on the fire. When the flames flared up too high from his pile of briquettes and newspaper, out came the Stream of the Gods. The water inevitably brought a cloud of smoke, prompting squirts of charcoal lighter to restore life to the fire. I just wanted it to be over. I hoped Mandisa wouldn't show up in the middle of this barbecue foolishness. She wouldn't be impressed. We were under attack and Red Eye was stressing over getting those briquettes a "perfect gray."

"It's all ready," he finally told me. "Just needs one more squirt."

As I came out the back door holding the bowls of the marinated steaks and chops, I watched the flame back up the trail into the can, then blow it up like a little bomb. Red Eye flew back like Tommy Hearns caught him with a haymaker meant for Marvin Hagler. He kept his feet for a moment, then staggered three steps backwards. The third step landed him in the pool.

For some reason I decided to jump into the pool to rescue Red Eye. The chef's hat was floating in the deep end and I didn't see his head above water. I went in feet first and by the time I looked around Red Eye was striding toward the stairs, Charlie Brown's smile bobbing in and out of the water.

"That was a helluva bang," he hollered. I'd never seen anyone laugh with singed eyebrows, beard, and arm hair. He started splashing me. As I jumped back to avoid the splash, slices of jalapeno floated to the surface in a puddle of red sauce. I'd forgotten to let go of the meat before I leaped into the pool.

Red Eye submerged himself, came up with a chop in his mouth and threw it onto the pool deck. Just as the meat plopped on the concrete, Mandisa arrived at the gate. She took one look and beat a retreat.

"I'll come back later," she said, rushing toward the front yard. I dragged myself out of the pool and sloshed after her, but I couldn't get up any speed in soaking wet jeans. By the time I got to the front yard she was driving away in a yellow Chevy. I stood there for a few seconds and watched her car turn left and disappear around the corner. Then a gold Jaguar with tinted windows cruised past and turned left at the same corner. I couldn't decide if Newman was tailing her or they were in this together.

CHAPTER 26

Though I was beginning to doubt Jeffcoat was our man, the next morning Red Eye insisted we had to find out about Peter Margolis. "Once we find out about him," he said, "we can start putting the screws to Jeffcoat. If he didn't do it he can point us in the direction of who did."

I was too crazed from the brick through the window and seeing Newman to disagree. I had become a passenger on Red Eye's bus. He decided that the starting point was Joaquin, a friend of his from the pen who needed a few bucks, had a car and no distinguishing features like a harelip or being sleeved up with everything from NLR to naked ladies performing lewd acts on smiling men.

Joaquin's task was simple. All he had to do was shadow Jeffcoat— find out his habits and his haunts. Red Eye said we needed a way to catch him out of his comfort zone, away from those panoramic views and pushbutton security guards.

"You can squeeze the balls of the high and mighty and they'll scream just like anybody else," was how he put it. "You just need to get them to a place where you can get a good grip on their *huevos*."

It took no time at all for Joaquin to discover Jeffcoat's major haunt— the Cavalier Bar, an upmarket downtown joint that served those seven-dollar drinks with fancy names and parasols or bears carved from ginger sticking out of them. Jeffcoat went there every night after work. But the place was more than a watering hole. According to Joaquin, lots of aspiring young ladies frequented the place.

"They're not hookers," he said, "just gold diggers."

I wasn't sure there was a difference, but that wasn't the point. Joaquin assured us that Jeffcoat liked to buy the young ladies a few drinks.

"He's real friendly," Joaquin said. He didn't need to explain any more. We already knew Jeffcoat's Achilles heel lay between his legs. If we could catch him with his pants down, he'd melt. All we needed was the right woman. Red Eye and I would handle the rest.

Olga took some convincing. Not that she was adverse to our scheme and she liked the sound of the new name on the drivers' license I'd gotten her, "Maria Kournikova."

"They will think I'm the sister of the famous one," she said. "So exciting."

The problem was she couldn't quite comprehend that the attire for the Cavalier had to be understated. She was used to micro miniskirts and massive cleavage displays.

"These are wealthy gentlemen," I told her. "They have the same desires but they require more discretion."

Olga may have understood the dictionary definition of discretion, but she had a hard time applying the concept. It was more than a language problem.

"Let's go shopping," I told her, "I'll show you." She didn't require convincing about making a trip to the mall to shop for clothes. We started at a little boutique called The Eternal Rose.

I picked out a long pink skirt with a slight slit, reaching just above the knee.

"This is discretion," I explained. "Still sexy but leaving something to the imagination. A little mystery."

She pulled a black leather micro-mini off the rack and found some gold stiletto heels to match.

"Trust me," I said, "that's not the ticket. We're going upmarket."

A round-neck white blouse went perfectly with the pink skirt. No cleavage but a suggestive button to be left undone.

"You wear this, you'll catch him," I said. "Wear one of those thin bras that give him a suggestion of your nipples. Like you're already hot. It'll drive him wild."

"American men are crazy," she said.

"I'm paying," I said. "I call the shots."

She pouted for a moment, then tried a sexy finger touch to my sensitive regions.

"You want my honey pot," she said, "buy me black leather. I go animal."

"Not today," I said. "Today is all business. I'm paying you a flat rate. A thousand dollars plus clothes." She was beginning to understand. "And you don't tell a soul about any of this."

"That's not hard," she said. "Olga may not speak good English but she knows how to keep a secret."

We picked a Thursday night to strike. We were prepared for success. We'd paid a friend of Red Eye's who he called Jimmy the Geek, to use his San Leandro apartment for the evening. It took a lot of air freshener to get it ready. I even bought a new pink bedspread and some matching throw pillows, then added a couple landscape paintings for the wall. It wasn't a suite at the Hyatt, but plenty good enough to trap a scumbag millionaire. We bought some vodka for entertainment purposes, though we didn't want Jeffcoat too drunk to be scared.

Red Eye and I sat in the Volvo with Olga just down the street from the bar and waited. We listened to the Eagles and waited for Joaquin to give us the high sign.

Once he phoned us and said Jeffcoat had just gone into the Cavalier, we turned Olga loose in her tasteful round-necked blouse.

She phoned us in an hour and said she had Jeffcoat wrapped around her finger.

"He's horny but not bad-looking," she told us as she got in the car. He was supposed to meet her at the apartment in about an hour. A married businessman couldn't be seen leaving a bar in the company of a strange woman with erect nipples. As I'd told Olga, discretion was currency.

As we headed off toward San Leandro, Olga started to complain.

"I can't make sex in these funny clothes," she said, "and in a strange place. Not a good idea." Everyone has their line in the sand. We'd found Olga's. I told her I'd throw in two hundred bucks more and she got back on point. We also promised her not to leave them together for too long. We got there before Jeffcoat, giving me enough time to fluff up the pillows and take the Oakland Raiders team photo off the wall. Don't know how I missed it the first time around. Red Eye was busy going through a little leather suitcase, making sure all our equipment was ready. It was going to be a long night. The only problem was that Jimmy's apartment was a studio—no place for us to hide. When Jeffcoat buzzed at the downstairs door, Red Eye and I headed for the roof. We promised Olga we'd be back in ten minutes.

"Just long enough for you to get his pants off," I said.

"No man has ever refused to let me take his pants off," she boasted.

We sat up on the roof and smoked a joint. Red Eye pulled the steam iron out of the suitcase and held it up in the air.

"This works every time," he said. "The minute you plug it in, they start shaking." I couldn't wait.

Jeffcoat was in his boxers when we barged in, guns drawn.

"Good evening," I said. "Is this a bad time?" Olga quickly pulled her hand away from Jeffcoat's rapidly deflating manhood.

"What the hell is this?" he shouted as he reached for his pants. Red Eye got there first. He picked up Jeffcoat's black slacks and threw them across the room.

"Your dick seems to be getting you into all types of hot water lately," I said. "Maybe you should learn where it belongs."

Red Eye summoned his most gravelly WWE voice to order Jeffcoat onto the floor. The pantless CEO crawled off the sofa and lay down on his back on the hardwood floor.

"Not on your back, fool," said Red Eye. "Roll over."

Jeffcoat moved onto his stomach. Red Eye tucked his pistol into his belt and pulled a pair of handcuffs out of the leather suitcase.

"Definitely don't want to scratch our boy's Rolex," Red Eye reminded me as he moved in to put the cuffs on Jeffcoat. Once they were in place, Red Eye peeled off the watch and put it on.

"Quarter past seven," he said, admiring the watch face.

I kept my Walther pointed at Jeffcoat's head. Despite our surprise appearance, Jeffcoat had regained his calm, save for the telltale dribble of sweat on his upper lip.

Red Eye brought out the duct tape. Initially I'd been against it but we'd had long talks the night before. Red Eye's persistence won out.

He'd also talked about swords, piano wire, electrical cable, and electric drills. My AK-47 fantasies had faded slightly so I managed to limit his toolbox to the steam iron and the curling iron.

"Mr. Jeffcoat," said Red Eye, "we can do this the hard way or the easy way."

"Do what?" Jeffcoat asked.

"You tell us everything you know about the death of Prudence," said Red Eye, "that's all."

"And about Peter Margolis," I added.

Red Eye reached into the backpack, pulled out the steam iron and plugged it into the wall.

"This is the hard way," said Red Eye holding up the iron. "I press your cheek like it's a Van Heusen. I'd hate to have to do that."

"I've told you everything I know already," said Jeffcoat.

"I've also got a curling iron," said Red Eye. "You've probably never felt one of those."

"I don't have anything else to tell you," said Jeffcoat.

"Tie him up with the tape," Red Eye told me. "And get her out of here," he added pointing to Olga. She didn't need perfect fluency in English to understand where this was headed. She'd already seen too much, at least enough to know Red Eye wouldn't be adding creases to Jeffcoat's slacks with that iron.

Olga scrambled to get on her high heels. I gave her an envelope with the $1,200 in it, thanked her, and she was on her way. I wondered what chance there was that she'd never tell anyone about this, like we'd agreed.

Red Eye plunked Jeffcoat down in a wooden chair. I wrapped the duct tape around him to make sure he didn't go anywhere. His gentlemanly forehead was suddenly enveloped in sweat but he maintained his ignorance about Prudence's death.

"And I suppose you still don't know anything about strange middle-of-the-night events at my house either," I said. He went silent.

"Don't worry," I told him, "we've got copies of all those tapes."

"If you did," he said, "we wouldn't be here." Part of the power of any successful businessman is finding the hole in your counterpart's argument. Jeffcoat had found ours in about ten minutes. I hated him for it. Red Eye's approach was winning me over.

"You've played your hand," he said, "now you've got nothing on me. I didn't kill that girl but I couldn't leave you with those tapes. You could have blackmailed me for the rest of my life."

The iron started to make that tapping sound. I wanted to put it right in the middle of Jeffcoat's face. Where me and Red Eye grew up, we used to fantasize about moments where we had clean-faced pretty boys like Jeffcoat begging for mercy. I thought I'd moved beyond those boyhood fantasies but I had to admit that this was way better than stealing lunch money.

"Let's stop this game before it gets out of hand," Jeffcoat added. "You don't want to kill me, and you don't want me for an enemy. Even two morons like you aren't that stupid."

I hated a smartass in a $2,500 Armani suit without his pants talking tough. Though the duct tape was wrapped around him, he had us tied in knots. The steam iron suddenly didn't seem like such a hot idea.

"If you didn't murder her," said Red Eye, "then who did?"

"How would I know? I wasn't the only man she ever climbed into bed with. She was a horny little slut."

"Shut the fuck up," I screamed. "Don't come with any of your high morals. You're a cheap whore yourself. Olga lit your dick up easier than turning on the Christmas tree lights." I wanted to knock him and his silk-tie ass across the room. He'd probably never been hit in his life.

Suddenly Red Eye looked scared.

"Let's talk, Cal," he said, motioning me out the front door. "Our boy's not going anywhere."

We stood in the hall and closed the front door halfway—enough to keep an eye on Jeffcoat.

"We're backed into a corner now," Red Eye whispered. "We've got nothing on him. The burglary at your house wasn't even reported."

"But he could be a killer," I said.

"We played our hand too late," said Red Eye. "If you want to ice him, we can. But we're gone. Remember, the cops already know about that lottery caper. We'll be prime suspects. A slam dunk for the DA. Plus the broad will rat in a heartbeat."

I wondered why I'd let Red Eye talk me into this heavy-handed session in the first place. Or maybe I talked him into it. As if he needed persuading. My memory was fading fast, along with my buzz.

I looked in on Jeffcoat. He still had that pompous air. On a gut level, killing him had its appeal. But I wasn't crazed enough to ignore what a bad idea it was. Not yet.

"Don't bother trying to get loose," I hollered at him. "Just be patient. We've got it all under control."

"With my fate in the hands of two geniuses, why should I worry?" he replied.

I charged back into the apartment, grabbed the duct tape and slapped three pieces around his mouth.

"Easy, Cal," Red Eye warned. With him playing the calm voice of reason in our partnership, we were entering very deep waters.

Jeffcoat mumbled through the tape. It sounded like something about not being able to breathe.

"Use your fuckin' nose," I said.

I toyed with spitting in his face but I left it there. Confusion, anger, and heartache were proving to be a lethal cocktail for me. Not to mention a shot of sheer foolishness.

Red Eye and I went back out into the hall and talked for another five minutes. We could have rattled on for hours and it wouldn't unravel this mess. I thought I was being righteous finding the murderer of my wife. Now it was all coming back on me. It wasn't Prudence's killer or this lowlife Jeffcoat who would end up in prison here. It was me and Red Eye. There's no justice for an ex-con finally trying to do the right thing. At least I had one card left to play. I brought out the list of names, explained to Red Eye what I knew about Peter Margolis from his widow.

"So we tell him I know about his settlement with Margolis. I figure he's been doing the same thing with these other people. Taking their money and not paying it into their insurance."

"We can't give him the whole list just yet," said Red Eye. "Always keep something back for a rainy day."

"Feels like it's pouring pretty hard right now to me and we got no umbrellas."

"This is just a sprinkle," he said. "We may be in the middle of a hurricane before this is over."

"Yeah, the one called Hurricane Three Strikes and You're Out." We loosened Jeffcoat's wraps and barked at him a lot about Peter Margolis.

Then I rattled off more names from the list: Sean Cutler, Ralph Jacobson, Earl Sadlowski. Jeffcoat's arrogance deflated a little each time I mentioned a new person.

"You've taken these people's money," I said. "Their life savings, their futures."

His eyes suddenly got real big. He didn't even try to mumble a reply.

"Sometimes getting caught with your pants down hurts more than a hot iron on the cheek," I said. For the moment, our business with Jeffcoat was over.

Red Eye put his hand in front of Jeffcoat's face, rolled it into a tight ball, then promised him that the next time the gonads of a great financial adviser would be inside that fist if Jeffcoat said anything to anyone about "our little night on the town together." I peeled off most of the duct tape, just leaving enough so it would take a few minutes for him to get loose.

Red Eye gathered up all our torture paraphernalia and put it back in the bag. We just might be pulling off a clean getaway. I was glad we hadn't used that iron.

"Don't contact anyone or go outside for half an hour," I said. "If the police find out about this, I've got lots more names where those three came from." At least this man who loathed ineffective business practices so thoroughly had learned to lie on his stomach instead of his back. Life is full of important lessons.

We had enough on Jeffcoat to keep him off our backs. The problem was, after all that drama, we weren't any closer to knowing who killed Prudence.

CHAPTER 27

J ust as I got to sleep after our night out with Jeffcoat, someone banged on the front door.

"Police, open up." The voice was deep, unfamiliar. I couldn't believe it. Jeffcoat had already blabbed.

I peeked in on Red Eye before I answered the door. He was wide awake, chambering a round into a Glock under his pillow.

"Get in the closet," I said.

He climbed down gingerly, pulled all the blankets, sheets and pillows off the bed and stuffed himself inside the closet, Glock and all.

"Winter, we've got a warrant for your arrest. Open the door or we're coming in." This was a different voice, one I recognized. Officer Carter. Something was wrong here. The Oakland Police didn't announce themselves. I tiptoed over to the door and checked the peephole. Carter and a short, well-built Hispanic stood alone on the front porch. More weirdness. The OPD came through your door in numbers, not in pairs. Overkill was the name of their game, even more so when dealing with ex-cons.

"Let me get dressed," I said.

"Later for that," Carter said, "open up now."

At least I sleep in boxers when I'm alone in the bed. As soon as I opened the door Carter's hand was in the middle of my chest driving me backwards until I stumbled and fell, not more than five feet from where Prudence had laid on the carpet. I hoped I wouldn't end up in the same state. They say history has a way of repeating itself. At least I could swim a little bit.

"Hands behind your back," Carter shouted, "you know the drill."

His heftily muscled partner had a big black automatic trained on my forehead.

I rolled over and Carter put on the plastic cuffs. If experience was anything to go by, I'd probably lose the feeling in my hands after a few minutes. Lots of fond memories were coming back.

The two pulled me to my feet and read me my rights. I was under arrest for obstruction of justice—helping people enter the country illegally. I had no idea where this came from. Could have been Olga, but if this had to do with immigration I expected the Feds. At this point, though, jurisdiction questions wouldn't help. It wasn't like I had a choice. Didn't matter that much anyway. The locals gave you less time but the Feds served better food. Some Fed joints even had free soda machines.

Carter's partner stuck his head in the door of the second bedroom. All he saw was an empty bed. And I'd wondered why Red Eye took all the blankets with him. Sometimes I didn't give him the credit he deserved.

Middle of the night isn't my favorite time to be arrested. The holding cells are always filled with the nightly cohort of drunks and defeated street brawlers soothing their wounds.

I had to climb over a guy who called himself "Crazy Jerry" just to get myself a little piece of plank bench to sit on. Jerry boasted that this was his "golden anniversary"—his fiftieth drunk and disorderly arrest. I hoped he wouldn't piss in his pants but the stains on his jeans didn't suggest the odds were in my favor.

I sat there in my boxers until some Skinhead offered me a t-shirt. I didn't like his politics but I was freezing my ass off so I took the shirt. Three hours later, just after dawn, our sack "breakfast" arrived—baloney sandwich, a mustard pack, an apple, a pack of cheese crackers and a half pint of warm nonfat milk produced in a prison farm near Fresno. I finished it all off in five minutes. It took them a whole day to give me a picture ID, have some nurse ask me if I heard voices and get my county issue clothes—an orange jumpsuit, a T-shirt and the black canvas shoes that we call "Jap flaps." It had been several years since I'd had the pleasure of looking down at my leg and seeing the word "prisoner" in six-inch black letters.

When I got to court the following afternoon, the DA said I was a notorious trafficker who had served federal time.

"He's a definite flight risk, your honor," he added. "The state opposes bail."

Justin, my youthful public defender who had introduced himself to me about three minutes before the hearing, leaned over to me and asked what I had to say in reply. After our conversation, Justin managed to point out that I was a "homeowner and lifelong resident of Oakland."

"Except for his time in federal prison," the judge interjected.

"Yes, your honor," Justin said, "but that was more than a decade ago."

The judge, a man in his fifties with a brown mustache and a horseshoe hairstyle, asked Justin various questions about my employment and other sources of income. Justin and I had more little conferences. I told him about my transport business and several other ventures involving "printing and publishing." There were grains of truth imbedded in the information I supplied but I wasn't ready to give him the whole picture. What was I supposed to do, say I did matchmaking for crackpots in Idaho looking for desperate young Filipina women? The fact that I owned two trucks didn't leave the judge overwhelmingly impressed. I didn't mention they were sitting in a wrecking yard being sold for spare parts.

"I'll set bail at $50,000," he said, drawing his gavel down and looking through the papers for the next case.

Even though a parolee isn't supposed to have contact with inmates, Red Eye came to visit me after court. We spoke through a metal screen in the visiting area. He said he'd already talked to Jerry Carney, a former heavyweight boxer who ran a bail bond business. I knew some of Jerry's associates from my time in the Feds.

"Jerry says you'll be out by the end of the day," Red Eye told me.

"And you'll get violated for coming here," I told him.

"My PO's cool," he replied. "Don't trip."

It took an extra twenty-four hours but the following day I was shedding that jumpsuit for the Bermuda shorts and Walter Payton T-shirt Red Eye delivered.

My next task was to scrap that wet-behind-the-ears public defender and get a real lawyer. We call public defenders "dump trucks." I didn't want to become a freshman lawyer's dumped load, especially since

I still didn't know exactly why I'd been charged, let alone what the evidence was. I did know one thing, though: I didn't have long to figure it all out before the whole house of cards crashed down on me and Red Eye.

CHAPTER 28

Two months before graduation the dean of students summoned Tarisai to his office. She didn't make too much of it. The head of the Biology Department, Professor Chawanda, had once called her in. When she got there, she found he wanted to ask her out for a drink. He was sixty-three years old. She had no trouble politely refusing. She still ended up with an A in his course.

Other professors had issued similar invitations. The girls in the hostel encouraged her to accept these invites but Tarisai always declined. Cephas would not tolerate her being in the company of other men. The girls in the hostel kept reaching the same old conclusion: Tarisai was a hopeless bookworm doomed to a life of biochemical experiments and celibacy.

Tarisai was fully prepared to offer a range of excuses when the dean popped the question. She was confident her diplomacy would ensure she wouldn't end up in an unseemly chase around his desk. Other girls had such problems, not Tarisai. She'd learned to act in a dignified manner.

The dean was a tall man who sat very erect behind his desk. Unlike most of his peers, he devoted an hour each morning to physical exercise. The grounds staff at the university were used to seeing him huffing and puffing along campus roads as they made their way to work early in the morning. He claimed to have run the London Marathon in 1979.

The dean had shed his jacket for the meeting with Tarisai, paring down to his crisply ironed yellow shirt and brown tie. His handsome, slightly aging face bore the sheen of imported lotions.

He greeted Tarisai in the traditional Shona way, clapping his hands quietly in front of his chest. He spent a few minutes asking about her family and her progress with her studies. This was the African way, finding out about a person's welfare and their relatives before conducting any business. The dean didn't do it with everyone but in this instance he felt it was important.

Once the greetings were finished, he reached for a green piece of paper inside a manila file with Tarisai's university registration number written on the cover in black marking pen.

"Miss Mukombachoto," he said, "you have compiled an impressive academic record during your time here. I have spoken with three of your professors. They all express the utmost confidence that you are on the road to becoming the first black woman in Zimbabwe to earn a PhD in biochemistry.

Tarisai thanked the dean. She was almost blushing. She'd never received such praise from someone this important. Despite such kind words, she couldn't quite relax. The belts around her middle were squeezing tight. She'd adjusted them in an extra notch for this meeting with the dean. She couldn't let him find out her secret. He was predicting a bright future for her.

"On the basis of this I have engaged in extensive discussions with the executive committee of the university. Unfortunately they have been made aware of your condition."

The dean almost swallowed the word "condition" he said it so quietly. It struck like a bolt of lightning to Tarisai's heart. Suddenly her mind started to race through scenarios of disaster. How could she talk her way out of this?

"I have tried to convince our committee of the need to make an exception in your case. However, they have overruled each and every effort on my part. They have insisted that the rules be followed to the letter. Therefore, I have the unpleasant task of delivering this to you."

He handed her the green piece of paper. It was a typewritten letter on the stationery of the Office of the Vice Chancellor of the University of Zimbabwe.

The dean continued. Tarisai was too frightened to even look at what the paper said.

"I regret to inform you," he said, "that as of today, you are expelled from the university. You have twenty-four hours to collect your things and move out of the hostel. I am sorry that we were not able to reach a more amenable and realistic solution. If there is anything I can do to assist you in your attempt to further your studies, do not hesitate to call on me."

Tarisai sat in silence. Who had betrayed her, torn her heart from her chest, crushed the dreams of her parents? Who could do such a thing? Probably one of those rich girls in the hostel had found out. She hadn't told any of them. She'd even waited every night until her roommate went to sleep before she got undressed. Still someone must have noticed the belts, the change in her style of dress. They couldn't stand a poor rural girl who was more beautiful and more clever than they were. Then she had a more disturbing thought: it could have been Cephas himself, wanting her out of his life. She didn't want to think about that possibility.

Ever since high school she'd lived on one track: her studies would carry her to success and she'd carry her family with her. How many times had she envisioned a team of local builders at the family homestead as they began construction of her parents' three-bedroom brick house, complete with a generator, a tin roof and ceilings in every room? Now it had all fallen apart. She went into a brief daydream, seeing herself climbing aboard the blue and yellow Matambanadzo bus, riding home in shame, sharing a seat with a woman carrying a live chicken on her lap or putting up with a drunken old man spilling sorghum beer on her dress and trying to touch her bare knees.

"Miss Mukombachoto," said the dean, "I'm so sorry. Is there nothing I can do? Do you need transport for your things?"

"I don't know," she replied looking past him at an obscure vision of her future. "I don't know what I'll do. Thank you, professor, for trying on my behalf."

She stood up and for some reason she curtseyed, like she used to do when she was a small girl waiting on the old men in the village. She went for a long walk around the campus, finally finding her way back to the hostel. Her roommate had gone to town to do some shopping. Tarisai locked the door and cried until her eyes were dry. It was almost dark by the time she staggered out of the room.

"I can't go home," she thought. "Never. If I leave town I'll end up as one of those thousands of rural girls who spend their life looking after children and maize fields. Men with a third-grade education will send me to collect firewood. I can't live like that."

She caught a bus to town and knocked on the door of one of her few friends from university, Dorcas Ncube.

Dorcas had graduated the year before and taken a low level job in the accounts department at Lever Brothers, one of Zimbabwe's biggest companies. She had a one-bedroom apartment in the Avenues, a sea of high-rise blocks on the edge of Harare's city center. The Avenues had a reputation as the sugar daddies' playground. Entire blocks of flats were full of attractive single women who entertained the prosperous men of Zimbabwe, married and unmarried. For their services, these "avenue girls" received various rewards: trinkets, stipends, and whatever else they could bargain for. Some had their rent paid. Others bought new lounge and bedroom suites from the sugar daddy's purse. A few got "ladies' cars"—Renaults 5s, VW Golfs, Mazda 323s. Shopping baskets, they called them.

A handful of avenue girls sought substance in their relationships. They looked for love, family, and future. If this meant stealing the coveted prize from an aging wife, so be it. Wealth and romance were in short supply. Competition was often intense, sometimes ugly. One night a girl two doors down from Dorcas woke up to a gang of thugs sent by her sugar daddy's wife. The girl ended up in hospital for three days.

Dorcas avoided this drama. She walked to work, did her job faithfully, and returned home, always careful to be behind her locked door before sunset. She lived only with her young cousin, Caroline, who had just started high school. Dorcas spent most evenings either helping Caroline with her homework or watching the one local television station. The highlight of her week was Sunday evening when her favorite program, *Dallas*, came on. She loved to hate J.R. Ewing.

Dorcas had patience. She knew one day she would rise in the ranks of Lever Brothers or some other company. Black women with accounting degrees were rare. Within a few years she'd have a house of her own, a nice car. Love would come to her naturally, through meeting someone at work or being introduced by friends. She would never become an avenue girl. She was attractive enough to compete, though not beautiful like Tarisai. Dorcas was slim and short, her complexion clear and dark. On special occasions she put on perfume and polished her nails. Otherwise, she didn't pay much attention to such things. Like Tarisai she had always relied on being clever, not glamorous.

Tarisai found Dorcas watching early TV news, eating a dinner of the green vegetable they called "rape" and the traditional maize porridge, sadza. She only had meat on the weekends.

Dorcas immediately noticed the panic in her friend. In the entire two years the young women shared a room in the hostel, Tarisai never carried this expression. She looked like her eyes would never close.

The two greeted each other in the carefully crafted way before Tarisai explained why she had come.

They talked long into the night, well after Dorcas's cousin had gone to sleep on the kitchen floor.

Tarisai told Dorcas the whole story, from her first meeting with Cephas to her expulsion from the university. They cried together at times, then planned how Tarisai could avoid that fateful, humiliating bus ride back to her rural home.

The next day Tarisai packed her two suitcases full of clothes, blankets, toiletries, photos, and her few pieces of costume jewelry. While everyone else was attending morning classes, a taxi came and took her away. She didn't have the courage to tell the other girls at the hostel what had happened. They'd figure it out themselves.

The taxi dropped her at Dorcas's. Tarisai arranged her things in one corner of the living room. She'd sleep on the sofa until she had enough money to buy a bed. Dorcas offered to share her double bed with Tarisai but she didn't want to trouble her hostess. The next day Tarisai would go to various companies and offer her services. She was sure she'd find something. After all, she'd gotten all A's in accounting in high school.

After two weeks she managed to secure a job at a small import-export company. She answered phones, filled out orders, and helped with the bookkeeping. They paid her $600 a month, a pitiful sum, but enough to help Dorcas with the food bills and rent.

At her job Tarisai didn't have to worry about tying belts around her middle. Her employer wasn't concerned about pregnancy as long as it didn't interfere with work. He figured Tarisai would do what most women did, work up until the day she delivered, take a couple days off, then be back at her desk. Maternity leave was almost unheard of in Zimbabwe. People still boasted that African mothers were strong, not "dainty and fragile" like their European counterparts who stayed at home for six months after giving birth.

While Tarisai easily completed all her duties, the long walk to and from work proved exhausting. As she got into her eighth month, she found herself laying her head down on her desk in the office and taking brief naps. When she arrived at Dorcas's in the evening, she did nothing other than collapse on the sofa and fall asleep.

One day on her way home from work she saw three girls from the hostel walking toward her. They looked so lively and happy. In just a few weeks they'd be graduating.

Tarisai ducked into a hardware store and waited for them to pass. The paint fumes made her nauseous as she concealed herself behind a display of Dulux high gloss enamel. Finally she heard their raucous laughter in front of the store. They were talking about a party at some company director's house the previous weekend. Apparently the imported whiskey had flowed like water. Finally the girls passed.

Tarisai spent several more minutes in the hardware store before she went back onto the sidewalk. She knew her former friends were gone but seeing them drained her energy. They were all a year younger than her, yet their life was on course. They reminded her of all that she had lost.

A month later she delivered a baby girl at Parirenyatwa, Zimbabwe's biggest hospital. She named the girl "Netsai," which means something like "troublesome." Despite the name, Tarisai loved the little girl and doted on her when she came home from work in the evening. During the day, Netsai stayed with Mabel, a sister of one of the avenue girls in the building. Tarisai paid Mabel $30 a month plus some food.

Several weeks after Netsai's birth, Cephas appeared at Dorcas's door. "I've come to see my child," he said.

Tarisai suppressed her anger. If he knew where she was, why had he waited so long to come? She handed him the baby. A child had a right to know her father, even if the man showed her no love. Cephas smiled and chucked Netsai under the chin.

Half an hour later when he left Cephas gave Tarisai $800 to buy a "few things" for his daughter.

It would be almost a year before Cephas would see his daughter again. By that time Tarisai had a new job and had moved out of Dorcas's apartment to her own place. Her life goals had changed as well. She was solidly on the road to becoming an avenue girl.

CHAPTER 29

You couldn't call George Tsiropoulos Oakland's premier lawyer. He alternated between flashes of brilliance and alcoholic binges. But he was affordable and wouldn't sell me out for another client with deeper pockets. I'd used George before. He saved me from ten years in the Feds back in the day. He stood his ground and got the prosecutor down to thirty months. He was no dump truck.

I hadn't seen George in a while and time hadn't served him well. His once slightly pudgy body had matured into full-fledged obesity. He labored to breathe and multiplying chins were putting serious pressure on the top button of his shirt.

His office furniture was in a similar state. The nicks at the corner of his veneer desk were starting to shred and the fabric on his client armchair had dwindled down to a few threads. Probably wouldn't even qualify for the Goodwill show room.

"We have to wait for discovery before we know what they have on you," he said. "Right now the DA's talking five years, one year for each count of trafficking. I could probably get him down to two or three if you want to deal."

"I need to know what they have," I said. "There's something fishy. What are these five counts all about?" I explained the complications with Jeffcoat. I left out the details about Olga, just said that Red Eye grabbed him and threatened him with an iron.

"What planet are you guys living on? You're lucky not to be looking at kidnapping," he said. "This isn't the Oakland of the 1970s anymore. There's a new sheriff in town."

"I still don't like it," I said. "See what you can find out."

Tsiropoulos phoned the next day.

"You know an Olga something?" he asked. "Russian sounding name, like that tennis player, the big blonde."

"Yeah."

"She rolled on you."

"What'd she tell them?"

"Don't know yet. She got caught in an immigration raid. Some strip club. I'll keep pushing for more info. I've got a friend in the DA's office."

I told him I had a few more things to explain, things that wouldn't go down well on the phone.

He got the point. That afternoon I unloaded all the all the gory details about our night with Olga and Jeffcoat at Jimmy the Geek's. George wasn't happy.

"How can I defend you if you don't give me all the facts?" he asked. "Jesus, you think I'm going to snitch?"

I spent five minutes massaging his ego, assuring him that I trusted him completely, that omitting the information about Olga was just another one of our "random bad decisions."

"Red Eye and me, bad decisions are us."

Tsiropoulos didn't crack a smile but he was simpatico. He could always find a way to forgive. Fuckups like me and Red Eye made his life interesting.

"It doesn't look good," he said. He was right. If Olga told them about our session with Jeffcoat, it was curtains. She'd be a witness to a kidnapping. With her and Jeffcoat on the stand, we'd be toast. She'd probably even wear a discretion-inspired outfit in the witness box.

I was still gambling that Jeffcoat wouldn't want to pursue it but the balance was shifting. He had the option of moving from adulterer to kidnap victim. We could only hope that the Peter Margolis card could hold him at bay. But something else about this was smelling rotten. When I showed up at Jeffcoat's office with the lottery story, I got a strange visit from Carter and partner the next day. Now this. Too much coincidence.

I phoned Red Eye on his cell. For once he picked up. He told me he'd be staying with a friend for a while. I didn't ask who.

"Olga rolled on me," I said. "If she spills her guts, you might want to think about that vacation in Brazil or Belize." I avoided spelling out the whole list of countries that didn't extradite to the United States over the phone. Red Eye would get the idea.

I told him we had to meet. He said he wasn't sure he could fit it in.

"I'm trying to get in the zone," he said. "The Greeley is this afternoon." Amidst all this, Red Eye was worrying about a hot dog–eating contest. Of course, this wasn't just any old hot dog–eating contest. This was the Greeley. He'd been thinking about it ever since last year when he suffered a "reversal," as they call them at the forty-dog mark, and lost his title. He was hungry for revenge.

"You might be sitting in some county jail somewhere by then," I said, "if we don't get this straightened out."

He caved in and we agreed to meet later at what we still called DeFremery Park. They'd renamed it after Bobby Hutton, some Black Panther kid who got killed by the police in the 1960s. Oakland just couldn't leave well enough alone.

Once the word "kidnap" stopped bouncing around my head like a beach ball in the wind, I looked more closely at the facts. If they had me for a kidnap, they wouldn't have granted bail, at least not for anything less than a million. Also, they'd have been looking for Red Eye, pressuring me to tell them where he was. And they would have torn my place apart.

Olga probably just told them I got her the drivers' license. But there was one thing about snitches—once they started telling, they usually ended up revealing the whole story, adding a few embellishments for good measure. They might protect their mother or child, maybe even a lifelong friend, but forgers and financial backers for small scale shopping sprees were definitely expendable. Olga had entered a complicated game. A good cop would have that sixth sense to know when she was holding back. They'd keep pressuring her. If she had to tell each and every detail to avoid that flight back to Belarus, she'd let it all hang out in less time than it took her to get Jeffcoat's dick hard. But maybe that wasn't the game here at all. If Jeffcoat was working with the cops, this was just a plan to get us out of the way. Still, if that was the game, how was Jeffcoat dumb enough to think we wouldn't rat on him about Peter Margolis? I needed to talk to Red Eye.

DeFremery Park, or Bobby Hutton Park or whatever you want to call it, was a bad choice. I'd played baseball there but that was thirty years earlier. It had been reincarnated as a drug-dealing haven. Red Eye and I would also probably be the only white faces there, not an ideal way to conduct a secret meeting.

As it turned out, I was wrong about being the only white faces. The place was crawling with undercover cops of all colors, sizes, and shapes. They must have been expecting a big bust.

Red Eye looked agitated.

"I was trying to focus today," he said, "to visualize that fiftieth dog going down the hatch." He was wearing his Greeley contest T-shirt from the year before. The drawing on the front showed a huge set of teeth devouring a frightened hot dog. Drops of ketchup, mustard, and pieces of relish flew in every direction.

"I wouldn't have bothered you if it wasn't important," I said trying to keep my cool. I didn't understand how he could be thinking of stuffing hot dogs down his gullet with a nice little trip to the pen on the table but that was Red Eye.

"It's not rocket science to figure out where this will end up," he said.

"And they probably don't have hot dog–eating contests in Belize," I said.

"Maybe it's time to make amends with Jeffcoat," he said.

"What should we do, send flowers and a sympathy card? Tell him our thoughts are with him in his hour of grief. All we've done is kidnap him, terrorize him with a steam iron, and vow to send some tapes of him banging Prudence to his wife. Oh yes, and accuse him of murder and threaten to tear down his business with our little list of names."

"Don't trip," said Red Eye.

"One of us better trip," I said. "A kidnap charge can get you the lethal injection." The seriousness of the matter wasn't registering. He was staring off into space.

"And I thought this was going to be my year," he said.

"Your year?"

"Yeah, that fat Irishman who won last year's Greeley got stomach cancer. He's out of the running. He was a hell of an eater."

"Have you thought about leaving the country?" I asked. "How does Brazil sound? Beautiful beaches, even more beautiful women."

"Won't help, homeboy. If they want you these days, they go and get you. The law doesn't matter anymore. Besides, I don't speak Spanish."

"Portuguese."

"Whatever. Still a foreign language. I only speekee dee English," he said, "and you know what?"

"What?"

"I've never been on a plane. Don't even like going up ladders. Does Greyhound go to Brazil?"

I wished weeping was my style. This was a perfect moment for uncontrolled sobs. Instead, we stood there for a long time behind a couple of trees in the park that were supposed to provide shade for the swings and the jungle gyms. What a waste. The swings were broken, and the jungle gym looked like someone had ripped out parts for scrap metal, probably to make shanks and machetes. A kid would be safer walking on a bed of nails than playing on that thing. Anyway, the only child in sight was a toddler holding his mother's hand while she paced in a circle in front of the park waiting for her connection. She was so out of it, she didn't even notice the dozen or so undercover cops trying to blend in. But then who was I to talk? I'd chosen this park and hadn't run away when I saw all the heat.

I kept talking about options. Red Eye's fear of flying dissipated a little when I told him they spoke English in Belize. But my efforts to convince him to leave didn't really seem to be making headway. He was Raider Nation to the core. He'd never live anywhere else. Couldn't really. His runs for me to Mexico were the only time he'd ever been out of California.

As I pondered Red Eye's boundaries, I examined my own. Brazil, Portuguese or Spanish, didn't look too bad when I set it next to fifteen years in the penitentiary. Half the guys in the pen spoke languages I didn't understand anyway. And all that talk about federal pens being like resorts was as exaggerated as the length of the salmon that got away. Any prison is hell for me. I didn't want to go back, would probably rather shoot myself in the head than end up doing life.

I told Red Eye I was thinking about making a fake passport for myself, just in case. He looked a little surprised, like I might leave him behind. If I did, he'd have to ride the whole beef. I couldn't do that. I offered to make him a passport as well, but he wasn't biting. Oakland held a magical mystery for him. He couldn't cut it loose.

When two cars stopped in front of the park and the white guys inside in the one-way sunglasses started looking our way, it was time to leave.

To my surprise, they didn't follow us. I guess they just wanted us out of their turf. We were happy to oblige. Neither me or Red Eye were going to Brazil, Belize, or anyplace else. I was as tied to Kenny Stabler, Al Davis, and Jack London Square as Red Eye. I just wasn't as quick to recognize it. Red Eye and I were bound together. We'd just have to find a smarter way than lottery schemes and steam irons to find out who killed Prudence. But for the moment our biggest problem was keeping our asses out of prison.

CHAPTER 30

bout ten blocks from Bobby Hutton Park, we picked up a tail. An unmarked car followed us for six more blocks before we shook him at a red light. I jumped on the freeway and headed south for San Jose. Paranoia was setting in and it wasn't even nighttime. The Eagles' "Take It Easy" didn't calm my waters. I tried Tower of Power, the greatest group in my city's history. Even their best album, *Back to Oakland*, couldn't ease the stress.

I phoned Tsiropoulos on the cell and asked him if he had any news about warrants for me or Red Eye. Probably a stupid thing to ask over the phone. He didn't know anything. By the time that Tower of Power album finished we were on the outskirts of San Jose and had run through every option from catching the next flight to Guadalajara at the San Jose Airport to renting a car and driving to Oklahoma to lay low for a few weeks.

Then we started tripping on the cell phone. We both knew a mobile could be a tracking device. I'd heard that taking the battery out removed the tracking capacity but I never believed technological rumors. Red Eye had heard the same theory so he encouraged me to throw the phone away for "safekeeping." I pulled into an AM/PM and told him to toss it in the dumpster out back. He followed my instructions after he set it on the pavement and stomped on it about twenty times with his boot. It's good to have thorough partners.

After the demise of the phone, we felt much better. An extra large coffee and a chili dog bolstered our spirits and sent us back toward Oakland. The Greeley might be Red Eye's last act as a free man but at least I'd try to get him his chance to bring home the gold. I had to hurry. I kept it at 85 all the way, darting from lane to lane like a runaway rabbit. When the traffic slowed me down, I slid along the shoulder and prayed no cops were looking. With a replay of *Back to Oakland* to inspire, I couldn't lose. Like Red Eye always said, "When in doubt, put it to the floor."

We pulled into the parking lot of the Oakland Coliseum with ten minutes to spare. A distant blue banner with the same logo as Red Eye's T-shirt gave us all the directions we needed.

"I shouldn't have eaten that chili dog," he said. "It could make the difference between the gold and the silver."

"Don't trip. You got it in the bag."

This was my first Greeley, and the crowd was impressive, about five hundred hysterical gluttony lovers and several teams of TV cameras. The fans were a cross section of WWE supporters, Ultimate Fighting aficionados, and the normal inhabitants of the Black Hole. Not a highly sophisticated Oakland hills gathering where a barely audible burp could draw glances of derision. A solitary black security guard policed the crowd. The Raiders could have used him on their offensive line.

Red Eye had the luck of the draw—spot number seven. The year before they gave him number two, which he said was "the same as rolling snake eyes." I never thought of it quite that way.

Most of the contestants sported bellies that bounced, rolled, and swayed in their battles with the dogs and buns. I didn't know exactly how best to support Red Eye's efforts. Very stout wives in halter-tops used the scream-in-his-face approach.

"Chew, Johnny, chew. You can do it. Eat that motherfucker up."

"Keep it down, Big Louis, keep it down."

They hollered like their heroes were breaking tackles at the Super Bowl and dashing for the winning touchdown.

At seven minutes a hefty bearded gentleman in blue bib overalls suffered the first "reversal" of the competition. At least he was in spot number three. Red Eye told me that a reversal right next to you could be fatal.

"It's contagious," he said, "like when you see someone yawn and you suddenly can't resist the urge yourself."

True to form, a bulky teenage white boy in spot number four vomited just a few seconds after his neighbor. The epidemic stopped there.

Eighteen solid competitors kept shoving in dogs and buns at a frenetic pace, adding just the right amount of water to flush the food along its downward path.

The scorekeepers were bikini-clad women poised behind each competitor. They flipped over a numbered card each time their contestant finished a dog. High-tech digital displays hadn't struck the Greeley just yet.

After nine minutes the bleached blonde standing behind Red Eye was flipping over card number thirty-seven, good for third. Lightning Johnny, in spot number eight, was in second place, one dog ahead of Red Eye. Johnny wore a Hell's Angels vest with no shirt to hide his ink web of choppers and naked women with huge boobs. Red Eye looked like a blank slate by comparison. Two biker chicks were doing everything but eating the dogs for Lightning Johnny. When they weren't screaming encouragement, they were miming grotesque chewing and swallowing movements or advising him to belch to "make room for more." I didn't know how to match their efforts.

The leader was a slim, Asian teenager named Rodney who wore a slick black tracksuit and an SF Giants cap. He was a clean, almost compulsive eater, even dabbing the grease from the corner of his mouth from time to time. He was two dogs ahead of Red Eye with three minutes to go. That's when the Hell's Angel began to falter. He had that overstuffed-pig-about-to-fall-over look on dog thirty-nine. The once vibrant motion that forced full dogs into his mouth in one enormous shove had slowed to an occasional half-hearted poke. He sat motionless for a few seconds, then succumbed to a mighty heave that covered his eating area and sprayed a few errant drops onto his nearly weeping female fans.

Red Eye plodded on, unfazed by his neighbor's misfortune. While Rodney was steady, Red Eye had a final kick. At eleven minutes and fifty seconds they were both on dog number forty-two. Rodney had an adoring young female fan who provided him with mild-mannered statistical updates of his competitors' progress.

"Stop eating," she said. "He can't finish his. With the extra space you'll win the eat-off."

Her strategy was brilliant. If they both ate the same number of hot dogs, there'd be the Greeley's version of sudden death. Whoever ate five dogs first took the gold.

The young man instantly followed her advice, throwing three quarters of a hot dog on the table and turning to look at Red Eye.

"That's your margin of victory," Rodney's advisor told him, pointing to the discarded hot dog.

Red Eye was still battling with number forty-two. With five seconds left, he took a sip of water and went for broke, trying to stuff the entire dog in his mouth. He couldn't manage. His chewing had slowed, as if he had a mouthful of rocks instead of a 100 percent pure beef dog sanctioned by the International Federation of Competitive Eating.

Red Eye held his palm under his chin, like he was trying to keep an overstuffed suitcase from popping open. He took a big swallow but his cheeks still bulged. With two seconds to go, the suitcase burst. Just after the twelve-minute buzzer, balls of chewed hot dog meat and bun plopped out of Red Eye's mouth onto the table. A dead heat.

The youngster took deep breaths while his female handler relayed encouragement.

"Focus, focus, focus. Visualize yourself eating five dogs in less than thirty seconds," she told him. "Think about how that would look, how it would feel."

Red Eye laid his head on his arms while his body convulsed with massive belches. They didn't allow anyone to touch the contestants. Otherwise, I would have been pounding his back and trying to get a few more precious cubic inches of gas out of his stomach. If a man could expire from eating too many hot dogs, Red Eye was at death's door.

"Ten seconds," came the warning over the loud speaker. The biker chicks had moved over to Red Eye's spot.

"Whip that little gook," one of them said.

"Give Red Eye a little quiet time," I said. "He needs to concentrate."

They complied and went silent.

I looked behind us. The man-mountain security guard had appeared.

"Is there a problem here?" he asked, looking at the two women. "Remember this contest is about eating, not color." He put his hand on his billy club. The women didn't beg to differ.

By the time Red Eye raised his head to confront that plate of five dogs in front of him, he looked fresh.

"Good luck," he said to his young competitor, "but you're history." Red Eye held his opponent's stare until Rodney's handler drew his attention away. Red Eye's glare had put doubt into those youthful eyes.

Red Eye beat Rodney by a dog and a half. The title was coming back where it belonged.

He lay down in the back seat all the way to my place, holding the Golden Dog trophy atop his massive midsection mountain of forty-six hot dogs. He must have belched a hundred times.

I remembered I had a bottle of champagne in the fridge. We could use it to celebrate Red Eye's victory. As I pulled up in front of my place, I realized it might be a while before I got to pop that cork. There were two guys I'd never seen before sitting in a white car two doors up the street. No one else in my neighborhood drew the heat. They were waiting for me.

CHAPTER 31

ed Eye couldn't get out of the car by himself. I grabbed his hands and pulled him into a sitting position in the back seat. From there he levered himself up to his feet with the armrest. I walked him to the front door like a football player with a torn-up knee. Each step brought more belches. I was hoping the inevitable wiener projectiles wouldn't fly from his mouth until we got to a bathroom inside.

The two men in the car observed our movements with great interest but they didn't get out. Likely there were considering a range of criminal activities that could have precipitated Red Eye's incapacity. Excessive hot dog consumption wouldn't have made their list.

I put Red Eye to bed, leaving a five-gallon plastic bucket at his bedside to accommodate any reversal. The trophy from the Greeley sat on the nightstand where he could look at it as he lay on his side. The topknot was a hot dog inside an undersized bun.

"I'm going to get my name engraved on the Golden Dog this time," Red Eye said. "I should do the other trophy too though I'm not sure where it is."

He moaned as he tried to adjust his position to get a better view of his prize.

I delivered a glass of Pepto Bismol.

"Don't think that will help," he said. "I'm beyond medicine. I just need a gigantic puke and a good sleep."

With that he held his head out over the edge of the bed, pulled the bucket into place and stuck two fingers down his throat.

The vomit came in waves. I stood back, trying to avoid the splash and stink. Out came gallons of greenish hot dog waste, a few pieces of skin floated in the pool inside the bucket. I should have put some newspapers or a towel down to protect the carpet.

"That's the best puke I ever had," he said when he was finished, "better than sex."

I needed to apply my matchmaking skills to Red Eye when he recovered. I hadn't been as good a friend as I thought. How could puking be better than butterin' the muffin? Red Eye was no Tom Cruise but somewhere there was the perfect match for everyone if you just looked hard enough.

He picked up the lid of the bucket and sealed the top, making sure all of the edges were pressed down tight. It didn't do much to stem the stench. At least I'd kept distance enough to stay dry.

"Sorry, bro," he said. "I'll dump it out in a minute. Just need to let my stomach settle." I couldn't argue with his offer. I wasn't going to touch that bucket.

"I'll get you a glass of water," I said. "You might get dehydrated."

"Gatorade would be better," he said, "helps with the electrolytes."

"Sorry, don't have any."

"Then give me a glass of water with a teaspoon of sugar and a quarter teaspoon of salt."

"Is that recipe from the Greeley's cookbook?"

"My personal trainer recommended that," he said.

"You don't have a personal trainer."

"Nowadays every champion has a personal trainer."

"Yeah, right."

I went to the kitchen to prepare his concoction. I was wondering what scent of freshener would clear the air. Hawaiian Hurricane might be a contender or the old standby, Fresh Lemon. I could hear Red Eye in the bedroom still laughing at his joke about the personal trainer. I hoped it wouldn't lead to another set of convulsions. With the lid on that bucket, a second round could bring disaster to my carpet.

As I stirred in the salt and sugar, the doorbell rang. I didn't have a hard time guessing who it was.

Carter's pal the Weasel was holding a thumb inside his belt and pushing his sunglasses back up onto the bridge of his nose. His very tall partner wore a suit and was high on something. Crank would have been my guess. His hair was kind of frizzed up and stuck in place with grease—a guy in his late forties chasing the fountain of youth. He'd taken a wrong turn. His wingtips needed a shine, the morning shave was pretty spotty. But I forgot all that once I looked at his mouth. Harelip. Thirty years ago he'd been wearing number 74 in that picture of Jeffcoat's high school football team. The dots were connecting.

The harelip reached into his pocket and pulled out a pair of handcuffs. Though he was running interference I suspected the same old quarterback was calling the plays.

"I'm parole agent Washkowski, looking for my client, Mr. Theodore Cornell. I believe you know him as Red Eye." Washkowski had that nasal sound to his voice. In another situation I would have sympathized. That talking through the nose was one part of the harelip experience I'd avoided.

"If you have a message for him," I said, "I'll deliver it. He's slightly under the weather at the moment."

"I'm afraid I'll have to see him in person," Washkowski said, moving forward. "Step aside." I closed the door a little to block his way.

"You got a warrant?" I asked.

"Don't need one. This is a parole search. According to our records this is Mr. Cornell's place of residence. He and his residence are subject to search any time of the day or night."

"He's very sick," I said without moving. I opened my phone and hunted for Tsiropoulos's number. I kept getting messages instead of the address book. Cell phones are confusing when the pressure's on.

"I'm calling my lawyer." I said.

Just as I got Tsiropoulos's number on the screen, those two alien bodies barged through the door. The Weasel pulled out his billy club and waved it at his side. It was one of the new kind, with a little cable dangling at the end to whip you with. I could feel the blood dripping from a slash in my cheek and he hadn't even hit me yet.

"I suggest you take a seat," he said, "and put the phone away."

"Red Eye," I hollered, "some asshole PO named Washkowski is here to see you. He's on his way in."

I heard Red Eye's feet hit the floor as the Weasel slammed me to the carpet with surprising power. As I tried to block the stench of the Weasel's excessive use of Right Guard, I heard Red Eye struggling with the lid of the bucket. I could understand why a PO showing up was enough to make Red Eye puke. I wished there was something I could do but with a knee in my back I wasn't going to be much good. I could see Red Eye through the open bedroom door, struggling to stand up.

"What's that smell?" Washkowski asked.

"It's this bucket," said Red Eye. "Let me move it out of the way." As Washkowski yelled at Red Eye to get down, my partner in crime reached for the bucket. In one surprisingly swift motion, he picked it up and hurled the contents at Washkowski. Little bits of hot dog stuck to the parole agent's hair while others dotted his not-so-new suit. I didn't want to think about my carpet. That show was worth the cost of three good steam cleanings.

The Weasel jumped off of me, pulled out a can of pepper spray and charged Red Eye. Washkowski was gagging. I hoped he wouldn't vomit. Red Eye tried to pull his T-shirt over his face to block the orange spray. It didn't work. I heard him coughing. Then my eyes started burning and I couldn't breathe. I tried holding my breath but it didn't help.

"My eyes, my eyes," Washkowski screeched, "that fuckin' shit is in my eyes."

I didn't know whether he was talking about the vomit or the pepper spray. Hopefully both. He streaked for the front door, leaving a trail of vomity footprints along the way. The Weasel had enough presence of mind to get the cuffs on the choking Red Eye and call him a few choice names.

"I'll phone Tsiropoulos," I promised Red Eye as the cop escorted him out of the house.

"What are you taking me in for?" Red Eye asked.

"You have the right to remain silent," said the Weasel, "you have the right to an attorney. And I have the right to kick your fuckin' ass."

"What's the charge?" asked Red Eye.

"Shut the fuck up," was the Weasel's only reply.

Washkowski had found my garden hose and was washing himself down on the front lawn. Red Eye and the cop marched past him. Then Washkowski threw down the hose and trudged a pukey path back to the patrol car. I heard him mumble something about letting that "fuckin' asshole clean up his own messes."

I closed the door behind me, got my car keys, and headed for the local U-Haul rental center to get a carpet shampooer. It would take a couple of hours to process Red Eye at the station, maybe longer. Time enough to get out the worst of the stains. That carpet would never be the same. I should have stuck to hardwood floors.

I phoned Tsiropoulos on my way to U-Haul and summarized the day's events. I don't think I made that much sense but at least he got the important thing straight: he had to get down to the police ASAP to check on Red Eye.

"He's a candidate for a serious beating," I said.

"I wouldn't want to say he made a bad decision," said Tsiropoulos.

"You had to have been there," I said. "Red Eye didn't have a choice."

It took me three hours of vacuuming, shampooing, and scrubbing to remove most of the stains. I figured it would get rid of any evidence that might incriminate Red Eye plus the Right Guard stench from the Weasel. I expected more cops to come and search the place but they never arrived.

I doused every room with Hawaiian Hurricane and Pine-Sol and left three fans blowing, This house of mine had to be cursed. Karma was coming to get me I guess. I strove for suburban tranquility and order. Yet there was always some unwanted invasion from somewhere. Maybe I wasn't meant to live this kind of life. I'd have to give it some thought. In the meantime, I hoped they hadn't beaten Red Eye to death.

CHAPTER 32

One of the conditions of my bail was no contact with "known criminals." Since Red Eye was now in jail, presumably visiting him would be classified as "contact." Probably living with him was also an issue, but they hadn't said anything about that. I thought of using one of my fake IDs with a disguise to visit but decided I wouldn't fool anyone. I had to wait for Tsiropoulos's report and hope no one arrested me first.

They'd picked up Red Eye for violating parole. He wasn't supposed to leave Alameda County without permission. He'd reportedly been sighted somewhere near San Jose. How could they have known that? I was sure I had ditched the car that followed us out of DeFremery. Had to have been the cellphone after all. Or maybe they stuck some device to my car. I still lived in the eighties when you could rely on your senses. I used little tricks like driving around the block three times to find out if I was being followed. Or making ten consecutive right turns. But in the new millennium our senses were useless. Technology had left them behind. If someone really wanted to track me, they could do it from an armchair. Whatever tricks they were using, someone was watching. Still, if they were watching that closely they would have made Olga tell them everything. Then they would have just come and got me for kidnapping. To my surprise, she seemed to be holding her mud.

I met Tsiropoulos as he came out of the courthouse after his visit with Red Eye. The wrinkled suit pants were a bit of an irritant but I'd rather have integrity than finely pressed Gucci. Tony Serra was one of the great defense lawyers of all time. They even made a movie about him, but his shoulder-length hair always flew in ten different directions and he rode a bicycle to work. A courtroom is not a catwalk.

The dump truck defense attorneys of today have forgotten this is an adversarial system. They eat lunch with the prosecutors, play golf with them on the weekends.

At least if Tsiropoulos wasn't shooting straight, it was because he had too much whiskey the night before, not that he'd sold you to the D.A. to save some rich bastard whose son got caught with a bag of coke in his college dorm room. The best things in life don't always come in neatly wrapped packages.

"They've just got Red Eye on a violation at the moment," Tsiropoulos told me, "but they're asking him a lot of questions about you."

"What kind of questions?"

"About bringing people into the country illegally, arranged marriages. That kind of stuff."

"I don't do that anymore," I said. "Well, not the coyote stuff. Just a bit of matchmaking on the side to kill the boredom. Plus, the occasional fake ID."

"Red Eye's little stunt with the PO will probably get him an assault charge, though I've never heard of vomit classified as a dangerous weapon. I guess it's a toxic substance. God, you guys live in a different universe."

"We have our moments," I said. "The cops should know not to mess with an eating champion right after a contest. It's like playing with an angry bull."

"And that PO said a lot of nasty shit to Red Eye in the car. Tried to scare him into telling."

I wasn't interested in what a vomit-soaked PO had to say, though I did take the time to tell Tsiropoulos about the high school football team connection between Washkowski and Jeffcoat.

"So you're telling me this now?" he said. His face was turning a deep red. He didn't believe me when I told him I'd just figured all this out.

"You haven't figured out shit," he said. "You got no idea who killed the girl, no idea why you or Red Eye got picked up and you still want me to save your ass. Jesus."

I didn't know what to say. Sometimes keeping quiet is the best reply to a lawyer. They can always out-talk you, even when you're a con man. I finally promised him there wouldn't be any more secrets.

He laughed and started telling me what the next steps were. Red Eye would have to wait ten days to get a decision on his parole violation. They could give him up to a year. His bucket toss wouldn't yield any generosity.

"His real PO is a brother named Kirkland. I left a message on his voicemail. Red Eye says he's cool."

I laughed at Tsiropoulos calling Kirkland a "brother." I never quite got used to it all when it came to racial terms, though I knew which ones not to use. Still, there was no way I could bring myself to say "African-American."

"They beat the hell out of him, too," Tsiropoulos said, "kicked his ribs and knees. He could barely walk."

"Why doesn't that surprise me?"

Tsiropoulos shook his head told me he had another meeting inside the courthouse. As we parted he advised me that maybe when I grew up I should learn to only fight battles I had a chance to win.

"You don't get it, do you?" I replied. "I'm not Vince Lombardi. I don't fight to win. I fight because that's what life is all about. What else is there?" I stuck my chest out a little but me and Red Eye were in just about the deepest shit possible. And now all I had waiting for me at home was a half-empty bottle of Wild Turkey. I was almost missing the late-night soccer games.

I drove home to the Eagles' "Life in the Fast Lane," feeling a little less eager for this game Red Eye and I were playing. I was counting on the Wild Turkey to restore my zeal, but before I had a chance to knock back more than a couple of shots Tsiropoulos was at my front door. I didn't even know he knew where I lived. He was out of breath and looked a little confused. I offered him a hit of the Turkey but he declined, said he was on the wagon.

"I just came from a meeting with Jeffcoat and some slick-ass attorney of his named Jarvis. Young dude, $400 haircut and all."

I took a swig from the Wild Turkey bottle. Lawyers' haircuts didn't interest me.

"This is the story. Jeffcoat's got all kinds of connections with the cops. If you and Red Eye keep pushing this, he'll make sure you get put away. If you agree to back off, forget about the tapes and this Margolis, they'll leave you alone. I promised them an answer by tomorrow."

"What about the murder?"

"Jeffcoat swears he knows nothing about Prudence's death and that none of what he calls his team does either. They were all bonkin' her, getting blackmailed by her. But he said murder was not part of his repertoire."

"You believe that?"

"Don't know."

Toodles started meowing from the other side of the sliding door. I got up to let her in. She'd been hanging out at my place more and more lately. Could be it was the fresh halibut I kept giving her but I liked to think it was the company.

Maybe we'd been barking up the wrong tree all along. As much as I loathed Jeffcoat and all he stood for, he never felt like a murderer to me. I was getting confused. Then there was Newman, or could Prudence have had a whole other set of tricks we hadn't even stumbled on? Clearly she got around.

"Tell him we'll back off," I said. "The test will be if Red Eye gets out and they drop his charges."

"So I should phone Jarvis and tell him the deal's on?"

"Yeah. I'm sure Red Eye will go along with it."

"But does this mean you really are going to back off?"

Toodles jumped up on my lap. She was purring like my Volvo right after a tune-up.

"The official answer is yes. That's what I instruct you as my lawyer to say. Of course, under the protection of lawyer-client privilege my answer could be slightly different, but we won't go there, will we?"

Tsiropoulos shook his head as he opened his phone and speed dialed Jarvis. The deal was done.

An hour later Red Eye phoned me from his cell phone.

"My PO cut me loose," he said. "He was pissed as hell. I need a drink."

"How's your stomach?" I asked.

"The least of my problems," he said. "Come and get me. I'm thinkin' seriously about Rio." I couldn't wait to give him all the news.

CHAPTER 33

Harare, Zimbabwe, 1997

Thursday nights belonged to Nhamo Nyakudya, also known as Baba Charity, which meant "Father of Charity" in Shona. Charity was the name of Nyakudya's oldest child. This rotund man was one of a handful of black Chartered Accountants in Zimbabwe. A whiz with all things financial, he also used his acumen with money matters to secure the company of beautiful young girls like Tarisai Mukombachoto. Baba Charity was far from handsome. He wore black-frame glasses and wide ties, both of which had been out of style for at least a decade. Due to some disorder his doctors could not identify, he'd become afflicted with a rash of hairy facial warts as he entered his fifties. At first he had them removed with liquid nitrogen but after a while he just gave up. He didn't even bother doing anything about the one that had sprouted up two millimeters from the tip of his nose. He was letting nature take its course.

Luckily for Baba Charity, avenue girls didn't choose their partners for good looks or sexual prowess. Baba Charity understood that he was in a marketplace where the best product went to the highest bidder. He had the resources to secure Tarisai. She was top of the line.

Baba Charity didn't like those thin-as-a-fence-post fashion models, though a few had made themselves available. But neither did he look for a figure that was too traditional. His wife had one of those and then some. Tarisai was trim but had developed an extraordinary curvature of the lower spine, which allowed her most outstanding physical feature to provide a well-rounded display. As she became more versed in the avenue girl world, Tarisai acquired a keen sense of the power of her buttocks to open a pathway to the wallets of wealthy men. Through the gifts from her various partners, she'd compiled a set of skin-tight designer jeans and African-style dresses which emphasized the perfection of her backside. Not that the rest of her was anything less than astonishing. Her hair was always done meticulously with the smallest of extensions. She sometimes spent a whole day in the same chair to give her hairdresser time to achieve perfection. Her skin bore a translucence, as if she could glow in the dark. She used nothing but the finest imported creams and lotions from Europe. She'd come to abhor the slimy feel of the Vaseline she'd rubbed on her skin as a youth. She told her friends the petroleum smell of Vaseline was worse than the stink of rotten meat.

Just a little over a year as an avenue girl had brought Tarisai the façade of prosperity—a seventh-floor apartment overlooking the city with the rent paid in advance for three years by Baba Charity; a double sofa lounge suite from Mod Con, Harare's most exclusive furniture store, a massive Sony color TV and VCR plus a JVC stereo system with cassette, turntable, and CD player. Alberto Andireya, one of her suitors brought the stereo back from Germany, along with a Siemens stove. He was an airplane pilot. She dumped him after cooking him one meal on the stove. He was no competition for a chartered accountant.

On this particular Thursday Baba Charity showed up a little late and very drunk. She'd never seen him this intoxicated.

"Daddy," she said, "why do you come to my house stinking of this Chibuku? You know I don't like that smell."

The traditional sorghum beer called Chibuku had a sour odor. Tarisai said it smelled like a "baby's dirty nappy."

"I'm an African man," he reminded her. "An African man must drink African beer, not this clear urine the Europeans make."

"That's right, Daddy," she said, "you're my big strong African man." She knew that an ugly old creature like Baba Charity liked nothing more than to hear how good-looking he was. Money could buy the most marvelous words of false praise.

In some ways, Tarisai liked him better when he was drunk. He didn't last long. Sometimes she could get him to squirt with just a few quick flicks of the fingers, saving her the discomfort of him fumbling around trying to find her "sugar plum" and the snorting, grunting, gurgling, and slobbering that followed.

When he was on top of her, she reminded herself that she was doing this for little Netsai.

"My daughter will have no future if her mother remains a simple accounts clerk in Harare," was her thinking.

Baba Charity was slipping his pants off. She reached down to help him. Some nights they got stuck around his knees.

"Next month I'm going to Paris," he said, "the city of love. We can go together."

Tarisai had always dreamed of seeing the world. She'd read books of love and romance in Paris and London. She had a postcard of the Eiffel Tower that Alberto had sent her.

Baba Charity's offer prompted a vision for Tarisai. She saw herself coming through the customs at Harare Airport laden with dozens of plastic bags from duty free shops in Paris. She'd be carrying perfume, clothes for Netsai, and her dream of dreams: a full-length black leather coat with a fox fur collar.

A few weeks later Tarisai was lifting off from Harare International, her first time in the air. Baba Charity had the middle seat, pinning her against the window. As the plane rose into the night sky, her stomach rocked. She glanced at the lights of the city out of the corner of her eye. The cars looked like little fireflies moving down the roads. The inside of her knees started to sweat. In fact, she was sweating almost everywhere. The little round vent above her head kept blowing cold air but the flow of perspiration didn't abate.

One of the air hostesses, Svikai, was an avenue girl who lived on Tarisai's street. She slipped Tarisai and Baba Charity several extra tiny bottles of Johnny Walker Red. When Baba Charity took a trip to the bathroom, Svikai stopped by to chat.

"*Wakakecha mari*," she said to Tarisai, "you've caught a lot of money there. Taking you to France while the wife stays behind. *Uri tsotsi.* You're too clever."

"I pay for this," said Tarisai. "He has the face of a giraffe and the body of a hippo. I make him keep his trousers on. That way I can feel his wallet from start to finish. Makes it all worthwhile."

Svikai promised Tarisai more of those little bottles of whiskey.

"That way he'll be too drunk to think of anything but sleep tonight," she told Tarisai.

The two women giggled. Avenue girls were full of tricks.

In Paris Baba Charity spent most of his days in meetings. Tarisai played tourist and shopper. While roaming the streets she attracted the attention of dozens of men who spoke to her in French and halting English. Tarisai didn't understand a word of French but she learned a few phrases. Her mind was still as sharp as in those university days. She just applied it in different ways.

One handsome fellow from Congo invited her to meet him at the Club Congolais that night.

"Kanda Bongo Man is playing," he promised her. Tarisai and her friends loved Kanda. When they partied with their sugar daddies, they always played his cassettes. The rumba music gave them a chance to, as Tarisai liked to say, "unleash an optimum display of our assets."

After Baba Charity fell into his drunken snores at 9:30, Tarisai sneaked into a skin-tight leopard body suit and headed for the Club Congolais. She didn't find the man who had invited her but she had no shortage of partners willing to buy her drinks.

She wasn't looking for conversation or any quick sexual liaison. Her relationship with Cephas had hardened her against any notion of romance, even in Paris. As she always told her friends, "Relationships are a pragmatic affair. I get what I can from them. Let the old men spill their hearts. Mine is steel."

She danced the rumba the whole night, fighting off arms, hands, lips, and more intimate parts of her pursuers. The excitement of the music, the thrill of being surrounded by an energetic young crowd took her attention away from any notion of time. No one put on a better show than Kanda Bongo Man. Tarisai especially admired the two women who sang backup. Their tantalizing twirls and twists gave Tarisai many ideas about how to liven up her avenue girl routine.

By the time she finally looked at a clock it was nearly six in the morning. Baba Charity came from the old school: early to bed, early to rise. He'd have been awake for at least an hour by now; probably have taken a shower, shaved, maybe even have put on his tie and jacket. Ready for business. This morning, for once, business would not be uppermost in his mind. A much bigger issue would be plaguing him: where was his sugar plum?

Though Baba Charity was a calm, calculating businessman, he

tolerated no nonsense in his sexual companions. A girl who didn't show him proper respect was a bad investment.

By the time Tarisai dragged her sweaty, alcohol-reeking body through the door of the hotel room. Baba Charity had already swallowed three shots of cognac. The old guard drank early in the day. To top it off, Tarisai had forgotten that this was his day of respite from the meetings. He'd planned to walk through the streets of Paris with his showcase girl garnishing his arm. Instead he smelled the smoke and perspiration of other men polluting the luxurious suite his money had paid for.

"Sorry, Baba Charity," she said, "I couldn't sleep so I went out for a drink. I didn't want to disturb you. I'll shower and be ready just now."

Baba Charity didn't reply. He twirled his brandy snifter in his hand while she undressed for the shower. Then he set down his glass and loosened his belt.

Tarisai had never feared Baba Charity. He was a big, slow man. Methodical, not the type for violence. Along with his enormous pocketbook, his tranquil demeanor was one of the reasons Tarisai chose him over Alberto and the others. She never realized that the combination of jealousy, alcohol, and humiliation could transform her sugar daddy.

She wrapped a towel around her waist, her breasts bouncing freely as she searched for the shampoo. She sensed his approach. She turned to embrace him. A few touches to the right places and the old man would melt, especially when there was only a towel between him and the naked splendor of this young beauty. She could wash off his mess in the shower.

He caught her off balance with a flat hand to the chest. She tripped and fell onto the bed.

"Come to me, Daddy," she said, holding up her arms. If she could change the mood, everything would be all right. The belt cracked against her cheek. She could smell the blood. As she tried to retreat he hit her twice more across the back. She felt the buckle slice into the skin on her shoulder blades.

"You bitch," he screamed, "you don't take my money to make me a fool. When I pay, you stay in my bed."

The blood leaked slowly down her back as she scrambled toward the headboard and tried to regain control of the situation. Once sex was off the agenda, her naked state lost all its power.

Baba Charity's glasses had fallen onto the floor but he still had a firm grip on his belt. He moved around the bed. She slid away from him and ran toward the door. He caught her with a slash to the buttocks as she crossed the threshold to the living room. If the suite wasn't so huge, he would have pummeled her far more. While she fumbled with the chain on the front door, she felt his hands wrap around her throat. She twisted around enough to look him in the face. She saw only a monster. The whites of his eyes looked as big as soccer balls. Hatred flowed though him like an electrical charge. For a few seconds, she thought she might perish right there, naked in a hotel room far from her home and her beloved Netsai. She couldn't breathe.

She knew his body well enough to find his wrinkled up old balls and squeeze them with all the force she could summon. If she could deliver pleasure, she could also deliver pain.

As her hand tightened into a fist, he screamed and let her go. She grabbed a tablecloth and rushed back to the door, wrapping herself like an African princess in the elegant white linen on which they'd eaten *coq au vin* just a few hours earlier. Tarisai had even enjoyed the red wine.

As she closed the door, Baba Charity lay on the floor groaning and rolling from side to side like a wounded rhino.

Tarisai had little trouble convincing the hotel manager that her husband was the aggressor in what she called an "unfortunate domestic confrontation."

With the discretion of the French, the manager persuaded Baba Charity to depart from the hotel and arranged for Tarisai to get back into the room to retrieve her luggage, passport, and return air ticket.

As she gathered her things, Baba Charity informed her in Shona that she was now on her own. When she looked inside her wallet, she found he'd removed every cent. She was alone in a foreign country and flat broke.

The hotel manager offered Tarisai a free night's lodging in order to smooth over the cracks and ensure no untoward publicity emerged from the incident.

Tarisai considered returning to the Club Congolais and attempting to befriend some free-spending males in an effort to extend her stay. But she found the bustling world of Paris too difficult to tackle with an empty pocket and a language she couldn't understand. At least the hotel nurse attended to the gash on her cheek, applying butterfly tape. She promised Tarisai there'd be only a tiny scar.

Without the anticipated armloads of clothes for her daughter or the full-length leather coat, Tarisai got back on the flight to Harare the night after her encounter with Baba Charity. Her legs and back ached from where he'd swatted her with the belt and she had bruises on her throat from his choking fingers. She had, though, seen another world—a world full of glitz, bright lights, and elegantly dressed people. No one in Paris rode in a dilapidated Matambanadzo bus, walked barefoot on dirt paths, or drew water from a river. The trip had whetted Tarisai's appetite. She would find a way to pick the fruit of the tree of abundance that grew overseas. The future of her daughter depended on it.

CHAPTER 34

I drove Red Eye straight from the jail to my house and poured him a big shot of Wild Turkey. The three floor fans had made a little progress on getting rid of the stink.

Red Eye on the other hand looked like he'd been in ten train wrecks. Tsiropoulos neglected to tell me about his broken nose.

"We've got to get you to a doctor," I told him.

"I gotta sleep first," he said as he flopped down on the couch, Jap flaps and all.

"The body needs time to recover from hot dog overdose, then getting the shit beat out of you. I think I'm suffering from that disease the soldiers get."

"Post-traumatic stress disorder?"

"That's it. PTSD. I'm gonna sue their ass."

"You ain't gonna sue nobody," I said. "You told me you're going to Rio."

Red Eye tucked two of the sofa pillows under his head and stretched out like he was down for the count but his eyes were still wide open

"You overdid it with the Pine-Sol, bro," he said.

"Rio," I said, "what's up with Rio?"

He said he needed another shot of Wild Turkey, then we could talk about Brazil.

"It's scary," he said.

I set the Wild Turkey bottle down on the coffee table next to him and teed up another round. He downed it in one gulp. Red Eye never talked about "scary."

"Washkowski said we were going down for that African bitch," Red Eye told me, "said the next stop for you and me would be death row at Quentin."

"He's a punk. That's all small talk. Tsiropoulos was just here. He had a talk with Jeffcoat and his lawyer. They're gonna call off their dogs if we back off."

"You mean that's why they cut me loose?"

"Yeah."

He grabbed the bottle and took a big hit. Red Eye never liked glasses that much anyway.

"Kirkland was pissed as hell," he said, "told me Washkowski was on his own mission here. They're going to discipline him."

"You already handled that with the bucket," I said. "Besides, Kirkland's no big boy, just a squirrely little PO."

I let Red Eye hit on the bottle again before I told him about the connection between Washkowski and Jeffcoat.

"They go way back," I said.

The fans hummed quietly in the background as Red Eye rolled into a ball and started to fade away.

"At least you saved your carpet," he said as he drifted into a deep sleep. After a few seconds, he was snoring like a sick warthog.

He didn't even budge when I slipped the Jap flaps off his feet. No one had ever slept on my couch with their shoes on. It was no time to start compromising. In the meantime, the answers to my other questions would just have to wait; I still had the Jap flaps in my hands when the phone rang.

CHAPTER 35

Mandisa was calling me to let me know she got a reply from Garikai Mukombachoto.

"He's Prudence's brother," she said. "Told me how sad all the family was to get the news. How they would miss her."

"Sounds like a gut buster."

"He said she'd been their role model and provider for years, that things were getting harder and harder in Zimbabwe with the evictions and all."

I had no idea what evictions she was talking about. Were landlords on the rampage, throwing people's furniture off apartment balconies? I wasn't even sure they had apartments in Africa.

"So how was she a role model, hustling tycoons?" I asked.

"I told them she died in a car crash while driving her new BMW. It seemed easier that way." I didn't think Mandisa knew how to lie like that. You always have to keep your eye on a liar.

"Can I see the letter?" I asked.

"Of course," she said. "I've got something else for you too." She told me to visit her at work that night. "Newman's been bothering me again," she added.

"Be careful," I said, "he's a straight up j-cat."

"A what?"

"I mean like he's kinda crazy."

"Don't worry," she said, "I can take care of myself."

I didn't know what to say. Mandisa was good at resuscitating old men in the park but she'd be in over her head if someone like Newman got heavy with her. And if Jeffcoat was telling the truth, Newman could be a suspect again. But then could I really even believe what Mandisa was telling me? Maybe Newman was bonking her instead of harassing her, for all I knew. Why would an African woman worry about lying to a white ex-con?

Once I hung up, I remembered that the article I'd found under Prudence's mattress said something about evictions. I dug it out and read it again.

The white farmers in the picture were being evicted. Something about the government taking over all the white-owned farms and giving them to blacks. The article also said the army had driven off ten thousand workers on these farms. Most of them were sleeping "in the bush," wherever that was.

The farmer in the picture was a Francis McGuinn. He said he and his wife would be leaving the country, that there was no longer "a place for white people here." Sounded like some wild stuff. My dear old Oakland was tame by comparison

When I caught Mandisa in her office that night, she told me again that she could take care of herself and how she wasn't scared. People who tell you how they aren't scared too often are the ones who are secretly terrified. She kept up a good front.

"You a fourth-dan black belt or something?" I asked. "No offense but you're no giant and Newman is a half-crazed body builder. He could break you in half."

"At home my twin sister was raped. She got HIV. I vowed it would never happen to me."

"What does that have to do with Newman?"

"When I came to this country, I went for shooting lessons. I've got a Smith and Wesson 9 mm. All legal. I can put your eye out at fifty meters."

"Please don't try," I said. "Is your sister all right?"

"Alive and well. My salary pays for her medication. It's too expensive there."

"Does she look like you?"

"We are identical. She's thinner than I am. When we were little no one could tell us apart."

"So you're real good with that Smith and Wesson?"

"I keep it under my pillow. I can hit any man who comes into my room and I'm a very light sleeper."

Apart from our friendship with Prudence and the fact that we both told the occasional lie, Mandisa and I had something else in common— we both slept with 9 mm pistols under our pillows. It's a weird world.

"What if they get you when you're awake and away from your pillow?" I asked.

She patted under her left shoulder.

"I've got a license to carry it," she said. "I'm protected outside the bedroom as well."

The conversation died there. She picked it up by telling me a few more things about South Africa that I didn't want to know. Apparently the president there thought AIDS didn't exist, that it was all made up by the Americans and the British to destroy poor people in Africa.

"He's a big problem," she said.

I told her I'd had enough of African politics for one day.

"None of it makes sense," I said.

"I guess you have to want to learn," she said and handed me the letter from Garikai.

Another aerogram, the blue paper no thicker than a Zig-Zag. His printing was scrupulously neat, like he used a ruler to keep the lines straight. The *i*'s had the same clear circles for dots—just like Prudence's. Eerie.

Garikai wrote of how happy they were that Prudence had become such a "successful architect" in the United States.

"She was the pride of our family," he wrote. The last paragraph tore me apart.

"Please, madam, if you know someone who can help us we request your kind assistance. We have lost our two sisters so we now have six orphans to look after in our house. Our parents have been thrown off Mr. McGuinn's farm where they have worked for so many years. Prudence's money was keeping us all alive. We don't know where to turn and our dear sister lies buried overseas, thousands of kilometers from home. What can we do? It seems that God wants us to suffer here in our country. I don't know why. Please give us some advice."

"What did you tell him?" I asked.

"I haven't responded yet," she said. "What is there to say?"

"Do you know anything about her sisters?"

"They died from AIDS," she replied. "In southern Africa we all have relatives who died or are dying. It has become our way of life."

"Why doesn't someone do something?"

"I already told you about that. What can we do?"

"I don't know. Someone must send some medicine or something. Isn't there a vaccine?"

"Just expensive pills from overseas."

"Prudence had so many responsibilities," I said. "I had no idea. If I had known . . ."

"If you had known, what? Responsibilities make you strong or drive you mad."

"Prudence was strong and crazy at the same time," I said. For all I knew, I was probably talking about Mandisa as well. Like Fast Freddy said we all have a darker side. Some people just hide it better than others.

If I was a good Samaritan, a Mother Teresa or something, I would have written back to this Garikai and told him that he and all his orphans and parents could just come and live with me in Oakland. My house was probably bigger than all the huts in their village or wherever it was they lived.

But Mother Teresa I wasn't. I couldn't even recall the last time I prayed, let alone went to church. I don't think our memorial for Prudence counted as full-fledged church in the eyes of God.

The best I could do would be to send a few bucks to these Mukombachotos and find out who killed their sister though maybe they'd rather believe she died in a car crash driving her new BMW. A car crash was neat, clean, and kept their fantasy alive. They probably needed that more than the gory details of her death. The truth doesn't always bring what the police like to call "closure."

For some reason, just as I left, Mandisa handed me a key to her apartment.

"So you won't have to break in again," she said, "and if I ever need you, at least I know you can get in. Desperation breeds desperate measures."

I wasn't sure who was desperate, me or her. All I knew was that no woman had ever given me a key to her apartment before. Normally that meant something. But I guess it just meant me and Mandisa were up against the wall together. I guess that made us friends, though I really didn't know how to be friends with a woman. Of course, she could have given me the key to set me up for something. A con man never accepts anything at face value. It's the kiss of death.

I just put the key in my pocket and rubbed it for a few seconds with my fingers. I decided for the moment I had to let my paranoias rest. If you don't trust anyone, all the screws come loose.

"Thanks," I said, "we'll always be there for you, me and Red Eye. Watch out though, we may not be that much help. We're used to carrying guns but neither one of us can hit the broad side of barn."

She smiled and said she understood.

I exited the IHOP and headed home in the Volvo, thinking about this strange woman from South Africa. She'd given me a tiny glimpse into her life. That was fine but I didn't want to know any more. Some things are just too complicated for a harelip coyote to understand. I thought about that key in my pocket. As usual, I needed a shot of Wild Turkey.

I turned onto International Boulevard and tried to pick up the pace. A classic gold Jaguar with tinted windows pulled up next to me on the left. Unusual car in this neck of the woods. The driver confirmed my suspicions by sliding down the passenger side window and motioning me over to the side of the road. Newman was clad in the silver and black T-shirt of our nation but somehow I was sure we were on different teams here. He pointed a second time toward the sidewalk. I gunned it.

My escape effort didn't go well. The Volvo was no match for his Jag. Plus, half a block down a truck and trailer was blocking both lanes on our side of the road, trying to squeeze down an alley to get at some loading dock. Why did he have to be doing this at eleven o'clock at night? I thought about jumping the island, but the traffic coming the other way was too heavy to dodge. And I'd left the Walther at home. I was at Newman's mercy and I figured he didn't have too much mercy on offer.

As I ground to a halt, the Jaguar pulled up next to me. Newman almost tore the door off getting out and streaked toward my car like

Marcus Allen heading for pay dirt. I locked the door but I knew that wouldn't do much. Within a few seconds he was standing next to my car waving a long-barreled .45, telling me if I didn't open the door and get out, my brains would end up splattered against the passenger-side door. I doubted he'd have the nerve to do all that right out in front of all these people, but the look in his eye told me I'd better not take the chance.

As soon as I unlocked the door, he yanked it open, grabbed my arm, and slammed me to the pavement. He'd shed his businessman's demeanor. This was all about brute strength, never my forte. He set his foot right in the middle of my back and started screaming stuff about motherfuckin' con men being the lowest form of life, that no one ever conned a Newman and he wasn't going to let me be the first.

"You tryin' to set me up for this murder, boy?" he asked. "Well you'll be takin' the fall, not me, bitch. If I ever see your lame ass around my house again, I'll blow your face off."

He stomped his foot a couple times in between my shoulder blades just to emphasize his points. I was getting the power of the message, I just wasn't too sure why he was bothering to do this. On stomp number three I felt a shooting pain in my side. All of a sudden every breath felt like a spear through my chest.

"You come talkin' shit about millions of dollars, make me almost lose my wife. Con men are some sick-ass people. Sick as hell."

"What do you want?" I asked. Each word brought a new jab of that spear to my chest.

"The girl is dead," he shouted. "Let her rest in peace or you'll be resting with her." A few horns started honking, then it became a chorus. His foot came off my back. I looked up. The truck and trailer had disappeared down the alley. Newman's Jaguar and my Volvo were blocking the way.

Newman rushed back to his car while I struggled to my feet. I couldn't make it. The pain was growing with every breath. I crawled the few feet back to the driver's side and lifted myself up to the seat. For some reason, I started laughing uncontrollably. Each laugh brought a new jab of pain. There was nothing funny. This was hysteria. I laughed all the way back to my house, with each giggle bringing another round of spears to my side. I was cracking up, becoming a j-cat myself.

 I couldn't get out of bed the next day. I kept touching the bumps in my ribs. I should have gone to the doctor but he'd ask a lot of questions I wouldn't want to answer. Besides, I was pretty sure they couldn't do much for broken ribs except give you some painkillers so you could breathe. I phoned Red Eye for a little help. He was the only person in the world who knew where my stash was. I didn't even like him knowing but I had to get at that dope. With broken ribs, every breath is torture.

Though Red Eye wasn't in the best shape, he came right away. The first thing he told me was that I looked like shit.

"I had a hard night," I said.

"She must have been a little rough in the rack."

"I wish."

I told him to just get that bottle of Demerol out of my stash and I'd tell him what happened. Before I got too high, I explained about Newman, the Jaguar, the truck blocking the road, and the foot on the back.

"The man is a lunatic," I said. "I'd ruled him out, but if Prudence got on his wrong side, he could have thrown her in the pool."

"Blackmailing a lunatic with sex tapes is definitely getting on his wrong side."

The Demerol was kicking in. I could still feel the pain but it didn't really matter. I was carrying the load but the weight was on someone else's shoulders. I wasn't sure whose.

"How did he know you were visiting Mandisa?" Red Eye asked.

Something about the pain of broken ribs had kept my mind from asking the obvious question. Thank God for Red Eye.

"She set you up, homeboy. Had to be."

"I don't think so."

"Who else knew about you going there?"

"No one. The only other possibility is that he's listening to my phone conversations. He's a freak for spy stuff. His office is full of it."

Red Eye wasn't convinced but in my Demerol madness I hatched a wild scheme to trap Newman if he was listening in. We'd put it into play the next day, once I'd slept off the Demerol. I never took hard dope more than once at a go. The perfect way to avoid addiction. By the next day, I'd step it down to a handful of Motrin and just deal with the pain. Red Eye left me to sleep it all off.

Sometime in the afternoon I heard the doorbell rang. It took me a couple minutes to stumble out of bed. I found a big manila envelope with "Mr. Calvin Winter" written on the front sitting on the doorstep. Inside was that list of twenty-three names with Peter Margolis at the top. A series of post-its in Prudence's writing was attached to the backs of the pages. The post-its added names, addresses, and phone numbers of each of the twenty-three. There was also a "to whom it may concern" cover letter in her writing that said her "partner" had downloaded the names from Jeffcoat's laptop. I wondered what kind of partnership they had. Most likely, that partner was the one hitting her on tape number nine.

For each of the names, the post-its showed the amount Jeffcoat underpaid into their funds. The total was a little over $700,000. I wasn't sure if that was serious money to Jeffcoat or not. Only after I looked everything over for a few minutes did I shake the envelope one last time. A small piece of paper fell out. "Hope this helps, M" was all the note said. Why was Mandisa giving me this stuff now? She couldn't be doing this and setting me and Red Eye up at the same time. Maybe she was actually on our side.

As I tried to piece together a plan to get these lunatic millionaires off our backs, it suddenly dawned on me who that little kid was next to Washkowski in that football team picture. It wasn't anyone I knew in the joint. Those guys were teammates for life.

CHAPTER 36

The following morning I popped four Motrin, pretended that the stabbing pain wasn't there with every breath and made my way to the post office. I had to mail two things, just in case it all blew up in my face. I sent Tsiorpoulos the envelope Mandisa had dropped off. At least if the cops searched my house, they wouldn't find it. Then I counted out $2,000 in fifties for the bright-eyed young clerk and asked her to make out a money order to Garikai Mukombachoto. I handed her a piece of paper with his address on it and an extra hundred bucks for postage.

"Just make sure it gets there as soon as possible and keep the change," I told her and walked away.

"But, sir, we're not allowed to take tips," she shouted at me as I left the building. She'd figure out what to do with the money.

I got back home just in time for the phone call from Red Eye that would kick our plan into action. If someone was listening they were heading for a dangerous rollercoaster ride.

The first step was to lead the person listening in astray. Red Eye gave me an address off Ninety-Eighth Avenue. East Oakland, just as our script called for. That was the spot where we would pick up our supposed copies of the tapes, the only ones in existence outside what Jeffcoat had stolen. If Newman was listening, he'd definitely be interested. If it was someone else, Red Eye had added a kicker to the dialog—that his buddy had worked his computer magic on tape number nine and the face could now be identified.

We played it out, me driving to E. Ninety-Eighth, then complaining to Red Eye on the phone about how dangerous the neighborhood was and redirecting him and his imaginary buddy to Mandisa's. I knew she was working double shifts these days. Maybe not the reason she gave me the key but what the hell. We'd be waiting for our mystery man there.

Red Eye met me in front of Mandisa's building. I told him to let me go in first.

"Just to make sure Mandisa's not there," I said. "I'll signal you from the window." I pointed to the third floor where she lived, "keep an eye out."

When I opened the door, Carter was sitting on one of the couches in full uniform, 9 mm drawn. He'd come a long way since his days of being the short chubby kid on Jeffcoat's high school football team. The scheme Red Eye and I had cooked up had worked perfectly, except for one detail: we were supposed to get there before him.

"On the floor, hands behind your head," he said. I had the Walther tucked in my pants but he had the drop on me. Red Eye was my only hope. I just had to believe that if I never got to that window, he'd figure something was wrong before it was too late. I sunk slowly to the floor. When I got one knee down, Carter put his foot in the middle of my back and drove my nose into the carpet. I was getting a little tired of getting kicked around. Then he patted me down with his loose hand, pulled out my gun, and threw it across the room.

"Wanna make a move for that little piece-of-shit handgun of yours?" he asked. "Go ahead."

He sat back down in the chair.

"By the way," he added, "I've taken care of your pal Red Eye. Reported he was seen driving a stolen car in the neighborhood. The black and whites will keep him busy for a while."

"What's up here, Carter?" I asked. "Your promotion can't be that important. So you bungled an investigation."

"That bitch wife of yours tried to blackmail me like the others. We had such a good thing going, then she had to go and fuck it up."

I licked the sweat off my upper lip and gazed at Carter's foot. He wasn't really watching me now. If I struck quick I might be able to grab him by the ankle.

"We had a sweet thing, me and her," he said stepping back out of my reach. "I was the security and she was the bait. We split the profits. We could have squeezed Jeffcoat and that black dude for life. But she tried to cut me out."

"Then it wasn't Jeffcoat?"

"He wanted to get rid of her as bad as I did but he doesn't have the stomach for killing. A quarterback always needs a lineman to do the dirty work. He didn't even know I was in on the scheme."

I couldn't quite believe Carter's tale. He was the partner—banging Prudence, helping her film the other guys and splitting the take. An ugly devil like Carter could never have created a match made in heaven like that one.

"She only made one mistake, Winter. One time she let me know she couldn't swim. Oops. Had an accident. God, she loved it with me, Winter. She just got greedy. I told her not to fuck around. I had no choice."

"So you iced her."

"She would have been biting me in the butt for the rest of my life. I thought I could trust her but I was wrong. It's sink or swim in this world. Washky will snatch up the tapes when they get here. I'm not just any old fool, Winter. You forget that. I've got friends in high places."

"We've got another copy of the tape," I said.

"Don't bullshit me. I heard everything you said on the phone."

"We lied. We set you up," I said.

"The question is who set up who here? I'd say you're looking like the one with the boot on your throat."

He was right. He held all the cards now. Red Eye and I were like Larry and Curly playing detective. All we needed was a Moe to round out our team. Carter had to kill me now. He'd told me everything.

"Lucky me," said Carter, "I interrupted a burglary in progress. The intruder was armed. When the intruder fired two rounds at me, I had no choice but to return fire. One more scumbag bites the dust."

Carter stood up and walked over to pick up my pistol. He kept his eye on me, losing sight of the front door. I could see the knob turning. I coughed to cover any noise. Red Eye had arrived in the nick of time to save me. I hoped he had a gun. The door opened slowly. I coughed some more.

"Shut up," said Carter. His cell phone rang.

"Great job, Washky," he said. He put his hand over the speaker.

"Washkowski's got your punk friend Red Eye in front of the building. I smell the sweetness of revenge right around the corner." He went back to his phone conversation.

"I've got the rest of it under control," Carter told his spiky-haired former teammate. I wondered if Washkowski was still tweaking. The only other question I had now was if it was Carter or Washkowski in tape number nine. I couldn't really decide which one I preferred to have been humping my wife. Suddenly I saw the bare feet of a black woman tiptoe into the doorway.

"Impound the car and wait for me at the station," Carter said, "after you finish your business with that piece of shit."

Mandisa stood in the doorway, her 9 mm held in both hands right in front of her. Perfect form. Those shooting lessons had paid off. And I thought she was at the IHOP worrying about inventories and work schedules. She looked calm but her eyes didn't blink.

Carter slapped his phone shut.

"Drop it," she yelled.

"I'm a police officer," he said, "can't you tell by the uniform?"

She took three steps forward. The barrel of the gun was no more than four feet from his head. She'd gotten too close.

"If you don't drop that gun you're going to fulfill one of my dreams," she said. "All my life I've wanted to kill a white man, especially a cop."

"Don't do it," he said, "you'll rot in jail forever if they don't execute you."

"Either way I'll die with a smile on my face," she said. She took a step back.

The usual twinkle in her eye had grown to a glow. Her life was coming to a head here right along with mine.

"I heard everything you just said," she added, "and you're the one who'll rot in prison."

"They'll never believe an African girl," he said. "I can get you as easy as I got your friend."

"You have a three count," she said, "or you'll go out in a blaze of glory. This African girl will take her chances with the great American justice system."

Carter's gun and my Walther clanged to the floor.

"Take two steps forward and get down," she ordered.

I leaped to my feet, sweat sticking to my shirt. Mandisa tossed me her cell and told me to call the police. They were there in ten minutes, put all three of us in handcuffs and took us to the station. Now the lies and counterlies would start flying. The old saying holds that the truth shall set you free. The truth, in this case, would set no one free. No one at all.

CHAPTER 37

Harare, Zimbabwe, 2002

As the new millennium arrived, Tarisai was shopping in the global mall of Internet matchups. She found her fate tied to one Calvin Winter, a homely-faced man with a huge scar on his upper lip. When she first saw his photo, Tarisai thought maybe he'd been sliced with a knife. When she looked closer she remembered a condition she'd read about in university: cleft lip. Mr. Winter's was not as serious as some she'd seen in her textbooks or even among the rural people in Zimbabwe. She found it difficult to think of kissing those deformed lips.

But then she wasn't doing this for romance. He'd pay her $5,000 and all her travel expenses to Oakland, California. More importantly, marriage to Mr. Winter would get her that precious green card which would allow her to work in the United States. Maybe one day she could become a citizen. People told her that after a year or two she could leave this ugly man and launch out on her own. She hoped she'd only have to stay with him for a few weeks.

A friend of hers had a sister who lived in Colorado.

"It's a lonely life there," she told Tarisai, "but there's money. Zimbabweans are hard-working. With our good education we always succeed."

Her words filled Tarisai with confidence. She still dreamed of returning to university, of leaving behind a life of chasing men. Once she'd gotten rid of Mr. Winter, she'd send for her daughter, Netsai. Her child had to grow up somewhere with opportunities for all people. Zimbabwe was like that in the 1980s, just after independence. That was before President Mugabe went off the rails. In those days the government built schools and clinics to serve rural families like the

Mukombachotos. Children like Tarisai had a chance to reach university. Now it was only for Mugabe and his cronies. He'd declared war on the poor. In her community people went in the middle of the night and stole the doors and window frames off the school buildings to sell them for food.

On the appointed day Tarisai took Netsai to her rural home and explained to her relatives what was going to happen. She'd never told them what really occurred at the university. They believed she graduated. She even had a friend print a diploma with a gold seal to show off to her parents. As long as it had the gold seal, they wouldn't know the difference.

Tarisai's mother and father embraced Netsai wholeheartedly. They would look after her until their daughter found a place to settle in America. Besides, they saw it as a chance to teach the young girl some proper African values. Children who grew up in the city didn't know how to respect their elders and often preferred speaking English to Shona. They'd put Netsai on the right path.

"I've been offered a job as an architect in California," Tarisai told everyone. She didn't have to explain that an architect in America made more money in a year than anyone in her village would ever see in a lifetime.

Her parents were as pleased and proud as the day she graduated from Mutare Girls' High School. To top it off, their daughter had brought them dozens of presents from Calvin Winter's advance payment. Everyone in the family sparkled in new clothes, shiny leather shoes, and fancy hats. The family slaughtered a cow and Tarisai bought twenty crates of beer from the local bottle store. The day of her departure would become a major event in village legend, the day "we ate until our stomachs burst," her mother called it, "like we used to do when independence first came."

Tarisai was elated to bring a little happiness to her family in these hard times, even if it was based on a lie. Ever since the drought a few years earlier her parents had spent most of the year working on Mr. McGuinn's farm. They couldn't squeeze a living out of their meager plot any longer. The soil was exhausted. Their survival depended on the few dollars a month the white man paid them for planting, weeding, and harvesting his maize. Her mother and father were old, too old to still be laboring as farm hands, but nowadays things seemed to get harder each year for the people in their area. Worst of all, both of Tarisai's sisters were ill. Sores covered their arms. Their eyes had sunk deep into their sockets. Her youngest sister, Chiedza, had a huge lump behind her right ear. Tarisai was once a prize science student but it didn't take a scientist to see that AIDS was taking her sisters. Each had small children who the fathers had abandoned once they learned of the mother's sickness. All the more reason for Tarisai to go to America. There would soon be more young Mukombachoto children with no parents to support them.

With the image of Netsai and her hollow-eyed sisters in her head, Tarisai boarded the blue and yellow bus back to Harare. Tears trickled down her cheeks the entire journey. Life was unfair. She'd made one mistake and she had to keep on paying and paying. This was nothing like the future she dreamed about back when her grade seven headmaster told her that one day she would go overseas.

Two days later Tarisai was sipping Johnny Walker Red Label on the Air Zimbabwe flight to London. Once she landed in Britain, she'd spend two days in the South End where some connection of Calvin Winter's had arranged a British passport for her in the name of Deirdre Lewis. From then on, Tarisai would be a Briton. Everyone said it would be easier that way. She was thankful that her teachers at Mutare Girls' High had taught her what they called a "Cornwall accent."

New passport in hand, she'd take a Northwest flight to Oakland, California. In thirteen hours she'd arrive at the house of her husband to be. She hoped she could avoid consummating this marriage. With a daughter living thousands of miles away, a host of financial responsibilities, two sisters dying of AIDS, and the complex network of lies she'd knitted for herself, Tarisai Mukombachoto a.k.a. Deirdre Lewis a.k.a. Prudence already felt like she carried the weight of the world on her shoulders. The last thing she needed was to worry about the sexual urges of an ugly American husband.

CHAPTER 38

My cellmate was an eighteen-year-old psycho who called himself Bullet. He never slept, just paced up and down telling stories about stealing cars and cooking methamphetamine. Bullet weighed about a hundred pounds. I tried talking to him, reminding him that he wasn't the sole inhabitant of that little concrete and steel box.

He kept speed rapping. After about four hours I concluded only one thing would shut him up—a good beating. I contemplated pulling him off his top bunk in the middle of the night and kicking his head a few times. With my luck I'd probably crack his skull and end up with a murder charge. Just as I started cramming toilet paper into my ears to block out his inane monolog, they called me for an attorney visit.

Tsiropoulos wasn't exactly shining. And he reeked of cheap wine. At least he bought me an Almond Joy and a soda from the visiting room vending machines but I wasn't sure he was ready for all the news I had to pour out.

I had to admit that it all sounded far-fetched, Prudence and Carter working together to squeeze money out of Jeffcoat and Newman. But there was another piece to the puzzle, Washkowski. He was no innocent lamb. Plus, if he was hooked on crank, he wouldn't survive much pressure.

Tsiropoulos just shook his head when I told him Carter's story. I reminded him that truth was always stranger than fiction.

"Especially when it comes from you and Red Eye," he added. He said he'd try to talk to Jeffcoat's lawyer and see if the Margolis stuff would get us any leverage. I told him to wait until the envelope I'd mailed him arrived.

"Then you'll have some real ammunition," I promised.

"Right now I'm just firing blanks and Carter'll probably get bail in the next twenty-four hours," Tsiropoulos added. I freaked. Once he got out, Carter would cover his tracks and make sure I never set foot outside an electrified fence again.

The three of us had our bail hearings the next day. They released Carter. No charges. He wasn't even on suspension.

They set Mandisa's bond at $5,000. They'd only charged her with unlawful possession of a weapon. If I knew her, she had all her gun registration papers in order. At least she'd be free. I was sailing in a different ship.

My bail was $1.5 million. Newspaper reports alleged I was under investigation for the murder of my wife. The prosecutor called me a "lifelong criminal and definite flight risk"; probably right on both counts. I didn't see myself waiting around to be a target for whatever Carter and the DA had in mind with Jeffcoat as financial backer. I couldn't think of a way to ensnare Carter in his own web.

The only thing that went my way was that when I got back from the bail hearing I had a new cellmate—Elmer Jones. They called him L'Amour since he'd claimed to have read all two hundred plus of Louis L'Amour's shitkicker novels. Elmer's reading days were behind him for the most part. Even with the strongest glasses the jail commissary offered, he could barely make out the print. After about five minutes of squinting he'd drop off to sleep. The Rip Van Winkle approach to doing time. It suited me perfectly.

After the bail setback I was, as they say, "hard-timing"—worrying myself sick. I couldn't take my mind off the horrendous possibilities that lie before me. Hours would pass and I'd do nothing but lie on my bunk and stare at the graffiti scratched into the cement ceiling. "Fatal, July 1998"; "Rabbit, June '87"; "Orange Julius, Xmas '83." Everyone had a nickname they'd left to posterity. Would my only legacy be what I scrawled onto a prison ceiling?

The following morning I dragged myself to the phone to call Tsiropoulos. We had an arrangement. If he had any news, he'd accept my call. If not, he'd refuse the chance to spend $3.89 to say "hello" and offer meaningful words of consolation. Not even the Hyatt Regency could top jailhouse rates for a local call.

He had some news. He said he'd gotten the envelope and was going to take it to a meeting with Jeffcoat's lawyer.

"Can't say more on the phone," he said. "I'll be by as soon as I find out something."

After the phone call I went back to hard-timing. I must have walked five miles just pacing up and down in my cell while L'Amour snored himself into oblivion. There was no way I was going to survive another fifteen years of this. No way at all. When you've been out for a while, you start to think that because you handled it once, you could handle it again. But if they got me this time, it would be for keeps. I'd be doing all day as they like to call a life sentence in these hellholes. And I didn't have enough money to make bail and sneak off to Brazil.

Just as I finally got to sleep the sirens started screeching. Something was jumping off somewhere. A cell fight, a suicide. Not much else can happen in the middle of the night. By morning, we were on lockdown and the rumors were flying around the pod about what had happened. I didn't pay any attention. A few minutes after I finished gobbling up the hard-boiled egg and stone cold oatmeal breakfast, the guard came and told me I had an attorney visit. We were on lockdown, so he put me in waist chains and leg irons and I shuffled off to learn my fate.

EPILOGUE

Since it was lockdown we had to visit through glass. No Almond Joys this time around. They didn't even take off the shackles. I was hoping for a big smile on Tsiropoulos's face when he saw me. No such luck. He looked hung-over, more like he'd come to tell someone their mother died than celebrate the DA dropping all the charges.

One of my Jap flaps came off as I scooted onto the round iron stool that passed for a chair. I kicked it out of the way.

"Get those cuffs and leg irons off my client," Tsiropoulos told the guard.

"We're on lockdown, counselor. That's the rules." The guard trundled away.

Tsiropoulos put a pile of papers on the counter in front of him. "You want the good news or the bad news?" he asked.

"Just shoot."

He went on one of those long, closing-argument kinds of speeches where he told me how once he showed Jeffcoat and his lawyer the list, that new versions of the truth started to emerge and Jeffcoat's loyalty to his teammates started to fade fast.

The reworked official story portrayed Carter as a "rogue cop" who got carried away when he realized a clever African girl had outsmarted him so that instead of making money off her seductive powers and getting free sex to boot, he might end up owing her for the rest of their life.

"He was just supposed to scare her," Tsiropoulos said, "but he got carried away."

Somewhere along the path, Washkowski had also joined in the fun, either driving the getaway car when Carter pushed Prudence into the pool or throwing the brick through my window. None of this was really a surprise for me. I told Tsiropoulos to cut to the chase.

"You're not walking on this one, Cal," he said. "I think I can get you out of the murder rap. Hopefully, that's going to be Carter's beef. Jeffcoat has agreed to give a statement to the police and testify in exchange for immunity on all counts. If the DA will agree and we can get Washkowski to roll, it's a done deal."

"So Jeffcoat will just walk away, apologize to the old lady and go back to the fourteenth floor?"

Tsiropoulos nodded. Then he told me I was looking at two to five years for the obstructing. "I don't think I can do better than two," he said.

I started thinking about the sound of that cell door sliding open every morning as I got ready for "another day in paradise." I could make two years, seven hundred and thirty morning cell door openings. Five was a push. For the first time in my life I was counting on a millionaire and a snitch cop to save me.

~

Three months later I was on the bus to Old Folsom, the place Johnny Cash made famous. Back in the day it used to be a killing field but it had mellowed out. The young bangers and haters who loved to rock and roll ended up at Pelican Bay, High Desert, or New Folsom. Old Folsom was a place where I could just do my time reading a few books, slapping down some dominoes and walking the track.

A few weeks later, Carter's trial hit the headlines with Jeffcoat as the star witness. Carter's counterpoint, trying to cast Jeffcoat as the "quarterback" of the operation failed when Washkowski came forward and recalled the events that day when he drove the getaway car from my house. As they pulled away, Carter supposedly informed Washkowski that "African bitch" wouldn't be bothering them anymore. Washkowski told the jury he was "shocked," that he never expected Carter would seriously hurt Prudence, let alone kill her. The jury bought it. Cops are just like anybody else except an old school convict—they'll do whatever they have to do to save their ass.

Jeffcoat came on the news the night he testified with his solemn-faced wife at his side. He told a press conference how he'd made a mistake of marital infidelity for which he would be "eternally regretful" to his family but that he never agreed to violence. He didn't take questions.

The jury found Carter guilty of second-degree murder and he got fifteen to life. With some luck he'd be eligible for parole after thirteen years. Luck wasn't likely to be on his side. Cops don't survive that long in prison. Convicts have long memories when it comes to remembering who kicked their ass, stole property from their home, bullied them in front of their families and friends. Carter had plenty of those skeletons in his closet. Besides with politics being what they are in California prisons, his little sojourn with an African woman would gain him the title of "race traitor" among the white gangs and quite a few of the guards. For once it seemed the impossible had happened: Karma had visited the justice system.

In the end I decided two years in the state pen was a small price to get justice for Prudence. To pay Tsiropoulos and erase bad memories, not long after Carter's trial I sold my house. When I got out, I'd buy an apartment in a neighborhood where I'd fit in a little better. I wasn't quite sure where that would be. Maybe Red Eye would get us a place once he finished doing a year in some state ranch for violating his parole.

Selling the house also gave me a little extra money to fund a trip for Mandisa to Zimbabwe. I gave her $15,000 to hand over to the Mukombachoto family and told her to give them all the spectacular details about Prudence's meteoric career in the world of California architecture before she died in that tragic collision in her new BMW. Some myths deserve to be perpetuated, like the myth of my wife, Tarisai Prudence Mukombachoto, the African Princess.

ABOUT THE AUTHOR

James Kilgore was a 1960s political activist in California, who ultimately became involved with the Symbionese Liberation Army. In 1975, he fled a Federal explosives charge and remained a fugitive for twenty-seven years. During that time, he rejected the politics of small-group violence and built a life as an educator, researcher, activist, parent, and husband in Southern Africa. Using the pseudonym of John Pape, he earned a PhD, authored a number of academic articles and educational materials, and coedited the acclaimed 2002 anthology *Crisis of Service Delivery in South Africa* (Cape Town: HSRC; London: Zed Books). Authorities arrested Kilgore in November 2002 and extradited him to California where he served six and a half years in state and Federal prison. While incarcerated, he worked as a teacher's assistant and also completed drafts of several novels and a screenplay. Umuzi Publishers (Cape Town) released his first work, *We Are All Zimbabweans Now*, in June 2009. It was republished by Ohio University Press in 2011. He is also the author of the 2011 novel *Freedom Never Rests: A Novel of Democracy in South Africa* (Johannesburg: Jacana Media).

He currently lives with his family in Illinois where he is a Research Scholar at the Center for African Studies at the University of Illinois.

ABOUT PM PRESS

PM Press was founded at the end of 2007 by a small collection of folks with decades of publishing, media, and organizing experience. PM Press co-conspirators have published and distributed hundreds of books, pamphlets, CDs, and DVDs. Members of PM have founded enduring book fairs, spearheaded victorious tenant organizing campaigns, and worked closely with bookstores, academic conferences, and even rock bands to deliver political and challenging ideas to all walks of life. We're old enough to know what we're doing and young enough to know what's at stake.

We seek to create radical and stimulating fiction and non-fiction books, pamphlets, T-shirts, visual and audio materials to entertain, educate and inspire you. We aim to distribute these through every available channel with every available technology — whether that means you are seeing anarchist classics at our bookfair stalls; reading our latest vegan cookbook at the café; downloading geeky fiction e-books; or digging new music and timely videos from our website.

PM Press is always on the lookout for talented and skilled volunteers, artists, activists and writers to work with. If you have a great idea for a project or can contribute in some way, please get in touch.

PM Press
PO Box 23912
Oakland, CA 94623
www.pmpress.org

FRIENDS OF PM PRESS

These are indisputably momentous times—the financial system is melting down globally and the Empire is stumbling. Now more than ever there is a vital need for radical ideas.

In the four years since its founding—and on a mere shoestring—PM Press has risen to the formidable challenge of publishing and distributing knowledge and entertainment for the struggles ahead. With over 175 releases to date, we have published an impressive and stimulating array of literature, art, music, politics, and culture. Using every available medium, we've succeeded in connecting those hungry for ideas and information to those putting them into practice.

Friends of PM allows you to directly help impact, amplify, and revitalize the discourse and actions of radical writers, filmmakers, and artists. It provides us with a stable foundation from which we can build upon our early successes and provides a much-needed subsidy for the materials that can't necessarily pay their own way. You can help make that happen—and receive every new title automatically delivered to your door once a month—by joining as a Friend of PM Press. And, we'll throw in a free T-shirt when you sign up.

Here are your options:

- **$25 a month** Get all books and pamphlets plus 50% discount on all webstore purchases

- **$40 a month** Get all PM Press releases (including CDs and DVDs) plus 50% discount on all webstore purchases

- **$100 a month** Superstar—Everything plus PM merchandise, free downloads, and 50% discount on all webstore purchases

For those who can't afford $25 or more a month, we're introducing **Sustainer Rates** at $15, $10 and $5. Sustainers get a free PM Press T-shirt and a 50% discount on all purchases from our website.

Your Visa or Mastercard will be billed once a month, until you tell us to stop. Or until our efforts succeed in bringing the revolution around. Or the financial meltdown of Capital makes plastic redundant. Whichever comes first.

Send My Love and a Molotov Cocktail: Stories of Crime, Love and Rebellion

Edited by Gary Phillips
and Andrea Gibbons

ISBN: 978-1-60486-096-2
$19.95   368 pages

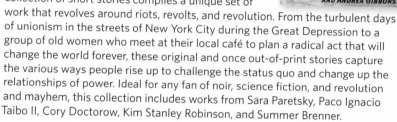

An incendiary mixture of genres and voices, this collection of short stories compiles a unique set of work that revolves around riots, revolts, and revolution. From the turbulent days of unionism in the streets of New York City during the Great Depression to a group of old women who meet at their local café to plan a radical act that will change the world forever, these original and once out-of-print stories capture the various ways people rise up to challenge the status quo and change up the relationships of power. Ideal for any fan of noir, science fiction, and revolution and mayhem, this collection includes works from Sara Paretsky, Paco Ignacio Taibo II, Cory Doctorow, Kim Stanley Robinson, and Summer Brenner.

Full list of contributors:

Summer Brenner
Rick Dakan
Barry Graham
Penny Mickelbury
Gary Phillips
Luis Rodriguez
Benjamin Whitmer
Michael Moorcock
Larry Fondation

Cory Doctorow
Andrea Gibbons
John A. Imani
Sarah Paretsky
Kim Stanley Robinson
Paco Ignacio Taibo II
Ken Wishnia
Michael Skeet
Tim Wohlforth

The Jook

Gary Phillips

ISBN: 978-1-60486-040-5
$15.95   256 pages

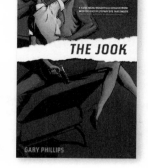

Zelmont Raines has slid a long way since his ability to jook, to out maneuver his opponents on the field, made him a Super Bowl winning wide receiver, earning him lucrative endorsement deals and more than his share of female attention. But Zee hasn't always been good at saying no, so a series of missteps involving drugs, a paternity suit or two, legal entanglements, shaky investments and recurring injuries have virtually sidelined his career.

That is until Los Angeles gets a new pro franchise, the Barons, and Zelmont has one last chance at the big time he dearly misses. Just as it seems he might be getting back in the flow, he's enraptured by Wilma Wells, the leggy and brainy lawyer for the team—who has a ruthless game plan all her own. And it's Zelmont who might get jooked.

"Phillips, author of the acclaimed Ivan Monk series, takes elements of Jim Thompson (the ending), black-exploitation flicks (the profanity-fueled dialogue), and Penthouse *magazine (the sex is anatomically correct) to create an over-the-top violent caper in which there is no honor, no respect, no love, and plenty of money. Anyone who liked George Pelecanos'* King Suckerman *is going to love this even-grittier take on many of the same themes."*
— Wes Lukowsky, *Booklist*

"Enough gritty gossip, blistering action and trash talk to make real life L.A. seem comparatively wholesome."
— Kirkus Reviews

"Gary Phillips writes tough and gritty parables about life and death on the mean streets—a place where sometimes just surviving is a noble enough cause. His is a voice that should be heard and celebrated. It rings true once again in The Jook, *a story where all of Phillips' talents are on display."*
— Michael Connelly, author of the Harry Bosch books